Pr

Skin was aware of a deep sense of danger. But her fear made her more passionate for Tooth – her shaman mentor – and it seemed that he too was being driven by a hunger he had previously suppressed. She was aroused despite her trepidation. Her friend Wasp had been right: it did not bother Tooth that he was breaking the taboo, and that this sex was in no way a spiritual experience. It was then that Skin decided not to let it bother her, either.

Primal Skin

LEONA BENKT RHYS

Black Lace novels contain sexual fantasies.
In real life, make sure you practise safe sex.

First published in 2000 by
Black Lace
Thames Wharf Studios
Rainville Road, London W6 9HA

Reprinted 2000

Typeset by SetSystems Ltd, Saffron Walden, Essex
Printed and bound by Mackays of Chatham PLC

ISBN 0 352 33500 9

Introduction

Primal Skin is a work of fantasy fiction – and sexual fantasy, at that – mixing different time periods and traditions ranging from the Upper to the Middle Paleolithic. It is a bisexual utopia and a world in which gender does not limit ability. There is a great deal of artistic licence (such as red hair being a specifically Neanderthal trait), but much of the detail is based in fact and various archaeological finds, however displaced temporally and geographically. *Primal Skin* actually takes place quite recently: circa 31,000 years ago, at a time in which permanent art was first appearing. Neanderthal/modern hybrids really did exist: there is evidence for them not just in Portugal (25,000 years ago), but also in Stone-Age Iraq. People have even theorised that Neanderthals may have contributed, in a very small way, to today's gene pool. I do not personally believe that art was something which was limited to our own sub-species (we may simply have made the most *permanent* art) and, as such, all three peoples detailed here have their own integrity and their own forms of creative expression.

An excellent book that was of great use to me is

Timothy Taylor's *Prehistory of Sex*. I have to credit it for much inspiration, particularly for drawing attention to the double-dildo traits of the stone-age 'spear-straighteners'. Bruce Bagemihl's *Biological Exuberance* is another work that I have to acknowledge for both illumination and information. James Shreeve's *Neanderthal Enigma* was very useful for research in Neanderthal culture and life; I must acknowledge it particularly for the description of obsidian blades being so sharp that they can be as 'thin as a single molecule'. It is an excellent and encompassing book, even if there are points of theory on which I differ.

I would like to thank Simone for her love and support; Clive, Michael and Shawna for their enthusiasm and both Kerri and James for their patience, forbearance and laughter. Most of all I would like to acknowledge the work of Jean M. Auel, whose *Earth's Children* series first brought the Paleolithic alive for my teenage self and a million others, and to whom I owe a huge debt of both admiration and eternal inspiration.

Leona Benkt Rhys
February 2000

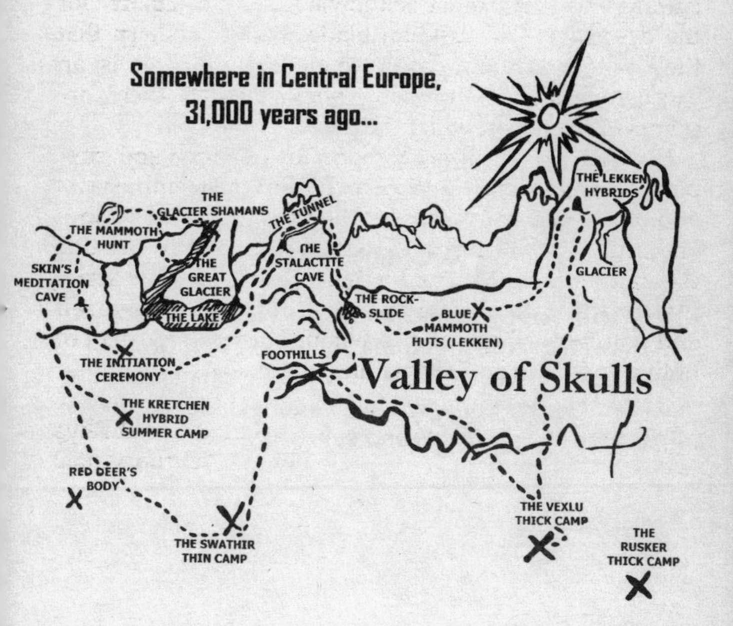
Somewhere in Central Europe,
31,000 years ago...
THE GLACIER SHAMANS
THE MAMMOTH HUNT
THE TUNNEL
THE STALACTITE CAVE
THE LEKKEN HYBRIDS
SKIN'S MEDITATION CAVE
THE GREAT GLACIER
THE LAKE
THE ROCK-SLIDE
BLUE MAMMOTH HUTS (LEKKEN)
GLACIER
THE INITIATION CEREMONY
FOOTHILLS
Valley of Skulls
THE KRETCHEN HYBRID SUMMER CAMP
RED DEER'S BODY
THE SWATHIR THIN CAMP
THE VEXLU THICK CAMP
THE RUSKER THICK CAMP

For Anne Vena,

with happy memories of Pee-Wee Herman,
dissected frogs, Soldotna ski slopes, *Real Genius*,
huge pizzas, slash, Chicago – Long Beach phone calls,
Edward Gorey, Conway Hall, Guinness, salt & vinegar
crisps and survival.

Chapter One

Skin was hungry.

A grass-covered plain spread over the horizon. Huge glaciers of blue ice, thick and opaque, licked at the edges of the steppe, a reminder even in hot summer of winter. Today the sun had melted a pool the depth of a finger on top of the glacier and the chilly, glittering pond surrounding the ice reflected an equally blue and cloudless sky.

But Skin was still hungry.

Usually, various beasts walked through the long grass: pale-brown horses with delicate hooves; ravens picking in the dirt, their black iridescent feathers shining in the sunlight; giant squirrels; enormous elks; bright-eyed rodents; sniffing wolves; wild cattle – and the tawny-skinned sabre-tooth tiger who stalked them all (except the raven). Usually. The earthquake thirteen days ago seemed to have frightened off some of the animals. Pickings had been abnormally bad this season anyway and the settlement hadn't eaten properly for a moon-cycle, but the lone mammoth that had been sighted earlier that morning would soon feed the whole Kretchen community. Already, Skin could hear the shouts of the hunting party. She had climbed up from her meditation cave to the top of the cliff in order to contemplate the great glacier, but now doubted that she would find any solitude here.

Her stomach continuing to rumble, Skin grew convinced she could hear the slow melting of the brilliantly coloured glacier below as she waited for the hunting crowd to pass by. Every year the ice was folding back on itself to reveal a cold new lake, receding more and more. The frozen mass of the glacier dripped slowly. Skin held her breath, waiting for the hunt to pass – and then suddenly there was a rush of colour and roar, blood and smoke.

'Watch out, Apprentice!' someone screamed – and finally Skin forgot her hunger for a moment, and the mammoth was nearly on top of her by the time she saw it. It ran towards her, closely followed by the spitting, shouting crowd. Someone else yelled, a high cry of exultation. The crowd that followed the injured mammoth continued to rush by even more rudely than the beast itself, nearly pushing Skin over despite her status.

She was left gasping and reeling on the path, trying to remember the jolting impression of what had just happened. Something momentous, a flash of inspiration, something important that she shouldn't forget. Skin covered her eyes with her hands and tried to think. Her heart was still beating quickly. It was the eye she had seen first. Huge, limpid, with multiple deep layers beneath the visible light-brown iris. She had seen it only for a second, but the image had been stunning: an enormous animal eye fringed with thick lashes. Trapped and still defiant, the eye had drilled right through her. But then the eye had quickly disappeared with the rest of the animal and now Skin stood transfixed on the path, caught in an endless moment. She had seen the under-eye, had seen what lay beneath the first. She had felt the whole strength of the animal and the force of its cornered spirit still trembled through her. She considered for a moment stopping the chase, but it was far too late for that.

Skin felt slightly faint, and her eyes flickered shut as she stood there, swaying on the trail. Closed, her lids still contained the after-image of that huge, beautiful eye. It was like it had burned into her brain in less than the time it took to blink.

She had seen the look of panic in the great, long-lashed globe before she had stepped aside, stumbling in her haste; before the enormous beast had thundered by. She stood quietly, the long green grass soft and rich and thick around her ankles.

I cannot help you, she thought belatedly. Skin reflected for a moment that it was humans who were the rougher of the two animals. Then she sighed, straightened some of the feathers that hung by strings from her leather waist-band and hurried along the path that twisted down the cliff. The soles of her feet, toughened by twenty years of barefoot living and only occasional footwear, were immune to the small sharp rocks of the bluff.

Even on the trail, she could hear the shouts and screams. She knew the animal was being prodded into confusion and would soon run in panic off the cliff. There had been something familiar in the eyes of the beast. Fear. She swallowed, her stomach still rumbling. Fear, and for the community, the first decent meal in three months. Then a great yell, a roar, and it had already happened; the beast had fallen – or been driven prematurely. Skin began to run too, faster than the mammoth, faster than the crowd. She had to get away quickly, get away from the sounds of the kill.

She reached the meditation cave that she so often used and crawled inside, attempting to push away the huge eye. The cave was a small, dank crevice where moisture glazed the interior surface of rock and where she was forced to sit; there was no room inside to stand. Yet she often found the darkness soothing, and eventually she calmed as she sat there, chanting slowly, concentrating on the duties she must perform in conjunction with the mammoth-kill.

She rubbed her hands together and her mind filled with a blank, vaguely face-shaped image. That would have to do for the time being, for it was today that she was to participate in a naming-ceremony, and it would be the first rite over which she solely had presided. There would be three young adults, all eager to attain a specific animal for their family totem. And it was Skin who had to choose. She buried her face in her hands, nerves churning her guts. She had experienced no visions yet, and the worst possible explanation occurred to her: perhaps she was not gifted with thoughtsight after all. Her stomach ached with hunger and anxiety, but she resolved to try: Tooth had always assured her that the details would come later, once she had chosen from the three candidates the correct features to match the rather amorphous visage she had just seen. That won't be too difficult, thought Skin, considering she had not really glimpsed much at all. She *hoped* it would not be too difficult. Even from inside the cave she could already detect the scent of the kill below and knew that the community would be expecting her to make an appearance very soon.

For a moment Skin lost her confidence again and despite her hunger began to shudder with a strange revulsion at the thought of the necessary slaughter, the demolishing of the mammoth's spirit. She pulled herself together by envisioning a litany of animal helpers – horse, tiger, bird – and eventually her heartbeat began to slow, even though the face that swam before her was still hazy. Times like this – when it was so necessary for her to remain calm – confirmed her need for the soothing agent of a personal totem.

What was it Tooth had told her last night? 'Don't lose your nerve, Skin. Confidence is everything. If you relax, then the visions will come to you; don't force them, but don't worry, either. The visions are there, and they will always appear eventually.'

'What if they don't come?' she had asked him angrily in response. 'What if I'm there in front of the crowd tomorrow, three initiates before me, and none of them are right? What if no visions come at all?'

Tooth had laughed then, his tan grizzled skin wrinkling up around his cloudy blue eyes. 'Well then, you can always lie and name an initiate regardless.'

For just a moment when he said that, Skin had been stricken with doubt. Was it all just an elaborate fakery? And for the first time she had doubted the motives of her mentor. But then Tooth had laughed again at her expression and had said hurriedly, 'I'm joking, Skin. If no visions come, then it is not the right time. And no initiates are named. It's happened before – not very often, but it's happened.'

And then Tooth had gone very quiet and soon after had left Skin with her meditations and preparations for the next day, left Skin feeling more nervous than before he arrived. He had been constantly preoccupied since the earthquake and Skin didn't know why: a few huts had been destroyed, but no one had been killed. He had not paid much attention to Skin as of late, but then later that night she saw that he had left his personal token behind for her, the flint-sharp tiger tooth. But she hadn't seen him since; he seemed to have momentarily disappeared. And it was this tooth she now felt through the pouch around her waist, hoping for a sudden inspiration. She had heard that some apprentices had had their naming visions even days before the actual day of the naming-ceremony – but this was clearly not going to be the case for her. Skin ran her hand down her braid ruminatively. Relax, Tooth had said. She would take his advice.

Skin took a deep breath as she sat there remembering in the cave, stroking the tiger tooth within its pouch. I am ready, she realised. My whole body is ready for the ceremony. The face would have to be filled in later, as it came to her. There would be no precognition. No obvious vision. Eventually, Skin dabbed green dots of paint on her cheeks, donned her costume, exited the meditation cave and raised herself to her feet, stretching her arms out on either side like a long-winged bird, feeling the afternoon wind cool on her face. Yes. She was ready. She could already feel the reverberating beat of the skin drums.

Before Skin reached the bottom of the cliffs, she collected herself further; this time in terms of outward appearance. She knew how she ought to appear to the crowd as apprentice shaman.

Skin also knew how she appeared to the crowd on non-ceremonial days, without costume: a jawline that was a bit too heavy for a Thin, a nose slightly too small for a Thick, a mass of healthy auburn hair. Sensual to all who dared to stare the apprentice shaman directly in the face: sparkling black eyes, smooth tender brown skin, full, smirking lips. In fact, she was considered over-sensual – she had just enough of a blend of both Thick and Thin to appear both exotic and familiar to everyone present – for even though all the Kretchen were hybrids too, most favoured either Thins or Thicks in terms of appearance.

Her grandmother was a Thick and this made Skin more muscular than the average Thin female, not that they ever saw many. Hybrids and Thins usually avoided each other. Skin also had a brow-ridge and a larger nose than the average Thin. But the trait that marked her heritage as particularly Thick was the deep fall of red hair. Her hair fell curling to her waist, but most of the time it was braided, as it was now for the ceremony. Particularly for the ceremony she had plaited the richly coloured tresses with stalks of bright green grass, so that a complicated pattern of green and auburn rolled down the length of her thick braid. Her red hair was important, she knew. The red hair reminded everybody present that she was a mix of both. A blend. A hybrid. Like them.

Skin cleared her throat as she moved into the group of people: hunters, skin-keepers, cooks, fathers, lovers, mothers. The Kretchen parted to let the shaman-in-training pass by, a seemingly confident young woman with an elaborate braid of green and red that shimmered in the sunlight. Skin's costume mimicked a bird: it was made of delicate birdskin – falcon – frail and translucent on this bright day, the sun exposing Skin's high breasts, curving hips and the dark delta of hair that covered her sex. Twenty huge, multicoloured feathers were sewn on to a wide, flat piece of leather that she wore over the back of her neck and which trailed down her back. She had a variety of bird talons strapped by sinew to the lower knuckle of each finger and her waist was fringed with an assortment of leather thongs and feathers. And she had already affixed the green, beaked mask that covered her nose and eyes. As she moved, the fragile bird-leather rustled. Ahead of her, the drums pulsed. For the first time, Skin started to feel the trance that Tooth had promised her she would feel.

A woman, heavily pregnant, ran up to her. 'One of them is my child,' she whispered into Skin's ear. 'The boy with the necklace. Be sweet with him.'

Skin nodded; the woman's words registered, but it was as if Skin were dreaming and accordingly she felt little inclination to respond. She could see them now. There were three of them. Two boys and a girl.

They all looked at least to have passed sixteen or seventeen summers and each would have made their puberty ceremony several years ago. For the chosen initiate, this ceremony would be more difficult. Skin knew it, the crowd knew it, and the three initiates knew it, too. Skin saw it in their watchful eyes, as her gaze briefly skimmed over them from behind the green mask.

She looked at the first of the two males. He was tall – far taller than she, and rather gangly with it. He wore a remarkable necklace of chunky black obsidian, and had a surly but handsome face. Skin looked at his arrogant expression, his still boyishly plump lips. His dark eyes met her own shining black eyes for a moment, held her gaze, and then finally dropped it in deference to Skin's power. Normally lacking confidence herself, Skin appreciated it in others and she felt for a moment a slight jolt to her sex, but she was already moving on to the next initiate, knowing instinctively that this young man with the dark red hair was not the one. It was honour enough that he had been put forth as a choice, and he would suffer no derision for his dismissal, only respect that he had in some small way participated. The dark-haired boy fell back.

The next was the girl. Skin could smell the scent of the already half-butchered mammoth, the fresh blood and the odour of the fire built high for its cooking as she moved to this second initiate. The girl did not move but stood frozen as Skin ran her fingers over the girl's high-cheeked face, over her jutting chin. There was little Thick blood in this one, with her light-brown hair's flicker of a rust shade and slight body. The smell of the now-sizzling meat caught Skin's attention and she looked away before finally returning her attention to the initiate. The girl was at most only three years younger than herself. Skin sighed, once again running eyes and fingers over the young woman's slender arms and unbelievably delicate digits. Perhaps. Skin released her hold on the girl and took several steps away.

The third and last initiate stood even stiller than the

girl had, but Skin could see that he was forcing his eyes to meet hers behind the mask. He too, like the girl, was slightly built. His eyes were pale yellow, with dark long lashes, and Skin began to feel the beginning of a shudder, the one Tooth had told her she would feel when a calling was apparent. She pushed down her instinct for a moment and stared at the boy. The meat continued crackling in the hot pits behind the crowd. A sharp chin, but a sharp brow-ridge as well. A slender-limbed body, but a large nose. Brown hair with a distinctively auburn sheen. She moved in front of the boy, ran her practised hands over the young man's lips, his face and neck. She could feel him trembling and she realised that she must be a terrifying figure to him, invested with all the power of her animal robes.

She wondered how it must be for him to be standing out here before the entire community, feeling the shaman's breath on his flesh as she fumbled towards a decision. Yet despite his shaking, he continued to look Skin squarely in the eye. Eye. Rich-coloured, heavy-lashed, and Skin felt herself falling deeply into the feeling she had suppressed, felt the heaviness and spirit behind the eye as she sought, and found, the second eye beneath. The hidden eye. The drums throbbed out their low rhythm. And again she felt the rumbling pull of certainty, as the image of the running, frightened, yet still defiant beast swam up before her. She felt a thrill rush through her, a near-ecstasy as she laid her palm against this third initiate and pulled him forward, named him for the crowd.

'Mammoth,' Skin cried, grasping the hybrid boy around his waist, feeling his joy as palpably as his taut skin. The girl fell back, blending swiftly into the rest of the Kretchen people, and there was only Skin and this boy and the scent of the cooking mammoth left before the crowd.

Skin felt a momentary flash of triumph. She had

fought her fear, gone with her instinct and the vision had come to her – just as Tooth had said it would. And if she was lucky and followed it through, the entire vision would be revealed.

A circle formed round Skin and the boy. Skin felt protective of the youngster. She glanced down at him, and he was still looking steadily at her. So, thought Skin, he trusts me, how about that? She waited a bit longer, and then motioned for the mammoth heart to be brought into the circle. She wondered where Tooth was; she could not see him in the crowd.

An older woman, clad in hunting clothes, brought the organ through on a flat plate of wood, the still-warm heart already staining the light-coloured wood of the platter to a dark rich crimson. The woman also carried with her a tiger pelt, and once she had placed both items on the grass near Skin and the boy she disappeared back into the group. Probably off to kill another mammoth, Skin thought bitterly – but with mixed feelings rather than bitterness alone, for she was hungry herself.

Skin drew the young hybrid man down on the pelt with her and positioned him so that he knelt before her, but not so that he sat back on his haunches. She tossed her long braid back over her shoulders, and then reached into one of the many pouches she wore, withdrawing the needle-sharp sabre-tooth tiger incisor that Tooth had lent to her, white and gleaming in her palm. It was the same animal whose pelt they now rested on, and Skin reminded herself to send out a special chant later for generous tigers.

The boy's eyes were enormous, just like the mammoth's had been.

'Be brave,' Skin whispered to him, her head bent down so that no one could see their covert communication. 'I will not truly hurt you.' How she wished that someone – anyone – could whisper the same words to her at a naming-ceremony.

From another fur-covered bag, Skin produced a clam-shell, closed and sealed. She pried it open with the tooth, and then spread the mollusc-flesh over the young man's bare, hairy chest. It was a local numbing agent, and would eliminate most of his pain. He would feel only a stinging.

Skin next took the tiger tooth in her right hand. She stretched out her left hand at the same time, holding it up in the air, palm flat out. She could still feel remnants of the crushed snail-like flesh beneath her nails, numbing the tips of her fingers.

'Watch my left hand,' she whispered to the young man. 'Keep your eyes on my hand, and don't look down.'

The young hybrid's eyes flickered up to Skin's hand. She knew he would keep his attention there. Balanced carefully, her other hand gripped round the sharp tooth, Skin began to scrape the skin on the boy's chest lightly, and then finally with enough pressure to break the skin beneath the thick sexual hair of his chest. A scarlet ribbon began to bead along the scratches etched into his chest, but Skin knew that it was unlikely that he was feeling much pain. She checked: he was still staring steadily at her left hand. She pricked out the necessary pattern: it was to be the intricate star of a snowflake, strung between the tiny erect points of his dark nipples. Then she stepped back, the smell of blood and fear and even mollusc blending strangely in her nostrils. Red. The colour of animals.

The pattern, delicate as a spider's web, was now scraped into the young man's chest in a series of tiny crimson rays, but still his eyeballs tilted upwards to gaze at Skin's palm, the yellow irises shining. Skin felt a certain amount of relief: he had not suffered, not in the slightest. The delicate embroidery of narrow lines of blood glimmered softly through his chest hair.

'Close your eyes,' Skin whispered to the youth. She didn't want him to see the cutting until it was completed, for fear that he might react unpredictably. Afterwards, of course, he would wear the shallow but expansive scar with pride. But for now, it was important that he remained calm. The cool, pungent scent of the mollusc continued to mix with the bitter scent of fresh red blood, distracting her slightly as she thought of the boy's unfortunate namesake. No. She had to be alert, had to urge both the vision and the ceremony forward.

Skin bent swiftly to the wooden plate near her, gazing for a moment at the red-haired boy, his eyes moving softly beneath his closed lids. She wondered what he was thinking. She was relieved: the difficult part was over; if the vision continued its course, it was pleasure from here on. Tooth would not have lied to her about these matters. Skin pressed her index finger against the huge mammoth heart. It was warm and soft and bloody and still very pliable. Then she raised her finger to the boy's chest and touched the edge of the shallow cutting. It was important that the blood mixed, and she now gingerly dabbed at each of the six points of the cutting. The mammoth blood would enter him now; now he was part of the animal. Skin exhaled slowly as she painted a red smear on his forehead, nose, each cheek in turn. She half-wished she was seeing her moon blood, so that she could blend that rich substance in as well. For a moment, the vision flickered on the edge of her consciousness again.

Skin drew back and looked at her handicraft, still kneeling before her. 'Open your eyes, Mammoth,' she said, out loud this time so that all could hear. 'You were already a man, but now you are an animal as well.'

The air was heavy with excitement; the warm rays of the orange-gold sun stroked sweat into the limbs of the shaman and her initiate. The Kretchen hybrids watched it trickle down Skin's back, beneath the feathers and the open birdskin to the leather thong around her waist. The mammoth meat roasted lazily in the pits. Within the crowd, mouths watered and no one knew if the cause was the charred, cooking, delicious meat or – perhaps – the promise of the more explicit spectacle that inevitably followed a cutting.

Then the skin-keeper came forth from the amassed group, holding in front of him the flayed, beaten leather underside of a mammoth pelt. The other skin-keepers with their pelts of wolf, horse and tiger had already stepped back in disappointment, knowing that it was not their turn at this ceremony. The mammoth leather was pale and yet looked smooth, soft as a baby's hand, perfectly tender for the imprinting.

The grizzled hybrid who held up the span of pale leather knelt gently before the boy. His manner was reverent as he carefully pressed the light leather square upon the snow-crystal design etched in red on the youth's chest. The older man closed his eyes in prayer, keeping palms flat on the leather against the initiate's chest. The hybrid youth also looked solemn, as if the more holy implications of his role in the ritual had suddenly hit him.

Then, the old man carefully began to lift the leather off the boy's marked chest so carefully that it was evident that he caused the boy no pain whatsoever. When the older man had completed detaching the soft tanned leather, he gave it a quick glance and then, grinning, held it up to the crowd, arms spread high in the air, spanning the width of the leather square.

On it was perfectly replicated the intricate six-point design of the cutting, an embroidery of human and mammoth blood now preserved for ever on the leather. The leather would become a relic, guarded carefully in a particular cave and handed down from generation to generation. Its red stain would fade, but its potency and the symbolism of the human–mammoth mix would not. And one day, the leather relic would be removed from the cave and used in ceremonies for the boy's clan – for henceforth this young hybrid and all his descendants would be known as Mammoth, and as keepers of the mammoth soul.

There had not been a named mammoth family for as many as thirty years, when the last one died out and a skin was made for the skin-keepers in the hope that one day there would be a new naming, so this naming-day was already remarkable. Most chosen initiates were predictable: generic birds, wolves, occasionally even a flower. A mammoth-naming was exceptional – and, what was more, Skin herself was exceedingly pleased. For the moment, there was no doubt in her mind that soon she would no longer be an un-named, un-totemed apprentice. She had performed admirably. It could only be a matter of time before she received the signs and portents that pointed towards her own totem-animal.

The youth's eyes were wide with wonder, and Skin could clearly see the pride in his eyes, the joy so evident in his expression. He made direct eye-contact with her now, finally, and their locked gaze established a connection that Skin was already feeling deep in her groin. Her hole was already growing wet and slippery, and she felt her clit twitch eagerly. She smiled to herself as she looked at the hybrid boy, decorated with the symbol of the ice and cold he must fight against with all his strength. Skin's eyes sparkled behind the mask, as she now pushed him back so that he sat on his haunches.

The heady odour of the charring meat was making her mouth water and her empty stomach tightened, nearly distracting her from the equally delicious sight of the beautiful young man with his elaborate scarification and hard eager prick. Skin was unsure which she desired more: sustenance or sexual gratification. She looked closely at the boy's limber, muscular arms, at the way the hair of his sex made a dark triangle of fur all the way to his navel: coarse, sexual hair. Sex, she decided. That was what she hungered for most. Until now, she had even forgotten to care whether or not Tooth was observing, and what he would make of the ceremony. He had always been in control before. But now, as conductor of this ceremony, sex was a privilege that was hers alone to take.

He was aroused as only a very young man can be – hard and stiff for her, she saw, with a medium-sized, thick cock already jutting up proudly. Skin again smiled, feeling her sex-lips sliding against each other, feeling the familiar warmth in her stomach. She liked it when the naming candidates were as excited as the shaman (or apprentice, in this case) – it made it more enjoyable for all concerned. She carefully removed the delicately linked sheath of bird leather, smoothing her hands over the sharp inward turn that delineated her waist from her proud full hips, and then unknotted the waist-thong, letting it all fall to the crowd. Tooth would be watching, too. She had a fair idea how the view of her plump, shapely arse would affect the group of Kretchens, but instead of the expected murmured rustling, the crowd went deadly silent. Skin looked up to the sky for a moment, tossed back her long red braid that tailed out from under her mask, and knew the silence for the heightened sexual tension it was. No one breathed as she looked down from the clear blue sky, stepped forward and straddled the new candidate's face, pushing her cunt down on his eager mouth.

Now the Kretchen stirred slightly, shifting forward to secure a better view of the scene before them: two figures held in a near-frozen tableau on the heavily oiled hairs of the tiger rug: one, the red-haired, black-eyed apprentice shaman who wore the beautiful green bird-mask, the other a newly initiated male, fresh from his name-cutting, his face obscured by the deep fragrant curves of the shaman's sex. No one in the crowd of nearly forty or so moved to touch themselves, not yet. The image being burned into their memories like a heavy torch-brand was too perfect, too full of promise. With an almost dispassionate yet eager hunger, the crowd silently registered the vision of the shaman's brown, fleshy hips and buttocks, so juicy and desirable; and the equally desirable sight of the young man's straining, muscular, adolescent thighs, sinews taut as he attempted to dip his whole face and nose deeper into the shaman's sacred aromatic cunt. She herself looked half-human, half-bird. But what a handsome bird she was. For a moment individual members in the crowd pondered what this rarefied sex-liquid must taste and feel like: sweet and pungent, clear as water. Yet despite their explicit ruminations, no one moved.

Then they heard Skin groan beneath the mask – a slight groan, but a groan nevertheless, and their own faces became flushed with active desire, as they felt the type of lust that inflamed, spurred action, and began to touch themselves, hands gripped round hard cocks, fingers sticky in holes – at first gently, and then feverishly.

Skin, on the other hand, pushed her cunt down further on to the youth's face, rubbing her hard clit back and forth over him, from his beautiful closed eyes to his exploring, eager tongue. She felt wet, full of magic, and she started to shake, to tremble with excitement. Sweat started to gather on her chest, across her full, dark-tipped breasts; she was damp underneath her armpits as the wave of pleasure made her groan again, a low rumbling sound. It was too soon; the orgasm wasn't supposed to come this quickly or easily. Skin felt as if her whole body was slipping into the rhythm of the boy's tongue as he drank at her; felt as if her whole body was turning to water as she trembled. It was too soon.

With an abrupt movement, Skin broke her crouch over the boy's mouth and stepped away, catching her breath, her thigh-muscles spasming from exertion and the necessary sexual control. But she *had* controlled it, she realised, looking up for a moment at the afternoon sky. She had delayed the pleasure. Tooth would be proud of her. Whether the remainder of the vision would come, she wasn't sure.

Oblivious to the lust-fascinated crowd, Skin looked down on the boy, who was still kneeling in position, eyes closed. Skin's sexual juices made his whole face glitter in the hot sunlight, the liquid even dripping down to mix with the blood of the ice-shaped scar freshly cut on his chest. Though she did not smile, it made Skin happy to see the two life-fluids mixing and blending against his young skin. His prick was still hard, too, fully erect and seeping with a pearl of pre-come.

Blood and sex-juice, thought Skin, caught in an odd fanciful moment of revelation as she prepared to dominate him once more with her cunt. Thick blood and Thin blood. Mammoth blood, human blood. Like Skin herself. Like the young man before her. Hybrid. And it seemed for a moment that the vision that had eluded her in the cave finally descended fully on her mind; the truth of it all, the answer to it all. And carefully, as the heavy beat of the skin drums began to sound again, the apprentice mounted the boy's wet, searching mouth and began again to feel pleasure and the joy of pure revelation pulse through her sticky, patient sex.

Only minutes after the ceremony had been completed – while Skin removed her mask and washed her face, body and cunt with clear, icy glacial water from a bowl proffered to her – a figure detached itself from the crowd and approached the assistant shaman.

'I enjoyed myself today.' He was a tall, slender Thin with night-dark straight hair that fell to his shoulders in a glossy tangle. Thins weren't often seen in the community.

'Thank you.' Skin looked down again, concentrating on scrubbing her body clean. Tooth had warned her that she would have admirers and hangers-on after ceremonies; he had told her that it was best always to ignore them and just to get on with the business at hand. She was in a hurry to find Tooth, too; she wanted to see what he himself had thought of the ceremony . . . she felt her face go warm. In fact, she had already said her good-bye to the young man she had initiated: he had looked disappointed but, judging from the circle of men and women surrounding him, he would have no shortage of eager sexual partners. And now, of all things, she had the bad luck to have a Thin as a suitor.

'Yes, for a first time, it wasn't bad at all.' His accent was guttural, a typical Thin intonation.

This time Skin jerked her head up to glare at the young Thin. 'Who asked you?' she snapped, forgetting Tooth's advice.

The Thin's eyes widened, his thick long lashes framing clever, gleaming eyes. 'I'm just admiring your technique, that's all.' He shaved, Skin saw, like all hybrid – and even Thick – males she had ever met. She wondered if he used a sharp blade of obsidian, as Tooth did every morning. He twirled a pouch that hung from a leather thong round his waist and smiled politely. 'From one apprentice to another.'

Oh, holy mother of all beasts. How could Skin have missed that? Her face immediately flushed nearly as red as her hair. 'I'm s–sorry,' she stuttered, her new-found self-confidence suddenly dashed. 'I didn't realise what you were.' She cursed herself for not spotting a fellow apprentice at first glance.

'That's all right.' The Thin kept smiling, putting Skin more at ease. 'I know you didn't realise. And I meant what I said.' He raked his fingers through his dark scraggly hair. 'Your naming of the boy; the cutting; the way you pushed yourself down on him and – well, just everything. You seem so confident.'

'Really?' answered Skin, hearing only this last sentence. She washed off the last of the grime and blood thoughtfully. 'You really think I'm confident?' She felt herself beginning to blush again, this time with pride. She splashed cold water on the back of her neck.

The Thin smiled in response. 'I'm from the Swathir – the Thin settlement a half-day away,' he offered. 'I just did my first naming-ceremony, too.' He moved closer to Skin, perhaps a little too close. She was wary of Thins – they were said to be obsessed with sex; they kept spouses purely for the sake of pleasure; they looked on hybrids as something both inferior and exotic.

She stepped back a little, unsure if she wanted to be in such intimate proximity to someone so soon after the ritual. Tooth had always said that it was best to get away quickly, to disappear somewhere where you could meditate in peace and let the visions simmer down. And besides, she was ravenous. Skin pointedly ignored the black-haired apprentice as she quickly wrung out the red length of her hair, but he still stood staring at her quietly, several steps away. She dressed herself again, this time in a simple robe that went halfway down her legs, her waist-thong full of pouches tied tightly. She gave her face one final splash and then shook her head in irritation.

Ignoring him didn't seem to make any difference and besides, it was a bad idea to make enemies with other apprentices.

'Have you had any of the meat yet?' she finally asked

grudgingly. She began to walk away, half-looking at him over her shoulder.

'Not yet,' the Thin countered, falling easily into step with her. He wore a long reindeer robe that had been tied up short. His legs were long and muscular, and a narrow tattoo of what looked like a series of bat wings wound its way up the back of each of his legs, from calf to thigh. Yes, of course. All Thins were heavily tattooed. She remembered this.

Skin noticed all this swiftly, and then kept her eyes forward as she walked back to the cooking pits, the irritating apprentice just one pace behind her. She squared her jaw: why was she burdened with this man? He was an apprentice shaman, so she couldn't just ignore him, as Tooth had suggested. But she hardly wanted to chatter lightly with him, either; and there he was, trailing at her heels like a trained wolf or an insistent child. Skin stopped suddenly, planting her feet in the dirt, and the tall, Thin shaman stumbled forward in surprise, falling flat on his rear in the grass, his long tattooed legs sticking out like those of an awkward insect.

The look on his face was so startled and offended that Skin broke out in laughter. He raised himself to his feet with dignity as Skin continued to giggle, and then finally smiled sheepishly himself.

'Bat,' he said at last, introducing himself as he stretched out to touch Skin's cheek and then kissed her brow in the customary greeting. 'Perhaps I should have introduced myself right from the beginning.'

'Yes, perhaps.' Skin stared at him, his face and body and the dark-brown pelt he wore all covered in dust. She hadn't realised how striking he was, until now.

'They called me that because I like to sleep during the day,' he said mockingly.

Skin found herself wondering whether they hadn't called him that because he was as well-endowed as bats purportedly were – entirely out of proportion to their rodent bodies. No, she supposed regretfully, it was probably because of his dark hair. The apprentice shaman had narrow green eyes in his angular Thin face and a smirking pair of red lips. Long lashes and arched brows, a straight nose and that wild mess of black hair. He wore a distinctive necklace of white bivalve shells. In fact, if Skin had had a taste for Thin men – which as a rule she didn't – she'd have been more polite right from the start; maybe she would have earned herself a lively bedmate for the night, too – Skin stopped herself. She didn't want to fuck Thin men; and apprentices never fucked each other. Nor did shamans co-mingle amongst themselves. It was an unspoken rule that there were no sexual relationships between shaman and apprentice, either, although Skin had often wished this were not the case. Still, it was that simple. But Bat looked like he might be amiable company, so at last she, too, stretched her fingers to his cheek and touched her lips to his forehead. 'Skin,' she said. People said a good friend was better than a bedmate, anyway. 'Shall we search out that meat?' Shamans – and apprentices, too – got the choice bits, after all.

'Certainly.' Bat nodded in agreement, and they both walked carefully up to the front of the queue for the delicious, tender mammoth meat, not looking at each other after the fragile truce they had mutually and silently agreed on. People tried not to stare, but it wasn't often that a full-blood Thin was in their midst.

Skin felt just a pang of sexual regret as she observed the young apprentice's slender haunches – so intricately tattooed – as he knelt to receive his portion of the kill, observed his sinewy brown arms flex as he carried it away. He was quite an attractive apprentice shaman.

Then she started suddenly. Speaking of shamans, where was Tooth?

* * *

Skin and Bat sat on a rock ledge some distance from the rest of the community, licking and crunching the delicious bones, their bellies finally full of the savoury well-cooked meat. But Skin found herself having a hard time concentrating on what the handsome Thin was saying, as he chattered freely on, offering details of his history, his family, the moment he had been chosen as an apprentice and what it meant to him. Skin vaguely gathered that he had entered his apprenticeship when his parents had died and that he had a cousin near his age, but her thoughts kept drifting towards Tooth: had he seen the ceremony? What did he think of it? Would he allow her to move forward to the next stage of her training? What type of training would that be?

'So, would you?' Bat was staring at her expectantly.

Skin blushed. 'Sorry, I didn't hear you.' Her fingers twisted nervously over her braid. Her body still felt heavy and satiated from the ceremony.

'I said, would you like to meet my cousin?' His green eyes flashed with a sudden intensity and he looked excited, eager.

'Uh . . . of course. Whatever.' Skin was embarrassed that she had been caught daydreaming. She rose and stretched out her arms (Bat had been talking for quite some time). It was now early evening, and most people were still gorging themselves near the fire, though some had already started cutting long strips of meat from the huge mammal for drying. And with Tooth missing, it wasn't as if she had a lot of opportunities for in-depth conversation. Most people balked at discussion with shamans, even apprentice shamans. And now that she finally had a chance to speak freely with someone, she was botching that, too, by being a bad listener.

'Let me meet your cousin,' Skin said abruptly, in an uncharacteristic burst of friendliness. 'It would be a pleasure to be introduced.'

'It's a bit of a walk.'

Skin felt reckless. Why not? Tonight she didn't have to answer to anybody. Why not meet his Swathir cousin?

As they walked away from the cooking pits, the sky turning orange and then red as the sun dipped lower into the horizon, Skin wondered suddenly why a Thin apprentice would make a half-day journey merely to view a naming-ceremony conducted by another novice. In a friendly tone she enquired what his mentor would think of it all and was shocked when Bat spun around angrily.

'I told you! Don't you ever listen? My teacher died thirteen days ago. She went missing one night, and they didn't find her body until after the earthquake. I think she was murdered, however. Not killed in the quake at all.' He glared at her as if she had caused the earth to shake herself.

'I'm sorry.' Skin could feel her own eyes beginning to narrow. 'I'm a bit preoccupied at the moment.' A terrible thought occurred to her. Maybe Tooth had been murdered, too. Maybe right this moment his mangled body was lying on the steppe, chewed by the great cats – no, it was too terrible to think. 'I should have paid closer attention to your words.'

Bat stood only a hand's distance from her face, staring into her eyes. He looked as if he wanted to say something, but then he suddenly bit his lip and walked away. Skin followed him, running to catch up.

'Again, I apologise.' Skin found the words uncomfortable in her mouth. 'And I am sorry for your teacher's death.' She forced herself to look him straight in the face. She could not read his expression.

Suddenly, Bat stepped in and ran his hand from Skin's neck to her chin, his palm cool on her throat. He held her face so that her eyes could not move away from his, and she found herself noticing odd details: the black ring of his iris surrounding his leaf-coloured eyes, a small mole near his left eyebrow. She could feel him breathing, his chest pressed against her breasts. Then all at once he was kissing her, his lips tender against hers, his tongue slipping coolly into her mouth. Skin felt not desire but emotion, something breaking open raw inside her. She closed her eyes as they kissed unhurriedly and it was unlike any kiss she had ever experienced. There was no lust exactly, but rather a detached, slow eroticism. Her hand went up to the nape of his neck and her fingers shifted the fine black hair that grew there. There was none of the rabid urgency she had felt at the ceremony with the young hybrid, but still Skin felt herself growing steadily, slowly wet. She drew back, and they looked at each other, their arms still around each other.

He spoke first. 'You don't need to apologise. You just need to listen.' He was half-teasing, Skin realised. 'You never listen, do you? Not really. You've got everything figured out.'

'Not everything,' said Skin, thinking of how her confidence inevitably failed her when she needed it most, today's ceremony being one of the few exceptions. And thinking how strange it was to be standing here with arms around the neck of another apprentice, one who she had met only this day.

Bat looked like he was going to say something else, then he appeared to change his mind. He gently removed his arms from around her waist and guided Skin in a detour around the cooking pits. She felt strangely at peace as Bat held her hand and they walked forward, felt no stirring in her groin aside from a warm sensation that spread up into her belly. The feathers still bound round her waist swayed slightly as they walked along. The Thin was obviously intent on something. What was it now? Ah yes, he wanted her to meet his cousin.

They approached another cliffside, on the other side

of the cooking pits from where Skin's own meditation cave was hidden. Bat began to lead her up a trail, one which Skin had followed often enough but not to its culmination. It led a long distance away, all the way up the mountain. There was such an odd silence between them. What am I doing? thought Skin. This was completely out of character – though maybe that was good. But Bat led her along the trail until the sun set completely and only the glow of twilight remained in the sky. It was not yet dark, but despite their exertion Skin was growing cold. It dawned on her that she would probably have to stay the night now, though that had not been her original intention.

'Don't worry,' Bat told her, as if reading her mind. 'We're nearly there.' Skin could still see the edges of the great ice-sheet that choked the cliffs, the pale-blue glacier etched with strange marks from the straining and pushing of the compacted ice itself. She shivered.

'Here!' Bat said, and none too soon, as he pulled Skin into a cave that she would have missed even if she had ever followed the trail out this far, which she hadn't. His arms were warm against her bare shoulders and she found herself thinking of their kiss, but she still longed for a pelt and a fire. What was she doing so far from home, anyway? And all for a moment's whim. She hoped this Swathir was trustworthy. Tooth would be worried. *Perhaps* he would be worried, she corrected herself mentally. He hadn't seemed inordinately concerned about the naming-ceremony for which he had prepared her so carefully – not enough to attend, anyway. Skin tried to make her eyes adjust to the dark interior of the cave. She could sense Bat still standing beside her. It wouldn't hurt to be away from Tooth for just one night. After all, she was nearly a full-fledged shaman and barely an apprentice at all, any more.

Bat, she realised, was waiting for her. She could now

make out his shape and perhaps the glint of his green eyes, but not much else of the cave. He began to walk further into the enclosure, however, and she followed him. He stopped before a pile of what appeared in the darkness to be various pelts and furs.

'You can sleep here,' he said to Skin, who was not feeling in the least bit sleepy, only very cold.

'But –' began Skin. It was all too strange. What was she doing here? 'What about your cousin?' Was she even safe with him? Perhaps it had been *he* who had killed his mentor. When would Tooth notice she was missing?

'You'll meet her tomorrow,' Bat said. 'Sleep for now.'

Skin tentatively lay down and covered herself with the warm furs with great relief. If he was to kill her, there wasn't much she could do about it now. She said nothing, but turned away from the Thin apprentice shaman and curled up amongst the pelts, surprised to feel very sleepy after all. It had been a long day, full of the hunt and the kill and the ceremony and the kiss, and now these images were swarming in Skin's head as she fell immediately into a deep, exhausted sleep.

Bat stood watching Skin for quite some time, and then withdrew to build a fire that would keep the hybrid shaman warm throughout the night. Then he returned to the lip of the cave, where at last he heard his cousin arriving. His cousin entered the cave quickly, knowing that she was late.

'It took me three days there and two days back,' Wasp whispered to her cousin, 'but I've located Wolf; we met outside her camp. I left at sunrise and she had planned to leave at sunfall – so I imagine she'll be here sometime before the sun is at its highest point tomorrow.'

After he greeted her, Bat paused for a moment to gaze at the world outside the cave: the black sky full of white bits of stars that glimmered like water. A curving bowl of obsidian with raindrops at the bottom. Inside, the fire-hearth glowed red and hot; the heat greeted the cousins as they stripped their bodies of clothes and walked towards the far end of the cave, past the sleeping hybrid.

'Well done,' whispered Wasp. 'I'm glad you found one. Why did you pick only an apprentice?'

'I didn't trust the shaman himself,' said Bat. 'And by the time I had reconsidered, he had disappeared. A handsome man, though.'

Wasp smiled at her male cousin. 'She'll be useful, I think.' Wasp was nearly a mirror image of Bat, complete with smirk, gangly limbs and green eyes. She washed the accumulated dirt and soot from her body in a pool near the cave-wall, and Bat did the same. Afterwards, he turned to look at Skin and the fire that would warm her while she slept. He and his cousin would spend the night on the ledge of the other side of the tunnel, touching each other under the stars. He looked over and met Wasp's green eyes. And with this hybrid's help, they would solve the mystery of Red Deer's death. He felt excited suddenly, and wanted to hurry. He watched bemused, though, as first his mischievous cousin crept up and kissed Skin lightly on the lips. The hybrid muttered in her sleep and turned away, burrowing further into the pelts.

'She's a grumpy one, isn't she?' his cousin commented, and Bat nodded. He smiled as he looked at Wasp. She was smiling back, her eyes gentle as she scanned his physique. He looked down at his body and then his cousin's: both were glowing red from the firelight. Water droplets still clung to their naked flesh from the wash; liquid captured on their skin: on their throats, their thighs, their merry lips. His cousin caught his eye and they both laughed out loud – for no other reason than happiness – as they knelt and pushed their limber bodies into the tunnel, their laughter echoing in the cave behind them.

Although it was not enough to wake Skin up from her dreams of blood and snowflakes. And mammoth eyeballs. And slow kisses that seemed to last through the long cold night.

Chapter Two

The cave was cool and dark, although eventually sunlight began to fork in from the entrance. Like an illuminated branch, it sought out particular corners and crevices, warming the dry dirt with its gentle morning heat. The cave was quieter at sunrise than it was at night: the nocturnal residents folded their wings or crept back into their holes and let themselves dream of blood, food and the next great night of powerful dark. Their slumbering hallucinations were of the dying heat of insect prey, the immediate joy of scattered morsels. They slept, and for a short while their reveries overlapped with the dreams of the day-animals: all asleep in the great dark cave where dawn was only trickling in, all dreams melding in a mass of want and comfort, tensed appendages and shallow breath, rest and the steady drip-drip-drip of blue-green stalactites. As the light hit them, the shimmer of these extended craggy growths was exposed and they turned radiant. The birdsong outside became more bold and slowly the air seemed to crackle, as insects began to click softly and a lizard stretched itself towards a sunbeam: the air in the cave still chilled, but now somehow fertile with intention.

Skin was the last being to wake up – long after the lizards and long after the birds lodged high up near the cave's sky-hole – and only when she had tried, fitfully, to bat the irritating rays of sun out of her eyes. At first she had resorted to turning over and burying her head, but finally she resigned herself to consciousness. She had the disconcerting feeling at first of not knowing where she was, or whose pelts she huddled under, or whose cooling hearth-stones (barely) warmed her feet. Her head still buried, she tentatively reached out a hand to feel for a bed companion, but felt no one, and yet she knew she was not at her own hearth. She was in a cave. The smell here was different, and she would never forget to block an entrance with skins so that she was not woken by the sun at the earliest possible moment. Like now.

A thought made her mouth go dry. What if a bear had managed to tear down the hides, and she was even now sharing cave and hearth with its uninvited presence? Slowly and carefully, with no jerking movements, Skin pushed her head out from the furs and, not daring to breathe, looked around the cave. There was no bear, she saw with relief.

So where was she? The reddish cave was flooded with light and she was unused to such early-morning brightness. She stood up and stretched. Despite the sun, the cold still made her shiver. She let the furs fall to the ground around her feet and bathed her body in the rays. She was just now dimly able to recall that a ceremony took place the day before, a sexually fevered one, yet despite this her sex was dry between her legs when she put her hand down to stroke at it. Dry, and yet she was aroused, the way she often was when waking from the most erotic of dreams only to find that the eroticism is a memory, that she was not as wet or lusty as she had been while dreaming, that somehow her physical body had not kept up with the slick urgency of the dreams. This was how she felt at present, and she could already tell that to bring herself to a completion would be a waste of time: at best, unsatisfactory, with only a hint of pleasure.

Still, whose cave was this? The question reared its ugly head and she looked around, just before yesterday's full events came flooding back to her: the skinny, black-haired Thin who had kissed her and the journey to this cave last night – only to finally sleep (it seemed impossible; she wasn't one who easily drifted off when faced with new environments); the mysterious non-appearance of Tooth. And now the inexplicable sensations of her dreams came back to her as well: huge irises that turned into dark lakes; dry unerotic kisses that were somehow still sensual and sexual: whisper-sex, like a dry hand on birch bark. Skin looked down at herself. She certainly looked ripe and sensual enough for such dreams. Firm, swollen breasts. Smooth skin. A lush forest of darkly red pubic hair covering her normally wet cunt. And yet she felt disconnected from herself, mind and sex divided, and she realised that rather than rub herself, she needed to meditate, to somehow once again connect her body with her soul. Her inability to physically react to her dreams was proof of it.

For just a moment, the chilling thought occurred to her that someone – who? some rival shaman of Tooth's? – had stolen her soul and left her with merely a body. She was here in a strange cave (although it felt safe enough) and Tooth was not here. She was gripped with a terrible fear of venturing outside the thick stone shelter before she found herself again; before she could regain her confidence. She would be safe enough here – try as she might, she could remember no intentional malevolence from the missing dark-haired young man. Bat. That was his name. And stranger in this cave or not, duties and mysteries awaiting her or not, she would have to first centre herself and bond her body with her soul. Else she would not be able to deal with that outside world – the bright, raging nature-world outdoors – at all.

By now the few hides hung over the entrance had let in so many rays that the cave's centre was fully illuminated and the hanging stalactites gleamed brightly. Skin forced herself to listen to their slow drip into shallow puddles on the cave's floor, far away from the flat dirt centre and the dry area where she had slept so soundly. Then she moved one fur to the centre and knelt on it, her face dappled with the jagged shapes of light. All was nearly quiet in the cave. Skin knew it was time to begin. She knelt silently, her naked body relaxing as she slid back so that her strong legs supported her weight.

At first she was aware only of the steady drip from the cave's ceiling and she made herself concentrate on that. In her mind's eye, she saw the whole living sculpture of the stalactites, green and blue, lavender and silver, shimmering with reflected light and the dull sheen of phosphorescent cave dust. Each a descending stone icicle, dripping down into a sister stalagmite at the cave's floor, each drop conveying sediment and colour. Deep in the first stages of her trance, Skin rubbed at her eyes. This was not the right mind-path; she knew this – Tooth had taught her to concentrate on the many at once, the singles with the whole, rather than the singles themselves. Exasperated, Skin discarded the individual imaginary stalactites for the moment. By now, she should have fully relaxed into the flow of spirit. Skin sighed, picked herself up and walked back to the furs in which she had spent the night.

Rummaging through the skin that made up her cape, she found the small leather pouches that she wore tied by rawhide round her waist. When her fingers touched the five small objects she kept stacked in a small pile inside one of them, her lips moved into a slight smile.

She withdrew the stack of five unbroken little half-shells and carried them in her palm back to the centre of the cave. She knelt again in the sunlight, but not before first placing each digit of her left hand into the cupped mould of each shell. The five shells fit snugly over the ridged tips of each finger and her thumb and when she raised her hand, palm down, the shells did not fall off.

'Concentrate on the many and one' – it was one of Tooth's favourite things to say, and Skin resolved to follow his advice. She had already been distracted by the singularity of the stalactites; now she closed her eyes in the sun and let the rich images inside her head began to flow. First, there was the smell of the cave itself, the dampness and the fur-covered ground on which she knelt. She let her mind seek out every piece of sand, every clod of dirt, and let the physical image of the cave's expanse hang there in her mind, where she left it suspended at some level. She would try not to imagine too many things at once: one time she had done this and had become quite confused, close to tears. She would reach back for the image of the cave when she next needed it; when she was ready.

Skin now concentrated on each separate finger and also on the grouped entity of her hand. She felt the smooth pull of each shell, and tried to imagine the colours: swirling, iridescent. She caught an impression, suddenly, of the sea-clams whose homes these shells had been: firm, crisp, shallow pebbles holding life and spirit, the pearly spirals of pale colour on the inside of each home pressed up against all that squirming life, as the shells now were again as they pressed on her own flesh.

As her mind turned towards the texture of the shells, stretching to conceive of their now-emptied vibrancy, Skin's hand turned to her body, stroking over her stiff nipples, down to the furrow of her navel, and then rested, pausing at the curving mound of sex-hair. The shells became animated in her vision, and Skin could feel their old vigour hot on each fingertip. And her other hand was hot, too, as it searched down into her wet depths and ran lightly over her clit.

Skin focussed on her right hand now, touching the softness and textures of her sex. Her fingers would be glistening, she thought, and a surge of heat ran down her spine, settled in her belly. She was hot and wet, in the midst of her trance; she had life connected on the end of each of her hands. This time she was easily able to envision the one and many, and for all that she was aware of the iridescent scalloped shells and her pulsing cunt, so was she also aware of the sensations on the end of each finger: creamy, pearly, shell interiors, wetness, hair, flesh. She had linked her soul and body once again. She was going to be all right.

A wonderful image occurred in her mind then, as she knelt with one juice-covered hand burrowing deep into her cunt, the other splayed back on the ground behind her, pressing so hard that the little shells were nearly cracking. The vision was of a huge spiralled shell, turning, slowly, bigger than the sky. And each part of the shell, each curve, was a different colour, and her eyes could not follow the curves, so intricate was the structure. Every time she tried to, the track along the huge shell's surface became something else. The shell was changing, and yet it always stayed the same. And Skin knew then, knew with certainty that, like other shells, this great shell would have layers under layers, more spirals, chains impossible to follow.

Skin rubbed hard at her clit, pleasure flooding through her. When she applied the many and one technique to this amazing vision, somehow she found that her brain *could* hold the shell's entirety, infinite though it was, and at the same time understand the singularity of its beauty. Everything began to merge into a slow lustful blend as she rubbed hard at her pussy, lost in the trance, but still never ceasing to feel her own wetness, her heavy sexuality, every pore on her body. This was her, too, the anomaly of hybrid within the whole: beautifully unique, plural. She moaned, her brow breaking out in beads of sweat, as she pushed herself down on her sticky hand, her ripe breasts trembling as her body strained with the effort.

The hybrid shaman was stunning, Wasp thought, as she watched from behind the curtain of stalactites, near the entrance of the tunnel from which she had just emerged. Her cousin had not exaggerated. Just watching her now made Wasp want to touch herself between her own moistening cunt-folds – or, better yet, touch the apprentice herself. That was anathema, of course. You could never disturb a shaman or apprentice mid-trance. Though they were desperate to talk to the hybrid, both she and her cousin would have to wait until the hybrid had finished the ritual. But as long as she was forced to wait, Wasp thought, nothing could stop her from taking vicarious pleasure. Nothing could stop her from admiring the tensed muscles of the woman's haunches, or from noticing how the apprentice's fingers went pale with tension as she pushed and rubbed them stiffly and frantically against her beautiful wet cunt. Wasp could even see a glimpse of the beautiful purple folds of the apprentice's labia, could see one delicate lip pushed out further than the other, could see the hybrid's shaman's cunt shining and glistening even from here, as the other woman plunged her hand hard against her ripe pussy, circling and circling the hard little bead of her clit.

Both Wasp and Bat watched open-mouthed as the hybrid's eyes closed in seeming ecstasy, and scarcely heard the faint cracking sound as she pressed down on the shells with such pressure that all five cracked simultaneously. They waited a respectful interval, then they approached the apprentice – whose eyes were still closed. Still, they assumed by her body's now-relaxed pose that she had exited the tense spell of the trance. Bat took a deep breath to speak, but then he tugged at his hair nervously, and remained silent.

Right, thought Wasp, that does it. As with most things, she would have to take the lead before her more tentative cousin. She cleared her throat pointedly, and the hybrid's eyes snapped open. Wasp watched as the hybrid surveyed her cousin with a glazed appraisal, recognised him, and then turned her gaze to Wasp herself. Wasp waited for the amazed gasp, the customary wonder over how two cousins of the opposite gender could look so much alike: the same dark length of hair, full lips and quizzical eyebrows. Accordingly, Wasp now raised one of said pairs of eyebrows, as Bat was doing, just to make the similarity more obvious. The hybrid apprentice didn't flinch.

'I'm Wasp,' said Wasp, striding forward to clasp the apprentice's hand – which she found was studded with small bits of broken shells. 'I believe you've already met my cousin. I – we – need to speak with you concerning a matter of unimaginable importance.' The superlative was silly; Wasp had little doubt that the hybrid was able to imagine whatever she wished.

The hybrid shifted and ran her hand along the back of her neck, thoughtfully lifting up the mass of red curls. 'Regarding what?' Her accent was sing-songy; all hybrids spoke with this musical inflection. Wasp could see that the other woman was scrutinising her tattoo: a hexagonal pattern like that of a wasp's nest, all the way up her left arm.

'Regarding –' Wasp looked helplessly at her silent cousin '– regarding a musical item. An item that makes beautiful sounds. Noises like a voice makes noises, like a calling bird when I blow into it, like this –' Wasp broke off here, and let out a trill that resounded through the dome-shaped cave interior.

'A flute,' said the hybrid. And rather rudely – Wasp was looking forward to illustrating the sounds; she wanted to explain their beauty, the sweetness that reached the ears with its pure, high tones. It was different from singing, but very similar.

So now Wasp faltered. 'Yes. A flute was found on Red Deer's body after her death. She was Bat's mentor.'

'I know,' said the hybrid flatly.

Bat finally stepped forward, as the conversation had become awkward. 'This is my cousin, Skin. This is who I wanted you to meet.'

Wasp watched as the apprentice folded her arms across her chest and said nothing. Wasp felt a surge of respect for her, hybrid or not. She wasn't giving anything away: Wasp had no inkling of whether the hybrid was pleased that she had been brought to this cave, or whether she violently objected.

'We've brought you here because the last thing Red Deer spoke of before she left our encampment was that she was going to be helping Thins, Thicks and hybrids alike. Has anything similar to a flute ever been found on the Kretchen site?' Wasp could see that the hybrid was deliberating whether to trust them.

'No,' she answered at last.

'Had you heard of Red Deer before I spoke of her?' Bat's voice was steady, patient.

'I think so,' said Skin hesitantly.

'She was a great emissary,' Bat continued, 'and it was she who periodically tried to make links between the Thicks, the Thins, the hybrids, so that the violence that flares up from time to time would not occur again.'

'Red Deer . . .' the hybrid whispered slowly. 'Yes. I have heard of her. My mentor, Tooth, has spoken of her. I believe they were friends, although I never met her myself.'

'We need your help,' Bat put in. 'It means peace between the communities. We have resolved to visit each of these communities and their shamans, one by one, just as Red Deer had done. We are going to solve the riddle of her death.'

'Are you sure it was murder?'

'Yes,' said Bat. His face grew angry. 'At first we thought it was just injuries from the earthquake, but once we looked closer we discovered that someone had . . . torn out, removed, both her heart and her lungs. So, yes – I am sure.' The hybrid's face softened in sympathy. Bat's explanation had been matter-of-fact, but effective.

This was what Wasp admired about her cousin. He was more thoughtful, so he came to his conversation points more slowly, but sometimes his slowness and carefulness proved more persuasive than Wasp's own direct nature.

'These . . . *flutes*, we want to know more about them. Can you help us?' His voice was polite, but Wasp saw the hybrid's face snap into anger all over again.

'And why would I be able to help you?'

'Well, you're part . . . you know, part . . . Thick,' Bat finished – rather lamely, in Wasp's opinion.

'And because I'm part Thick, I therefore know how to make the music? And because I'm part Thin, I'll easily tell you all those old secrets? Is that what you think? Well, I hate to disappoint you, my dear Thins, but I probably know no more of the art than you do yourselves –' the shaman took a breath '– and I would not be inclined, in any case, to share such secrets,' she concluded bitterly.

Bat's cousin spoke to the other shaman in a calm voice. 'You misunderstand, Skin. We have not come to steal music from the Thicks, or to insult you with assumptions. What we need to speak to you about concerns you, Skin, and it may even explain in part the disappearance of your mentor.'

'Why do you think that he has disappeared?' Skin asked in a sharp tone.

But Bat sighed. 'It is just a feeling. I could be wrong.' Wasp watched as her cousin's quiet words seemed to soothe the shaman. He had a gift, that was certain. His political gifts and his naturally flirtatious nature meant he would have made a good headman, but he had been given to Red Deer at the age of thirteen for training upon the death of his parents.

The hybrid moved her arms down from their defensive posture, and then grudgingly said, 'If you've no explanations, you had better give me better reasons to accompany you.'

'I will,' said Bat, and exhaled deeply with relief.

Skin sunk down to a squat. The morning sun now streamed into the interior, lending a cheerful glow to the faces of the two Thins in front of her, highlighting their sharp cheekbones and jutting chins. Skin didn't feel that cheerful, personally. Although she wasn't embarrassed about being nearly interrupted in the midst of a sex-trance, she wasn't entirely comfortable about the idea of other people watching her (unless it was a given situation, such as the mammoth-kill ceremony from the day before).

Still, the amazing vision of the shell, combined with the explosive climax she had experienced had combined to link her body and mind yet again and her head felt clear, a feeling that ran smoothly through her limbs, all the way out to her toes and fingertips.

Bat walked off to fetch a flat slab of rock from the side of the cave. He returned with it and joined the other two squatting on the dirt. He laid the slab down in front of the two women, and withdrew from his waist-pouch a stick of manganese. Skin knew he was going to try to draw with it, and she tried not to draw her breath in quickly in disapproval: for the Kretchen, the manganese crayons were ritually invested objects, meant for drawing art or decorating bodies, not for casual explanation. It was something they had inherited from the Thicks, she supposed, who she had heard regarded most art as something spiritual. Still, she held her tongue, recognising that the ways of the Thins were not her ways.

'Here,' said Bat slowly and patiently, drawing a thick red line on the stone slab, 'here is where we've travelled from. And here –' he made another coarse streak '– is the great glacier.'

It took Skin only a moment to realise that Bat's picture represented things by familiar objects – and then the onlooker can make them smaller, or bigger, in his or her mind. She knew the great glacier he referred to – she had seen the edge of it only yesterday, before the mammoth had been killed – and she knew where the nearest tribe of Thins lived and, by holding these two pieces of information, she could also tell how much the land had shrunk on to the representation on the pale-grey stone. 'And here,' she said, taking the chalky piece of blood-red manganese herself and drawing a stroke on the rock where she thought her own community was camped, 'here is where the Kretchen live.'

She returned the crayon to Bat, his hand on hers for just a moment.

'That's right,' Bat admitted. 'That's where I met you yesterday.' His face grew strangely pale with anger. 'And here –' he made another mark on the rock some distance between both the Thin and Mixed communities so that a triangle could be drawn between the three points, pressing down so hard on the slate that the crayon cracked and broke in half '– here is where my mentor was found dead.' His eyes were shut tight in grief, and Skin and Wasp exchanged a glance. It had nothing to do with confrontation, but instead a mutual concern.

And then a chill hit Skin, a fear so immense and heavy that she could barely stumble away to the entrance, where she tried to breathe deeply, but failed, and ended up gasping for breath. Not Tooth. This Thin shaman was surely not suggesting that the same fate had befallen Tooth. Not when she still had so much to learn. Not with the way she felt about him: her secret thoughts at night, the way his smile never failed to warm her. Not Tooth. She pulled herself away from Bat and Wasp and went to steady herself near the entrance, forcing herself to smell the different flowers outside: hollyhocks and dandelions, the warm scent of violets and summer grass still crisp from dawn. An insect buzzed by; she heard her own heart pounding quickly but solidly in her chest.

She did not hear Wasp whisper her name the first time, nor immediately was conscious that the woman had placed her fingers gently on Skin's naked shoulder.

When Skin at last turned, in control, the woman said in a low voice, 'We have guessed what it is that disturbs you. Your mentor does not necessarily share the same fate. There is more to Bat's story. Listen.'

Reluctantly, yet at some level touched by the fact that the woman had perceived the cause of her concern, Skin returned to the red-marked slate where Bat still sat. His eyes were no longer shut, but he was staring listlessly ahead at the flat rock, lost in his own feelings. When he eventually noticed that the other two had returned, he picked up half of the broken crayon, and pointed to the three main marks on the rock.

'Here, my mentor was killed,' he said with alarming ease in a numb, lightly casual tone, as if the words now meant nothing to him, 'here is our . . . the Thin summer site, here is the Kretchen encampment and –' he pointed again to the first place, where he said his mentor had been killed '– here a music item was found in her hands.

It looks as if they took her heart and organs and left this music item instead.'

'They're called flutes, not "music items". You should use the correct term.' Skin used a sharp tone, which she immediately regretted.

'Flutes, then. If that's the proper Thick name for them. But maybe you don't know the proper name, being only partly Thick yourself?' Bat gave Skin a sly, not-quite-teasing glance.

'I know enough,' she answered, without a glimmer of a smile. She was not going to give the Thin an opportunity to mock her parentage, no matter how distressed he might be over his mentor's evidently untimely death. Particularly if, as she suspected, he was about to lay the blame for his mentor's murder on the community of Thicks themselves. She did not know what Thins thought of Thicks, but she knew what they thought of hybrids: peculiar, exotic.

'This was what was found.' Reverently, Wasp passed a long white bone to Bat. 'I tried several times to blow in it,' she admitted, 'but so far the sounds are too piercing.'

'Let me see it.' Skin held out her hand and Bat laid the musical instrument in her palm. Her fingers curled instinctively around it; for a moment she relished the sensation of its cold, smooth texture. But then her curiosity took over, and she raised it up so that she could examine it by sight, as well. It was made of two beautiful pieces of bone, and the ivory-like sheen of the polished bone held the same luminosity as an egg-shell; Skin was sure the potential treasures held static inside this flute were as wondrous as those held inside the firm shell of a fresh egg.

There they were, the familiar holes she had all but forgotten; seven uneven spacings all the way up the length of the flute. She rubbed her thumb over the mouthpiece, which was fitted snugly into the rest of the instrument. It had been so long since she had seen one; she wondered whether she would still remember the melodies her grandmother had once taught her to play.

'What kind of animal is it from?' Bat stated the question without emotion – he surely knew the answer already.

Skin looked up with surprise. 'It's wolf, of course. You ought to be able to see that.' And he calls himself an apprentice, she thought, with no small amount of dismay.

'Is it always used to make items . . . flutes?' Again, it was the flat, emotionless tone, as if Bat already knew the answer.

'I wouldn't know.' It was the truth. Skin's grandmother had never discussed the making of the flutes, and Skin's own childhood visits to the Thick encampment had been hurried, fleeting affairs; brief and blurred trips with her grandmother that she only half-remembered making.

Bat started to say something, but Wasp cleared her throat pointedly and interrupted him. 'There were other . . . flutes found in Red Deer's possession, when her hut was examined upon her death – three, to be precise. They were smaller flutes – the bird-bone was so tiny that I doubt you could even make sounds on it.' Her fingers twitched as she spoke, Skin noticed, as if she herself were playing a flute made slowly of air. 'One was of squirrel-bone, one of fox.' She reached out to respectfully stroke the flute that Skin was still holding in a moist, tight grip. 'We do not know why she had this cache. The only ones who know how to make these flutes are Thicks.'

Skin's dark eyes flickered in thought. 'Then you must talk to a Thick.'

'Correct,' said Wasp triumphantly, and Skin felt a surging but entirely controllable impulse to slap the tall

Thin woman. 'And we have. Red Deer did not receive these flutes from either of the known Thick communities, neither the Lekken nor the Ruskers. Their source is a mystery.'

'Come with us, Skin,' Bat said hurriedly, noticing the angry gleam in Skin's eye. 'For Tooth's sake. And for the memory of Red Deer.' Skin could see how it pained him to mention his mentor shaman by name. Bat took a breath and continued: 'Red Deer often spoke of Tooth. She sought his opinion on many matters. You say that you know nothing of the flutes. Yet your master is missing, Skin. And there is another hybrid camp not so far away – the Lekken camp. We want to ask them questions, but without a hybrid with us, we have no chance. Do you want to help us?'

Skin was silent.

'Do you want to help your mentor?'

This time she answered softly. 'Yes.'

Bat bowed his head respectfully.

'Though I'm surprised Red Deer would stoop to seek knowledge from a hybrid,' Skin added in a dry tone. 'Unless the Thin thought she could bed the hybrid, too. I know what you think of us.'

'Why don't you listen to what he's trying to say?' Wasp snapped.

But Bat merely touched his cousin's bare arm and smiled sadly. 'Red Deer wasn't like that. She respected the intelligence of everyone and anything that gave her cause for respect: hybrids, Thicks, Thins, a hare running through the grass, a thoughtful horse, a bird as it makes its last cool flight in the sunset. She thought of Tooth as a valuable ally towards peace. And now Tooth has disappeared.'

'Yes.' The comment was light on Skin's lips, but deep in her body she yearned for Tooth. Puzzling matters like the present situation would have been referred to him, relieving her of responsibility. She was not sure if she could cope without him.

'We do not think Tooth is dead.' Bat broke into Skin's thoughts with a misplaced reassurance, reminding her gloomily of the stark possibilities of the situation. 'But perhaps he is hiding, or has even been stolen away.'

Skin considered what they were asking of her. Both cousins were observing her; she felt embarrassed, rushed; she didn't want it to seem as if she couldn't follow the implications of what they had been telling her; didn't want to enforce their certain bigotry regarding the intelligence of hybrids . . . She knew what it was that she had not realised. 'Do you think Tooth is in danger?'

'Yes.'

Skin thought: what is death? Even a tiger kills quickly, usually, necks crushed between huge jaws. Life might be short, but be it tiger or another human, you could at least assume that the blow would be quick, and that your soul would quickly become just another amongst the other dead animals shining in the firmament. But murder took longer, with more suffering. Murder was different from death.

Skin was suddenly aware that she was still uncovered. This was no bad thing, as she usually felt more confident naked, anyway. She turned towards the stalactite curtain, the long line of stone spikes faintly glowing in the morning light. She felt the sun hot on the back of her neck. A wisp of a spider, its slender legs dark as obsidian, rapidly crawled over one of the hanging pendants of the stalactites and disappeared.

'Is that where you came from?' With her eyes, Skin indicated the space behind the rock formation.

'Yes.' Wasp was watching Skin intently, and Skin had the uncomfortable feeling that she was staring at her lips. 'There is a tunnel there.'

This hardly surprised Skin, but it made her feel quite

uneasy in retrospect to think that she had slept in the pile of furs so near a tunnel from which anything might emerge. This was something she didn't like to do unless it was a cave she knew well herself. There was too much danger from bears, or tigers, or even other people. She was tangibly aware of the stillness between her and the cousins. They were waiting breathlessly for a decision from her, but trying not to show it. She was aware as well of perspiration still damp on her breasts and of the fertile, musky smell coming from between her legs. Outside the cave, a bird called. Everything was waiting. But to Skin there seemed no choice, only surety that she would seek out Tooth wherever she could. But there was no need to let this pair know that. She stroked thoughtfully at the mouthpiece of the flute.

'It's fine,' she said in hardly more than a whisper, 'I mean, of course. We can work together, and we can seek out the makers of this flute, and find the killer of Red Deer, and find my own mentor too, safe and whole.'

Skin did not expect to see both cousins break out into wide-toothed smiles at exactly the same time, but they did, and the effect was magical. One could clearly see at that moment how identical they were, with their matched and radiant smiles, despite the fact that the male seemed far more gentle than the female. Skin abruptly remembered Bat's strangely asexual kiss at the mammoth-kill, how sensitively their lips had met, and how neatly, gently, smoothly their tongues had intertwined: as if they had been seeking out secrets from each other with their mouths. She began to shiver. She was not sure that the cousins had told her the entire story, but it would do for the time being.

Skin carefully handed the flute back to Bat, who seemed adverse to touching it and passed it quickly to his cousin. 'What now?'

'Now we wait,' said Wasp. 'There is one more person

that you will have to meet whom this concerns. A magic-woman whom you do not yet know.'

'From which camp?'

'Are you willing to wait and see, Skin?'

Skin considered this. It made no difference probably, so she supposed she was. She nodded. A general feeling of quiet anticipation fell over the cave. Wasp sat down and settled into the patches of sunlight. Bat, however, drew close to the fire and Skin watched him push and prod at the stones with a stalactite that had fallen from the curtain. He blew at the coals, and they turned momentarily red and hot and vibrant with his breath.

Once she realised that Bat was not planning on conversation, Skin went over to examine the tunnel on the other side of the stalactites. She stood there for some time looking and the other two made no moves to stop her. Eventually she watched the same spider she had seen before spinning at a huge, intricate web and she forgot all about the other two. The spider's creation reminded her very much of the snowflake which she had carved into the young man's chest the day before, and she wondered vaguely how he was faring. When she peered into the crevice, she saw nothing; it occurred to her that the only way that you could see something would be to hold a living, flaming, stick in your hand. Ultimately, she emerged from behind the rock formation and found Bat still preoccupied with the fire. He had found some kindling somewhere in the cave, and was now blowing the coals into tiny tongues of agitated flame, though he had not yet managed to char the thick branches.

Wasp on the other hand was lying on her back in the sun and was completely nude; she did not seem to be aware that the extreme tattoo of six-sided shapes might cause some surprise. She had dragged a large horse pelt over to lie upon, and her eyes were closed. She still held the flute loosely in one hand crossed across her small breasts, and were it not for the fact that she was humming a melody, Skin would have assumed she was asleep.

Skin approached quietly, and sat down near Wasp's head, watching the other woman spin out a tune with her red lips pursed shut, the song buzzing out from her delicate throat. Thins were so spindly, thought Skin – she herself was quite robust. The bones of Thins looked as if they would snap easily, and they had no noses to speak of. Still, there was something attractive about the young woman's hair, all splayed out on the brown horse-hide like the glossy wings of a raven. Her flat brow made it easy to observe the curve of her lashes, as long as her cousin's, and each fine hair of those active eyebrows.

Skin felt puzzled – she had never been particularly attracted to Thins before she had met this enigmatic pair. But she supposed they were not like ordinary Thins – one was an apprentice, after all, and the other – well, she must be a musician of some sort, judging by her interest in the flute. Perhaps a songster, or someone who accompanied her male cousin's shamanic rituals with a drum.

Skin reached out and pressed her fingers against the bone flute. 'Would you like me to show you how to play?' she asked the Thin. Wasp's eyes opened immediately, her humming stilled in her throat.

The cave was full of sunlight now, all the way through the soaring interior. Bat had by now finally coaxed the fire into genuine flame and was busy skewering on to slender stalactites strips of meat and shiny globes of iridescent wild onion that he extracted from one of his many pouches.

Skin reached over and gently took the flute from Wasp, placing the fingers of her right hand over two of the holes and blowing out a shrill note. She then relaxed her lips as she held the vertical flute and let out a much lower tone without once moving her fingers. When she did move them, it was to play a quirky little melody her grandmother had once taught her, a song about waking early on an autumn morning for a walk, and about how the sun shines ice-bright on the brittle grass. She handed the flute back to Wasp.

'You put your fingers here, you see, and the notes go higher when you adjust your fingers like this. And you can make two sounds with no fingers at all, high and low. Here, I'll show you.'

But the Thin woman shook the shaman off, and quickly placed her fingers on the instrument, blowing into it. To Skin's astonishment, Wasp duplicated perfectly the melody which she herself had just played. Skin had no doubt now that the woman was an extremely skilled musician. She listened transfixed as Wasp mutated the little melody, adding extra tones and short pauses where there were none before. And then suddenly the early-morning song was an entirely different tune, one that made Skin now think of cold winter, when life was mainly spent huddling in caves, and how the sun still lit the day, but this time it was snow that shone rather than a thousand tiny blades of dawn grass. The music was beautiful and even Bat stopped his intent cooking to listen to the tune Wasp was producing from the simple bone flute.

For some time Skin sat there on the horsehide, basking in the sun and listening. The Thin's talent was boundless: it seemed that whenever she had mastered one string of melody, it would change, run into something more complex, then more simple, then suddenly reappear as fluidly as a salmon dipping through river water.

At last, though, the scent of the skewered meat pulled Skin towards Bat and she ate a morning meal of well-cooked meat, onions and dark mushrooms, all the while listening to the magic of Wasp's music; she had never met someone who played so well. The meat strips were nicely fire-charred – Skin chewed at them and stared thoughtfully up at the hole in the ceiling where the smoke exited the cave. She felt certain that the smoke sent a message to far away that there were people here, cooking and living. For just an instant she had a fleeting impression of Wasp's music exiting the cave as well, curling and fingering its way out of the ceiling-hole to the outside world, where it would hang there shimmering and vibrating slightly, a silver cloud of vapour eventually drifting away to where other people could hear it, too.

Skin asked Wasp quietly if she wanted something to eat, but Wasp shook her head, eyes still closed, and continued to play, lashes shut, fingers hovering over the holes of the flute. So Skin observed the cave around her to see if there was anything that had previously escaped her notice. There wasn't. She reckoned that this was not a living cave but a temporary one, where people would stay perhaps only three or four nights every cycle of seasons. When she had finished eating the last of the savoury meat, she wiped her hands carefully on the horse-hide and approached Wasp, who was now playing a violent if still beautiful melody on the bone-flute and staring fixedly at the line of stalactites.

'May I try once again?' Skin ventured. Wasp immediately stopped playing, smiled and handed over the bone flute.

Skin's fingers were momentarily nervous on the instrument; she was slightly concerned about how feeble her playing would be in comparison to Wasp. But her confidence increased as she remembered an old Thick hunting melody and, as she lost herself in the vivid jolts of both music and memory, she forgot to worry. She was gratified to realise that Wasp, like all truly gifted artists, was obviously not thinking about Skin's comparatively minor musical gifts: she was listening for new tunes, strands she'd never heard, and incorporating them into her head. No doubt, thought Skin dryly – but with admiration – already twisting and changing the melodies in her own skull. Bat also drew away from the fire and stood closer, listening to Skin play. Skin stopped after a particularly rigorous note sequence for a moment to catch her breath, lowering the flute from her lips. She was about to raise the flute to her mouth once more, when Wasp stopped her.

'Wait.' Slowly, ever so slowly, Wasp ran a finger over Skin's full lips to the sharp, long angle of her left cheekbone, all the way up to the edge of her scalp. Skin trembled, still breathless from the force of her own playing, unsure what to think. She found herself trying to count the hexagons on Wasp's tattooed arm.

She had a good idea of what was on the edge of happening, and she was unsure of whether it was a good or prudent thing.

But instead of moving away, she closed her eyes and felt Wasp moving her talented fingers through the rich mass of Skin's copper-red curls, pulling and stretching at the unpolished glory of Skin's tangled red hair. Skin sighed, and bit her lip, hard. She was well aware of Bat on the periphery of her vision and sensed him moving towards his cousin and herself.

Then Wasp's hand travelled all the way down to Skin's neck and Skin's heart began to thump wildly. She looked over at Bat and his green eyes held hers. They were not as dispassionate as they had been the day before, and his lips hung open: slack, full-lipped, expectant. Skin had not prepared herself for the rush of heat between her legs then – not in the company of two Thins, anyway. As she watched Bat move closer, closer, closer, Skin's insides felt watery and her legs unstable; the lashes of Wasp's green eyes brushed against Skin's lips as Wasp kissed her just on the side of her throat, under her chin where Skin was sure a pulse was beating away like the heartbeat of a tiny creature, just below the fragile membrane of her skin. Then Wasp's kiss turned hot and needy, her tongue seeking Skin's and thrusting, caressing inside Skin's mouth.

'Wait,' said Skin.

'Why?' Wasp's eyes were gleaming with excitement.

Skin wasn't exactly sure. She thought it was because there was something wrong, something different. 'I can't feel it . . .' It was difficult to express herself. 'I can't feel it . . . in my head.'

'In your head?' Wasp looked bemused, if slightly flustered.

With a certain degree of embarrassment, Skin realised that it would be difficult for her to explain that it was quite unusual for her to have sex without the spiritual aspect taking a huge role of importance in the act. Everything that she had ever been taught told her that it was best to combine the two. She had never seen Tooth engage in sex with anyone without the sex act being somehow attached to ritual and the transference of otherworld beasts and spirits.

In fact, now that she thought about it, the reverse was true as well: she found it difficult, if not impossible, to meditate without her body being fully connected to her mind, and the only sure way that she had ever known was through the immediate transport of orgasm. Hadn't she tried just this morning to spiritually connect, and hadn't she found that it was useless when body and mind were divorced? And now these two Thins wanted to have sex for – well, for what? Just for the sake of pleasure itself? The idea unnerved her. She had never pleasured for the pure sake of pleasure alone. She noticed abruptly that Wasp was watching Skin carefully, waiting for her next comment.

Skin's throat was raspy, dry with embarrassment. 'I find it difficult to think of sex without at the same time striving towards a vision.' Her words came out slowly, as she sifted through the thought that she wanted to express.

There was a muffled sound behind her and she realised that it was Bat, trying not to laugh. That infuriated Skin, but she attempted to explain further. 'It seems that not striving towards the spiritual – well, it's just physical then, isn't it? It's like something that the animals do.' As soon as the words were out of her mouth, she regretted them.

This time, neither of the cousins bothered holding in their astonished laughter. It was Wasp, as usual, who spoke first: 'I thought your entire profession involved communing with animals, not putting yourself above them.' Wasp was right, and Skin regretted her words even more, now. She felt ashamed at her lack of awareness, especially in front of a fellow apprentice. She knew in her heart that there were many lessons she had yet to learn, and perhaps the fact that she hadn't learnt them yet meant that Tooth had felt that she was not yet sufficiently prepared.

Wasp's voice was nearly bitter. 'What, do you think your precious mentor Tooth never rutted a pretty girl or boy just because he wanted to? Do you think he never got down and just *screwed* – do you think he never *fucked*?'

'No . . .' Skin's answer was barely a whisper. She had so much to learn. She closed her eyes. She knew in her heart of hearts that humans were animals, too; Tooth had always taught this, yet here she was trying to put one above the other.

Someone cleared their throat.

Skin opened her eyes to find both Wasp and Bat staring at her; Wasp's expression was the more speculative of the two, as if she were pondering Skin and finding her unfathomable. Then she stepped up to Skin and kissed her abruptly on the lips again, while at the same time scooping her hand under Skin's cunt, and leaving it cupped there. Skin squirmed away slightly, but Wasp's grip was fast. The female cousin continued to look Skin straight in the eyes; Skin tried to look away towards Bat, but she couldn't avoid Wasp's gaze.

'You feel lovely,' said Wasp, and she stroked Skin probingly where Skin was still very moist from her previous excitement. Skin's earlier embarrassment made her feel even more uncomfortable. Yet she felt herself going even stickier between her legs now, not wet beyond her wildest dreams, but wet nevertheless. She tried to reach out for some sort of vision, failed and sank back against the wall of the cave. Her legs could no longer properly support her, and she was so wet now, wet and full of heat. She stretched a hand out – she didn't think it was in protest, either – and she felt Bat's own hand then; hot, sweaty with urgency. Skin pulled him towards her and his cousin, and his cool lips sucked at her fingers. His sucking was so intense it embarrassed her: like a greedy, suckling infant. She felt it right in her cunt. Bestial. Animalistic. But this was right, wasn't it? She had to accept her own self as an animal, as well. Meanwhile, Wasp's hands probed down inside her, deeper and deeper. Wasp had her hand splayed right across Skin's cunt, rubbing her hard, two fingers half-inside her.

Skin exploded then, felt like she was going to piss herself, and forced out a stream of clear liquid all over Wasp's hand. It wasn't an orgasm, exactly, but it felt good – a release – and it made her want to get fucked all the more. Wasp stepped back, and Skin touched herself, her fingers rolling all over her stiff clit, over and over and over. Her mouth was dry with arousal, her eyes screwed tight. Two Thins standing watching her and she had no visions in her head at all, unless you counted dirty, heaving flesh and sex: soft tits and erect cocks and tender juicy pussies and soft limbs, her own hair hanging in her face, her breath coming out in quick pants. It felt good, and then it was better than good, fantastic, as she rubbed herself, masturbating hard, her fingers soaked from her own juice. She bit her lips, opened her eyes, and saw them both there. Wasp, panting, her green eyes animal-like with urgency, her whole face flushed; her nipples were erect, dark brown on her smooth long body; her pubic hair was dark and sleek and glistening.

She reminded Skin of a dark otter, and Skin kept Wasp's gaze as she masturbated, pleasure only once causing her eyes to glaze over and not see properly the dark-green depths of Wasp's flashing eyes. Skin felt herself close to coming, sweetness and need rolling over her. Her fingers pressed hard against her wet sex, as she felt how stiff her clit was, how erect, saw how her full, plump breasts jiggled when she looked down. Her body was breaking out in sweat, but the rhythm and movement were right, just perfect, slick and –

'Stop.'

Skin could have killed him.

Bat swiftly pushed his cousin aside and Skin's hand as well, and Skin did not know which was greater: the residue of lust still pumping through her body or the rage she felt at Bat for interrupting. She could feel her almost-orgasm dying away now, and with her veins overstretched first with pleasure and now adrenalin, she felt weak with disappointment – too weak to move or protest, in fact, or else she was sure she would have tried to strangle him.

He was still holding her hand and now he licked off the juice, and Skin could see his white shell necklace and his lips shiny with come, fluid and glittering, as if he had run his tongue over and over their delicate ridges, those soft vertical lines in lips that Skin scarcely ever noticed and oh fuck, she wanted him then despite her anger, wanted him and Wasp too: his cock inside her, spurting out come, or over her, it didn't matter; her own tongue licking along Wasp's hot sweet cunt, feeling Wasp's body begin to shake with need, watching Bat's hips, too, begin to shake involuntarily. She wanted them both.

Now Bat leaned in close to Skin and all Skin's anger was suddenly gone. Her cunt was in near-pain from lust, much worse than it had been before. And she realised now what Bat had done: he had stopped her so that she would feel it all the more later on; she would feel it deep down in her cunt as she felt it now, heat moving upwards through her whole body like a rapid dawn, as even her fingers began to buzz with warmth and lust. She forgave him mentally, gripped his cock with her free hand and slipped his foreskin back and forth, wanking him slowly and purposefully. She felt his cock begin to tighten once she had achieved exactly the right rhythm and she knew that she had hit the point now where everything she would do would be right and feel good for him. He groaned, and this made Skin groan too, so she pumped her hand over him more and more rapidly, a tight circle of fingers and thumb over his hard, pulsing prick. It made her so wet that her cunt twitched, wanting to be touched, but Skin's whole self was intent on wanking Bat, fast. She wanted many things at once: she wanted to fuck; she wanted him to shoot, hard and fast, and faster still. Skin felt Wasp's fingers fumbling at her cunt, and then what had to be another prick being pushed inside her, though of course this could not be true.

Skin looked down and saw what exactly it was that Wasp was forcefully pushing deep and deep again into her pussy. A long, smooth-ended stalactite was now wet with moisture, thick creamy girl-come, and wet with the clear fluid that she was ejaculating as well, over and over, so that rushes of fluid ran down the length of the smooth cool stone in irregular spurts as Skin pumped out come and then frantically, lustfully wanked Bat. His cock was so hard, his eyes screwed tight, he was ready; Skin could have touched him just as lightly with only the tips of her fingers and still she knew that he would come, that's how hard he was, and Wasp just kept pumping her with the makeshift stone phallus, her tattoos rippling as her arms moved, and Skin's heart was thudding, her cunt twitching with hunger for more penetration every time the dildo was pulled away, her clit throbbing as Wasp rubbed at it once again. Skin wanted to suck Bat, wanted to feel his cock stretching out her mouth, on the edges of her throat. She took his bursting prick between her lips, licked once, softly, at its deep-red head, and took him hard into her mouth and began to suck, hard as she could. Almost immediately he came, his come rushing into her throat.

Skin was desperate to swallow it, the sweet tangy taste of him so creamy as she swallowed the whole load, her throat full of liquid sex. It was delicious; she had to have more. She wanked him hard, milking out a few more precious drops and it felt like he was coming again, dryly this time, shuddering as he thrust and thrust his hips against Skin's mouth as she bent her head closer to suck at him and then finally withdrew. Throughout this Skin had been aware of Wasp's work at her sex below, but in order to concentrate on her sucking she had pressed it down, sublimated it.

Now the power of Wasp's fucking came back full force. Skin twisted down on the smooth stalactite, trying to force more of the tool up inside her, and it was always enough and never enough. Bat kissed Skin deeply, his tongue searching out the now-cool semen in her mouth, their mouths pressed wide open against each other, Skin's hand clenched round one of her over-tight nipples.

She felt what had to be Wasp's tongue flicking gently at her clit, and then Wasp straddled Skin there as she fell back against the cave wall and Bat bent over Skin, as well. Skin looked down and saw Wasp's beautiful arse nearly in her face. The deep dark musk of her cunt, the tiny puckered star of her anus, which was shining where the juice had run down in excitement. And Bat continued to kiss Skin, and Wasp continued to flick her tongue so delicately, so lightly between Skin's legs, and moved the heavy tool so deeply inside that the movement was a dull pain that was enormously exciting, an erotic ache. Bat reached his hand out then to rub at his cousin's anal star, and when Wasp began to jerk in pleasure Skin felt herself begin to come, too, and it felt glorious, wonderful to know that she was herself spurting liquid deep into Wasp's mouth, just as Bat had done with Skin herself.

Dizzy with her orgasm, Skin was still aware enough to hear and feel Wasp slurping up her juices, and she felt the pressure of the stone phallus give a little as Wasp released a hand only to bring it quickly to her own clit and juicily rub herself to a climax. Skin felt her clit begin to swell again in Wasp's mouth and Skin came again, her tongue thrusting and sucking at Bat's tongue – like an animal would do, she thought happily. And Skin felt, rather than saw, Bat spray again, all over her breasts and belly and his own cousin's sweet arse. Skin broke the kiss, rubbed her hand in the wetness flowing all across her breasts and then sucked ravenously at her fingers as the last twitches of her orgasm subsided.

Slowly, Skin sunk back against the wall, her arms still round both cousins, and they stayed there for some time, their breath slowing and heartbeats quieting. At some point, Wasp got up and walked away, still humming a snatch of one of the previous melodies she'd been playing, and it wasn't long before Skin could again hear the piercingly sweet melody of the bone flute. Bat soon detached himself as well and at last, with a sigh, Skin too raised herself up, stretching her muscles luxuriously and feeling the languor swim through her veins in a sweet, comfortable ache. She picked up the stalactite and rolled its moist stony weight in her hands and slipped out between the few skins at the entrance.

She didn't know how much time had passed until she looked out through the entrance of the cave and saw that the sun hung already at its highest point in the sky. She stepped out this time, and walked around the curve of the cave to the left, whereupon she saw the trail she had come in on, and a steep incline where the trail picked its way through craggy rocks, many of the rocks taller than she was herself. Her red curls were still matted damp on her broad forehead and the midday breeze felt good all over her body. Skin glanced down at the phallus she still held in her hands. Its smooth surface had been previously polished, she realised – this was not merely an implement that had fallen off the hanging row from the ceiling of the cave. It was still shiny, and Skin rubbed her thumb along the surface, feeling the slick moisture residue.

The colour of the stalactite was dark orange where it was damp and pale orange everywhere else; as she touched it, Skin felt a tiny thrill prickle at the back of her neck and just a spark of insight, a feeling which hinted at the thousands of years that this stalactite would have hung in a dark cave, reaching and dripping towards its twin stalagmite in the cave, drop after drop of careful sediment. She could see it hanging there if she concentrated enough, orange and sparkling and spinning and perfect. She could even see the bats that had flown by it; the animals which had lapped at the pool into which it dripped. She could smell the build-up of guano, which would eventually be burned with a sweetly acidic, dungy scent, smoke creeping haphazardly up to the crystal-topped holes at the top of the cave. Skin smiled to herself: she might not have had her regular ritualised sexual visions, but they weren't entirely gone, yet. As she grinned to herself, rubbing her fingers over the bright stalactite, Skin could hear the cousins talking loudly, though she couldn't make out their exact words. Perhaps it would be more civil to return; they were, after all, going to help her find her master.

Naked and cheerful, she turned back into the cave, swinging her arms, the fingers of her left hand locked firmly around the pale-orange stalactite. 'You've forgotten something, Wasp,' she started to say, and then stopped speaking in astonishment. Both Wasp and Bat were by the stalactite ridge, talking to a being that Skin could only assume had climbed in from the dark tunnel beyond the stalactites.

Skin was looking at the smallest and therefore the most repellent person that she had ever seen, and it filled her with distaste.

Chapter Three

There was a brief, rather terrible silence before anyone spoke. Then this incredibly, repulsively diminutive person – dressed head to toe in wolf skins, a satchel strung across its shoulder, a labret embedded in its lower lip – moved towards Skin with an outstretched hand.

'Skin of the Kretchen hybrids, my name is Wolf, from the Rusker Thicks. I am very pleased to meet you.'

With distaste, Skin realised that this dwarf was Thick and female. Skin also realised that the dwarf was holding out her hideously small hand to touch Skin's cheek in the customary greeting, but Skin tried her best to ignore this. How terrible to think that this ugly misshapen Thick already knew her name and had the audacity to speak to her as if they were equals.

Wasp coughed. Skin turned sharply towards her, nonplussed to see that Wasp's sombre expression had an edge of shame. As well there should be, Skin fumed: presenting her with exactly the type of person hybrids hated most – small, diminished human beings, evidence of misbreeding and fertility mistakes as opposed to interbreeding to make beings stronger, as the hybrids did.

Wasp coughed again, and then said quietly: 'Skin, you are making our guest uneasy with your hesitation.'

Skin felt dull horror begin to curdle in her stomach. Oh spirits, she prayed, my animal sisters and brothers, please don't let this abomination be the person for whom I have spent half a day waiting, albeit pleasurably. She turned towards Bat, seeking out his gaze in near desperation, but his green eyes were lidded, his long thick lashes covering whatever secrets his eyes might reveal as he stared fixedly down at the ground. *Oh please,* thought Skin, but Bat practically echoed his cousin's words –

'Skin, we are waiting for your response. Please do not disappoint us.'

There was absolute silence. Finally, Skin stepped forward and brushed the tip of her right hand against the dwarf's cheek for an eyelash of a moment, then kissed her brow as quickly as she could; the dwarf did the same to her. Skin exhaled as she quickly stepped back, feeling the sensation of tainted flesh tingling horribly at her lips. She closed her eyes, and forced out a lie of a greeting: 'I am pleased to meet you, Sister . . .' Damn, but she had already forgotten the abomination's name.

'Wolf. It is my totem-name. It's always been my nickname, but I received it officially a week before my final shamanic ceremony.'

The dwarf's response was so angry, so quickly abrasive, that Skin's eyes snapped open, and for the first time she looked it directly in the eyes. What she saw, unsurprisingly, was the spitting, angry, grey eyes of a furious Thick dwarf. It was quite disconcerting to see that it obviously felt an equal hatred and repulsion towards Skin herself. Skin quickly looked away and turned towards the other two for confirmation that this ugly, insolent female was indeed the magic-woman they had wanted her to meet. But even as she turned, a fleeting word registered in her mind: *ceremony.* The dwarf had had a *shamanic ceremony*. All spirits, this abomination was a shaman, as well.

'Wolf, too, is a shaman,' Bat confirmed gently.

Skin whirled around. 'I had already realised that,' she said angrily – then immediately regretted her tone as she saw Bat's face. He looked disappointed in her for some reason. Skin took a deep breath. Then it was up to her to speak to the dwarf; Wasp and Bat, it seemed, were not going to explain anything further than preliminary introductions. It was she who was going to have to be polite and mature, she who was going to have to reach past the simple matter of revulsion and tend to the tasks at hand. With dignity, Skin walked over to the furs and retrieved both her robe and her feathered waist-string, before returning to face the dwarf.

'I have been waiting to meet you. What connection do you have to Tooth's disappearance?' She directed the question to the ugly dwarf and made her voice sound light and casual as she re-knotted the leather string round her waist.

'Red Deer was a frequent visitor to my camp,' Wolf said, staring steadily at the hybrid shaman, not answering her question. The midget wasn't giving any ground at all, Skin realised. The Thick shaman ran her tongue thoughtfully over her lower lip. 'I intend to find out the cause of her death.'

Skin felt her whole body tighten with fear. Then she stared accusingly at the cousins. 'But Tooth certainly is still alive.' She heard her voice catch, but snapped her mouth shut. There was no chance that she was going to find herself exposing any weakness of emotion in front of a dwarf.

'We said it is unlikely that he is harmed, Skin.' It was Wasp who responded, in a cool voice. 'It still is unlikely. Yet Red Deer mentioned both the hybrids and the Thicks, and we must find out what that connection is.'

'And you contacted me because Red Deer knew Tooth?'

'That was the primary reason,' admitted Wasp. 'And also, of course, because you – along with Wolf – might know something of the flute. Although I asked Wolf yesterday, already.' It made Skin shudder to think of the shared Thick ancestry between herself and the dwarf . . . shaman. But she had to admit, taking a quick glance at Wolf's blazingly red hair and firm brow, that it was true. She was struck by uncertainty and abruptly felt very tired: she was surrounded by three people, two of them shamans, two of whom she had just had sex with, one of whom she had been brought up to despise on sight, and all three of whom were utter, utter strangers. She longed for the comfort of easy answers, of Tooth's reassuring pat on her shoulder. Her easy unfulfilled attraction to him had grown as predictable as the mental exercises she was supposed to practise as part of her training. But even as she wished for this she could hear Tooth saying, 'No easy answers, Skin. You already know this.' Exhaustion hit her, a blend of fatigue and depression.

She glanced up uncertainly, and was jolted to see that Wolf was still staring at her, but not with complete antagonism this time. With something that looked close to pity or – if Skin had been willing to put a kinder label to it – empathy. It didn't seem possible, but the red-haired dwarf was giving her a rueful smile. Skin looked away and busied herself with removing Tooth's pendant from one of her pouches in order to give herself time to think.

She was aware once again that they were waiting for her to speak; there was complete silence except for the faint rustle of some small cave creatures. Why do they always wait for *my* decision, she thought with frustration, touching the tiger tooth she had hidden away. It was meant to bestow courage. She had hoped to feel a link with the animal, a surge of totem-feeling, but this had not happened. She squared her jaw and looked the dwarf straight in the eye. 'What next?'

The dwarf answered as casually as if Skin had been politely asking her advice the entire time. 'Wasp and Bat have asked me here. We intend to journey to the site of the Lekken hybrids. We will have to journey immediately. I have spent all morning travelling; the day is half-gone, and we have at least a half-day's journey ahead of us. Are you ready?' asked the dwarf, directing the question to the dark-haired cousins. They nodded. Wolf turned back to Skin. The dwarf was, Skin saw, fingering her labret with what looked almost like nervousness. 'Are *you* ready?'

Skin nodded. And she found herself justifying her compliance: they would not miss her back home in the Kretchen group; shamans often took periodic spiritual journeys. Besides, she had to locate Tooth. Wasp and Bat were already bundling up furs and tying them together to carry.

'Here you go.' Wasp threw over a pair of thick, hard rawhide soles to Skin.

'Thank you.' Skin hoped this was not an indication of a particularly rough journey.

Wasp had the bone flute gripped firmly in her hand as if she would never let it go, and the dwarf Wolf was bending quickly to the ground floor to retrieve the orange stalactite where Skin had dropped it in surprise. Skin felt at a loss what to do and embarrassed that a dwarf was holding an instrument that had penetrated her so intimately. She already had her robe and waist-string complete with pouches; Wasp and Bat were carrying enough furs to keep all of them warm, and she had no other personal belongings. She strapped to her feet the shoes with tight leather strings.

But as the last bits of cooked meat were gathered back into Bat's pouches and the four of them were at last, rapidly, heading to the tunnel – with Skin observing with distaste the dwarf's inefficient, rolling walk – Skin began to hear a low rumbling sound, and she noticed the stalactites vibrating.

'Is that another tremor?' she asked sharply, stumbling into the tunnel, with Bat and the dwarf Wolf in front of her and Wasp following up behind.

'It's nothing,' said Bat up in front of her and Skin bit her lip to stop herself from saying more as Wasp shoved her on ahead in the tunnel.

'It might well be,' said Wasp under her breath. 'It means we ought to hurry.' It was completely dark and wet and it stank of bat guano and what Skin was sure was stale human piss. It wasn't long before they had to stoop to continue and finally to crawl, and always there was the same feeling of urgency. But whether they were hurrying towards or from something, Skin was not yet certain. Towards Tooth, she told herself, as her hands and knees were cut by small rocks and her breath came more and more rapidly; and yet still Wasp pushed at her from behind. Towards Tooth's pale, beautiful eyes and his gentle voice.

'Hurry up!' Wasp hissed to Skin at one point, and though the comment made Skin furious, she couldn't catch her breath to answer. Instead, she kept scrabbling on ahead through the damp grit, the only light a dim cloudy phosphorescence on the wet cave wall that did little to cut the blackness of the tunnel. She remembered thinking back in the cave that a torch would be necessary to negotiate this tunnel. Only a suggestion of Bat's leather clothes was visible before her. Worst of all, Skin was heartily ashamed that the dwarf's endurance seemed to be more prolonged than her own. It occurred to Skin that they were crawling upwards, rushing as much as they could on hands and knees. Skin could by now feel a stickiness on both kneecaps and smell the familiar sweet, metallic scent of blood. Her shins were scraped, her hands were aching, and she could swear that somewhere along the way she had lost several pouches off her waist-string. Whatever the reason for this speed, I hope that we are hurrying towards something, rather than away from something, she reasoned, as anyone would be able to trace the scent trail of blood and sweat that we're leaving behind – let alone the noise we're making as we scramble through this tunnel like four overgrown rats. Well, three overgrown rats and one moderately medium-sized one.

'Hurry! You're slowing down!' Wasp was as persistent as ever behind her, but Skin noticed that she made no demand to go in front and Skin was grateful for the apparent kindness. It was clear that Wasp had stayed behind to look after Skin's best interests. So Skin made no bitter reply in return and instead attempted to creep faster, but her hands and knees felt numb. For the first time, she experienced a four-legged affinity with animals that she had never once experienced in any trance or ritual. No matter how she had slathered the red ochre powder, the powder that symbolised beasts, all over her body and tried her best to think like one, she had never come close to anything like this.

The crawl-space was tightening, and now in addition to the stresses of urgency and discomfort, Skin was becoming quickly claustrophobic as the tunnel led ever upwards. Her hands and legs were certainly freely bleeding. She let out a slight whimper and afterwards hoped desperately that the others hadn't heard. Her breath in her chest felt like a long sliver of rock was burrowing its way slowly under her ribs. Skin tried to meditate but, unsurprisingly, it didn't work. She was firmly, irritatingly, stuck within the confines of her physical body and all the trials it now endured. What's the point in being a shaman then, she nearly found herself thinking bitterly. She smiled grimly, knowing well that shamanic powers weren't meant for occasions like these, but sometimes, just sometimes, selfish trances might be quite a sweetener in the shaman business. Her heart was beating so fast it felt like it was going to burst free of its bony, fleshy cage – red, brilliant and still pulsing.

'Please hurry,' pleaded Wasp behind her, yet again. Except, thought Skin, Wasp would probably make me leave my popped-out heart behind on the ground of the tunnel, and admonish me for the delay. Skin made herself speed up, her flesh gritting alarmingly on the sharp rocks adorning the trail. 'That's more like it,' Wasp muttered behind her.

'We're out!' Bat or Wolf gave a shout up ahead, and this gave Skin enough energy to push ahead around a curve in the rock, whereupon she could make out, at last, a spray of reflected daylight up ahead. It made the tunnel slightly lighter and she now could see both Bat and Wolf's heads up in front of her through a dim, eerie suggestion that was not yet genuine illumination. She scrabbled up ahead as suddenly sunlight glared into her eyes and she could smell the rich scent of conifers and fresh air. She blinked as she moved on, her eyes watering from the sudden difference in light.

Finally, she pushed herself out of the small hole that made up the exit, and Wasp did exactly the same behind her.

A huge valley spread out beneath them, and it was then Skin realised that they must have rushed straight through the pinnacle of the mountain itself, for the view here was entirely different, and even Skin, who had once travelled great distances with her grandmother in search of the Thick sites, did not know whether she had previously seen this particular view. There were pine and spruce trees all around them; the small spindly types that grow high up on mountain ranges. The sun was just short of its highest point; it was mid-afternoon and its rays reached and warmed far over the huge valley. From where Skin stood, still panting, she could see glaciers, rivers, steppes, even what appeared to be a canyon.

She took a deep breath of the fresh air and realised that she could make out at least three separate communities from where she stood, evidenced by columns of faraway smoke, one atop a distant mountain. A breeze lifted her hair slightly, cooling the sweat on her neck, and at last she turned to speak with her travelling companions – if that was how she now had to think of them. Fellow searchers, perhaps.

They too, even the dwarf, were staring out over the landscape. If Skin had been willing to credit the dwarf with emotions, then she would have acknowledged that Wolf's eyes were wet, as if she were either upset or particularly moved. But Skin chose to ignore this, and turned her attention instead to the cousins. Bat's hands were round Wasp's waist as she stood behind him. Wasp's cheek pressed against Bat's as they held each other silently.

Skin glanced down at her hands. As she suspected, they were scraped and bloody along with her knees, but not to the extent that she had imagined back in the cave tunnel. 'Where are we?' she asked the cousins softly, almost shyly. They were so engrossed in their own thoughts that they did not respond.

But Wolf answered. 'We are in the Valley of Bones,' said the dwarf, in what Skin thought of as her nasal accent – even though her own grandmother had spoken with the same inflection. 'I believe it is also called the Valley of Skulls.'

This time Skin flinched. This was a name she had heard her whole life: mainly in stories told to the children to warn them not to walk too far away from the camps. She had never suspected that it was actually a real place. Even once she had been given to Tooth for training as a thirteen-year-old child upon the death of her grandmother (she had never known her father and her mother had died in unsuccessful childbirth many years before), even then, from time to time, Tooth would bring up the old tales of the Valley of Skulls. And, now that she thought about it, Tooth had always referred to the valley as a real place, a concrete environment that really existed, and Skin had always put this down to his love of a good yarn and his twinkling resistance to ever admit that he was telling her a tall tale. 'If you persist with all your questioning, young apprentice,' he would say, 'then you, too, will end up in the Valley of Skulls, wearing human teeth for necklaces, so crazy with fear that your eyes will pop from their sockets and hang from strings of flesh, and you'll have to go around with only your feet and the ground to see all day long.' And Skin would shriek with frightened delight and try to make him promise her that the Valley of Skulls was not a real place. But he never would. And now here she was.

Casting a quick look back and seeing that Wasp and Bat were still dreamily holding each other, Skin forced herself to ask Wolf in a friendly, conversational tone, 'Is it true what the old stories say?'

'Which old stories?'

'The ones they used to tell about the Valley of Skulls, where people would wear necklaces of –' But Skin never got a chance to finish her question, because at that moment there was a huge roar and a rumble, and then it seemed as if the earth itself was being rent apart. It's a rockslide, thought Skin, not another earthquake, and as she thought this she was thrown up in the air, and she told herself that this was it now, her time had come, and she gave herself over to all the animal spirits that accompanied her. Even as she did this, as she was cast painfully against rocks and dirt and dust was forced in a gritty drink down her throat, it occurred to her sadly in this moment before death that she had still not been allied with an animal totem, as all other shamans and apprentices were – the right vision had simply never appeared – and this filled her with a violent sorrow as before her eyes she watched the ground burst out beneath Wasp and Bat, tearing them apart. Then the reverberation increased, and Skin herself was rolling, being shoved down the mountainside in a wave of uprooted trees, stones, grit, rocks, dirt and dust, so much dust. Then there was only pain, and dust in Skin's eyes, throat and nose. And then there was only dust.

The pile of rocks and rubble seemed immovable. Skin was weighted down; her whole self as heavy as dense rock. She did not care if she lived and for the moment it seemed easier just to lie there bleeding and let everything outside her dim away. She would not ache or grieve; eventually her body would seep away and rot richly into the rocks and become as insubstantial as ash. It went against everything that Skin thought she believed: that all things contained spirit. But it was easier to lie still than to twitch with pain. She did not try to calm her thoughts with meditation, either: there was no way anyone would be able to concentrate on Tooth's many-in-one in this condition. She could not even tell if her eyes were open or closed. She imagined a film of dust settling on the whites of her open eyes, just as ice does to streams – thin crisp transparent shells over moving water, just as snow solidifies in horizontal sharp layers over white soft mush. She would die here.

Then there was a noise, and Skin blinked, and her envisioned peaceful, still death quickly disappeared and both pain and her will to live returned, and she was struggling again, this time pushing a huge weight of rocks off her chest, her whole body livid with pain. Skin sat up, breathless, into an environment of piled cliffside, rocks and bushes with their roots in the air. The afternoon sun was still blazing hot. She stood up carefully and, though she was aching badly, it was immediately apparent that she had no broken bones.

'Skin.'

Skin turned. It was the dwarf Wolf who had spoken. Her ivory labret was scratched, Skin saw, and there was an abundance of earth and dust in Wolf's red hair, turning it nearly as grey as her wolf hides. Skin put her hand to her own auburn braid, and realised that in some ways they probably looked quite similar at that particular moment.

'Skin.' Wolf motioned Skin closer to where she herself sat, the sunlight highlighting the layer of dust on her arms. Skin limped over. Her mind had not started working properly yet, and though there were elements that she knew were wrong with this desolate environment of rubble and hot sun, it was not until that moment that she realised both Wasp and Bat were missing – or indeed even remembered the fact of their existence at all.

'Where are they?' Skin whispered as she reached Wolf. The dwarf too was unhurt, though she was sitting still with an alarming serenity of shock, stirring her fingers through the dirt. There was a twig caught in the mass of her dirty hair, and Skin found herself removing it before it occurred to her that she was actually in near proximity to a misbreeder. She threw the stick away with a flick of her hand.

'They are below; I saw them fall,' Wolf whispered equally softly, her voice uneven and shaking. She pointed several arm-lengths away from where they stooped, and when Skin looked she saw that she and the dwarf were not at the foot of a hill, as she had numbly supposed, but rather on a plateau half-way down the mountainside. She crawled to the edge and was overcome with vertigo. There below – much, much, further below – she could see a stream that ran off the mountain into the distance and a second heap of rubble, this time truly at the foot of the great hill. And as she looked, her eyes burning and tearing with dust and sunglare, she could make out the dark forms of two figures. One was moving, she saw with relief, although the other figure was lying inert on the rock-studded ground. She could not see who was in motion, Wasp or Bat, but the moving figure seemed to be pulling at something, and Skin realised that the prone and still figure was stuck, embedded in a half-grave of earth and rock. It was clear that they required assistance.

'Wolf,' Skin said, 'we must make our way down. They need immediate help.' Her own voice sounded questioning, frightened, and she realised that she was speaking to Wolf as if she were an equal, asking for advice and reassurance.

Wolf gave Skin a quick, rueful grin. 'You must help me first, in that case.' Skin saw then that Wolf's left foot was wedged under a great stone, bigger than half of Wolf's body, and that Wolf had silently, uncomplainingly, been digging herself out – not stirring patterns in the dirt, as Skin had thought. Wolf would have eventually succeeded, too, Skin saw, but she could speed up matters. Skin pushed back the rock, which was as heavy as water, and it moved quickly and easily with the leverage she attained from her height and vantage point.

'I would have managed myself after some point,' said the dwarf, rather than thanking Skin.

Skin was silent for a moment. 'I know,' she said finally. She checked Wolf's foot quickly for breaks or open wounds but, like Skin, Wolf seemed only bruised and shaken, not truly hurt. Wolf took a step and hobbled at first around the small plateau. But her gait became sure again, and she hurried over to the edge of the plateau.

'The incline to our right is less steep,' Wolf said. 'If we are careful, we can make it down, I think.'

Skin looked down over the edge herself. Far below

she could still see the two figures. The previously moving one had now stopped as well, and was a crumpled-up dark dot near the vertical line of the other.

Wolf and Skin exchanged a strangely sympathetic glance and moved to the right side of the plateau, after Wolf grabbed her small satchel that had been trapped underneath her body. It was still necessary to progress gingerly, but they went over the outline of the small flat overhang they stood on, Wolf first and Skin following, and began to make their way carefully down the mountain. They moved as quickly as they dared, and more than once Skin's foot slipped and the small avalanche of unearthed rocks she sent tumbling down the side filled her with horror and the too-recent memory of what they had only just experienced themselves.

At first Skin tried to keep an eye on the cousins below, watching for movement and life, but after the third time she did this and her foot slipped and vertigo seamlessly folded over her like a terrible, dizzying cape, she instead turned her attention to her balance and descent and no longer glanced below. Wolf was always several steps in front of her, and Skin remembered how much more surefooted than herself she had been in the cave tunnel. Wolf was as sturdy and determined as a goat; Skin wondered why she had always been told that misbreeders such as Wolf were said to be less efficient, weak and frail. Skin had to admit that so far on this day Wolf had proved herself to be far more efficient than Skin was herself.

'Oh no,' Wolf muttered. To herself, Skin presumed, because she didn't appear to be much interested in holding any conversations. Skin carefully looked down towards where Wolf's eyes were fixed. They had only a short distance down left, and it was now clear that it was Wasp who lay on the ground with Bat huddled beside her. Skin could hear Bat sobbing and a chill struck her; her throat felt like it was going to close up.

It seemed unlikely that Bat would collapse into tears while there was still hope – everything he had evidenced earlier made him seem dependable, logical; he was an experienced apprentice. Surely if there was something to be done concerning Wasp, he would be doing it. The sun was getting in Skin's eyes now, and the glaze of light made it difficult to see during this last ominous leg of their decent.

But by the time Wolf and Skin reached the bottom of the mountainside, it was obvious to them both that Wasp was dead and Bat was not to be consoled.

I hardly know these people, thought Skin, as she poked at the coals of their meagre fire. I am here with a bereaved and grieving Thin, and a misbreed to top things off, and yet I hardly know them. It seemed scarcely possible that she had set off on such an odd journey in the first place, scrambled through the middle of a mountain and had witnessed a death, all in less than two days. All for what? Skin wondered, bending in and blowing gently on the coals so that they and the twigs she had placed on them bloomed once more into flame. Was it really, she asked herself, only so that she could seek out Tooth? Regardless of what Bat and Wasp had told her, she had little doubt that the distinguished shaman would reappear at the Kretchen camp within several days. And she would feel the old inevitable pull towards him, as well. No, if she were honest with herself, there had been something else that had driven her into this situation. Something within herself, some question that hadn't been defined – or answered. Perhaps – it was a new thought for Skin – she would stop worrying over why she was here in this place right now, and instead see what transpired and what developed. Despite the tragedy, despite her own whirling insecurity, it somehow seemed right that she should be here. She would not, she resolved, spend any more time worrying about why she *was* here. She would accept it, and she would learn from it. This thought lightened, only slightly, her melancholy. Wasp: a woman she had known for half a day – in some ways intimately, in some ways as a complete stranger. She knew as well that her reflectiveness was a technique to push back her grief over Wasp's death. An apprentice was trained to be aware of her feelings, and Skin was no exception. But it didn't mean she had any easier a time dealing with them.

She went over to Wolf, who was kneeling over Bat's slumbering form. 'Is he all right?'

'He's gone to sleep at last. It's good; he was exhausted.'

Wasp's body was several paces away. Skin and Wolf had done their best to cleanse her body, cupping their hands full of water from the nearby stream. It was the same stream that had coursed down from the hill and they had drunk from it before they had rinsed away the dust and blood on Wasp's flesh, smoothed the grime away from her tattoo. Gestures such as these were easy, methodical, ritualistic, and Wolf and Skin did not allow themselves to dwell on the fact that it was Wasp whose cold and damaged frame they were washing. But when they had finished, it was too clearly the dark-haired musician laid out before them: her hair curling in inky waves around her pale face, her thick lashes shielding her now-vacant green eyes. The eyes were left open in death, as they should be, so that the dead would go awake into the afterworld. One couldn't see, when she lay like this, the deep injury to her mid-section that had caused her death. Even her lips still curved into a smirk; her fingers were tensed and curled. It looked as if she were ready to place her digits on a new, more challenging flute than the one she had played before. Skin's eyes had filled at the thought, and she had turned away so that Wolf could not see such weakness in a hybrid.

But a snuffling sound had confirmed that Wolf, too, was affected, and they had both wept quietly as they completed their ministrations. By the time they had finished, the sun had nearly set and the first sparkling smudges of evening stars were beginning to appear. And if she and Wolf had attempted to stifle their tears, Bat had wept the entire time until his voice was hoarse and broken. Then he had continued to weep silently, crouched into a little ball, rocking back and forth. Around that point Skin and Wolf, with a bit of foresight, had hurriedly begun to build the night's fire and break thick branches off the uprooted trees that had made the fall along with Wasp and fared no better. Under Wolf's direction and Skin's strength, they had dragged three entire large trees over before they had decided that this would be enough for the night. It was finally when the fire had been leaping and smoking high into the darkening sky that Bat had slumped into sleep and Skin had carried him gently to the hearth so that he could rest by its warmth. He had been surprisingly light and limp and if he woke up while she had moved him, he had given no sign.

Now both Skin and Wolf sat warming their toes while the evening deepened. The two of them chewed thoughtfully on some dried meat in near silence, speaking only when it was necessary to break off another branch into the fire. Skin shivered, listening to the fire crackle and watching its sparks burst up into the night. She and Wolf had hoped to burn Wasp's body before night-time with due ceremony – in the hybrid fashion, as it happened, burning the body in open fires. But, as they had not been able to discuss this with Bat, they had resolved to wait until morning. Still, it was considered dangerous to sleep next to a dead body out in the open with no shelter; Tooth had always told Skin that it was not the scent of blood that drew the bears and wolves and tigers, it was the scent of death itself. Skin did not know if this was true.

For several hours into the night they ruminated like this, their limbs slowly stiffening with cold and conversation kept to a minimum. This relieved Skin: although she was slowly growing used to being in close proximity to a dwarf, she did not feel comfortable having to converse with her. It was unlikely that they had much in common anyway. As she sat there, fruitlessly attempting to massage her hands into warmth, Skin found her thoughts endlessly repeating the climb and then the fall itself. It seemed even then that Wasp had known that they must hurry; that something terrible was to befall them. Skin felt for just an instant guilty that she had not hurried enough when Wasp had repeatedly urged her to do so. But then Skin reasoned that the rockslide probably would have happened anyway, and she knew that this was the truth, and also knew that she would feel no future guilt. Still, how curious it was that Wasp had sensed the disaster from the first rumblings deep in the tunnel. That reminded Skin of something Tooth had once told her.

'Wolf –' it felt so strange to address a misbred Thick by a totem-name, but Skin resolved to be aloof yet polite '– I was once told that when the earth shakes once, that other shakes will often follow. Perhaps this was what happened today. Perhaps this was what caused the rockslide.'

Wolf's face was sombre in the flickering firelight. 'I have also been told this. Yet I am not old enough to remember the last great quakes; it was in the time of my parents, several cycles before I was born.' With a start, Skin realised that she and the dwarf must be close in age. It was odd to think of having shared the same seasons with this over-short Thick, to think that they would both have been able to recall, for example, the period when for three winters there was no snow at all.

She peered closer at Wolf. The dwarf's face was grooved with lines around her mouth and eyes, but these – Skin conceded – could just as well be from laughter as from age.

'How old is Bat?' Skin asked abruptly.

Wolf's face shifted imperceptibly, and then she let a gentle smile shape her lips, her labret protruding as she did so. 'He too would not have remembered the quakes. Nor would Wasp have done so,' she added quietly, as if in afterthought. They both went silent again, and it seemed to Skin that in the cold blue night there was nothing but the roaring, spitting fire and their stilted conversation. They were vulnerable, too, she thought, still crouched near the side of the mountain – vulnerable if the mountain were once again to vomit its purge of earth and dust. The truth of the matter was that they were only two figures, one slight and one even slighter, cowering against the red light and heat while the entire unknown night stalked outside. Visible to predators. Unprotected in the event of new rockslides or earthquakes. Exposed to . . . Skin shuddered and pulled the fur of her cape close around her shoulders. She didn't know what they might be exposed to: the demons of Tooth's old stories, for all she knew. Skin stood up and stretched, checking to ensure that Bat still slept soundly. As soon as she stepped away from the fire, her teeth began to chatter, so she walked to where Bat lay to make sure that he was warm enough. But he appeared to be resting peacefully and strangely his flesh was warm to the touch, so Skin returned to the fire and Wolf's quiet company.

But Wolf had also risen to her feet and was staring out into the night. Skin had no idea why the shaman was attempting to do this, as the glare of the flames made the eye blind to almost anything outside the near circumference of the fire itself. 'What is it?' she asked the Thick uncertainly.

Wolf motioned for Skin to be silent and Skin felt fear begin to claw its way into her stomach. She was suddenly aware that the hair on her body was erect, like the mane of the great toothed tiger before it attacks. Perhaps it too is afraid, she thought inappropriately, as she began to listen to the night. She remembered suddenly her promise from the initiation rite to thank that specific animal – and she did so, but quickly.

At first she heard nothing except for the hiss and crackle of burning wood and the rapid, solid beat of her own heart. Then, as she watched Wolf's expression change to fear and felt then the same horror herself, Skin heard a long, drawn-out wail. It could have been a night-bird, she reasoned, or even a child crying for a parent, she thought irrationally. Maybe mating tigers. But she had heard all possible variations of all these sounds, and knew it was none of these. The wail came again, far off in the distance, and then Skin knew it for what it was: the unearthly, distinctive sound of a flute. But there was no melody to it; the very sound made her shiver. 'Wolf!' she whispered, needing some kind of human confirmation, even if it was only the partially human confirmation of a misbreeder. 'Is it a flute? Is that what we're hearing?'

But Wolf did not answer and instead moved quickly back to the fire and with great personal effort tugged the second of the great trees into the flames. Skin could see how she got her totem: she really was as secretive and strong, and somehow as courageous, as the animal whose hides she wore. Now there was only one of the trees remaining of those they had previously dragged over, the largest of the three. The shadow cast by the small shaman from the fire-source was nearly four times larger than Wolf herself, a long dark shade that wavered as fluidly as the white-orange flames that crackled up anew around the raw fuel. Then Wolf, as Skin had done, walked over to where Bat slept, although Skin did see her look once in the direction where Wasp's body lay. From the warmth of the fire, Skin watched Wolf bend down once to Bat and lay her hand across his flat Thin brow. Skin wrapped the fur around her even tighter. She did not like sitting alone by the fire on this frightening night, even if Wolf was only several paces away.

When Wolf returned to the fire, her demeanour was somewhat calmer than it had been while she had listened to those distant, eerie flutes.

'Shouldn't we wake him or move him in closer to the fire?' asked Skin. She did not like the idea of any of the three of them being separated. She blinked and swallowed hard. She also did not want to think about Wasp's body lying there cold and stiff. Wasp, who in the short time Skin had known her had been as lively and spirited as Skin liked to think she was herself.

'No,' Wolf answered. 'I think we should let him rest it out in peace for a while. He has a slight fever, but he should be sleeping easier now.'

'Why?'

Skin was sure that Wolf looked affronted, though the idea of a hybrid affronting a misbreed seemed too preposterous for thought. 'Because I felt it in his skin,' Wolf snapped. 'And while he slept I gave him a poultice of herbs to breathe in, which should calm his dreams and bring a temporary peace to his grief. At least in sleep.'

'Oh.' Of course, the dwarf was a full shaman. Healing – even for a misbreeder – required a great deal of skill, patience and memorisation and she was not very good at it herself, yet. She looked away uncomfortably. She had never been as skilled at herb-picking as Tooth had wished for her to be and had often found the necessary rote memorisation frankly tedious. She found herself vaguely irritated by the thought that a misbreed of her own age already had earned the right to call herself shaman, while Skin – and Bat, too, for that matter – still had to make do with the title of apprentice. 'When did you become a full shaman?' she asked, merely to be polite.

Even in the flickering firelight Wolf's grey eyes seemed to glare right through her own. 'Last winter. Even though I am slight, I was considered worthy, you see – Thicks do not share your own people's prejudices about the "misbred". And as you've obviously got a portion of Thick blood yourself, it's a pity a little bit of the tolerance hasn't worn off as well.'

Skin was astounded. She had made every effort to be gracious to the little wretch of a misbreeder and had disguised her discomfort at every point. She might as well have been bluntly rude right from the start, if this was how her politeness was regarded. She sniffed and turned away. Unfortunately, she turned right into the channel of smoke that skimmed the air above the fire in varying directions, and found herself coughing violently, her eyes stinging. She choked on the smoke for quite some time, and when she finally recovered she gave Wolf an indignant look. Some healer she was, not even attempting to aid her betters when they choked!

They resumed their uneasy, uncomfortable truce of near silence and sat there while the fire slowly etched away at the huge tree, the burn creeping further and further up its still-green, damp branches, transforming the pale wood to lurid bloody coals and then finally to dark hot charcoal. Skin found herself poking half-heartedly at old coals with a spare stick, as she tried to avoid Wolf's eyes. As she did so, she heard again a crunching, moving sound. Only this time, the sounds were all around them: surrounding the campfire, over where Bat slept, even over where Wasp herself still lay. Fear shot up Skin's neck and she felt her bladder weaken. She couldn't move, but her eyes met Wolf's. This time, the dwarf was every bit as scared as she was herself, and Skin could see that she had no plan of defence, either.

At that very moment there was a shout. Skin tried for the second time that day to organise her thoughts before death, but failed for a second time as well. It's all very well being told to order yourself spiritually, she thought rapidly, but it matters very little when all you want to do is save your skin. She looked in terror at Wolf, who had jumped to her feet and now stood paralysed, uncertain where to run or what to do. Without thinking much about it, Skin stepped towards Wolf and clasped the shaman to her. Their arms went round each other, Wolf's head nestled tight against Skin's abdomen, and they stood there in complete terror, eyes closed. Skin knew that if she were to die, at least she would die clutching at something she knew, however distasteful that thing might be to her in different circumstances. The fear overcame all that, and Skin grabbed Wolf's heat to her, her fingers sinking sharply into the dwarf's flesh as she did so, and Wolf did likewise, and they screamed and screamed and screamed into the dark night.

'Quiet!' It was a low male voice, and Skin opened one eye to see Bat standing there before them, staring with half-crazed eyes at the two of them clutched together and yelling for dear life. He was unsteady, his legs obviously unstable, and with some embarrassment Skin hurriedly detached herself from the dwarf's embrace. She noted that Wolf seemed equally eager to rid herself of Skin's comfort now that the danger revealed itself to be merely Bat, dishevelled and disturbed as he presently seemed. Suddenly, Skin found herself so relieved that it was only Bat who disturbed them that she didn't really care who thought her a coward. Even if it was Wolf. She stole a sidelong glance at the dwarf, who at the same time was also gauging Skin's reaction. When their gazes met out of the corner of their eyes, the strangest thing yet happened: they burst out in laughter. Suddenly, all that Skin could picture was the ludicrous sight of the two of them plastered together in extreme fear, screeching and yelling their fright into the darkness.

Bat stared at them uncomprehendingly. Unfortunately, this had the effect of making them laugh all the more, so that eyes grew wet and stomachs began to hurt. Skin found herself slapping the Thick's small flat back as if they were old friends, and when their eyes chanced to meet once more, they went off into gales of laughter all over again. When finally their chortles began to die away, and they wiped at their eyes still giggling slightly, Bat was still staring coldly at them.

'I'm sorry, Bat,' Skin said. 'I realise that this is no happy time, and –'

His stare was as cold as the night outside the fire's heat. Skin watched him try to shape his face into anger and fail. Unsure what to do, she reached out her hand and took his. He made no move to tighten his fingers; they simply hung there, limp cold digits. He said nothing, staring helplessly at both Wolf and Skin. With a flash of insight, Skin realised that his irritation was not personal. He was overcome; he could not even muster the strength for wrath. 'She's still there,' he said quietly, turning to Wolf. 'She's still there, and even when I sleep I can hear her calling to me.'

Skin watched how Wolf stared at Bat for a long moment. The dwarf's expression, while grave, was not unkind. 'Come,' she said finally. She reached for his other hand and took it. 'If my herbs did not help you sleep, perhaps there is something that will.' Wolf's gaze flickered over to the direction in which Wasp lay, and Skin then understood what it was that they needed to do. With Wolf and Skin each holding one of Bat's hands, the three of them walked slowly out of the wake of the fire and over to where Wasp's body lay in peaceful repose, the smirk ever-present, her sable hair disturbingly evocative as it fell in dark waves over the planes of her smooth, pale face.

The three of them carried her body back to the fire, and Bat, along with Skin, bore the weight of most of his cousin's body while Wolf cradled her head. Skin marked that Bat's eyes were still numb – even if now his body could, to some extent, function as an awake man's body should. He was silent, avoiding both speech and eye contact.

'Is it because we laughed?' Skin found herself whispering to Wolf, as they began to drag the last tree over to the fire. But Wolf reassured Skin that Bat's anger was not that specific. The three of them managed finally to shove the trunk of the uprooted oak into the centre of the fire, where at first smoke rose tremulously and no flames caught at all. But at last the great log started to catch fire in the hot coals and then it crumbled away, the hearth looming tall and spitting into the deep night. Bat helped to place his cousin's body on the flames, and then stepped back to watch her flesh be slowly consumed. Wolf began to chant in a low tone, and Skin too began a private ceremonial farewell. She sang a quiet song – Skin rather liked to sing – and tried to remember some of the tunes that Wasp had played. She emptied out several dust-covered pouches, finding a mass of broken clam shells. Remembering the morning in the cave – which now seemed so very long ago – she deposited the bits of iridescent shell into the fire, the mass of sharp broken pieces falling like dangerous, shiny snowflakes into the fire. They littered Wasp's burning body, looking momentarily like the crumbs from a hundred miniature abalone shells.

As Skin undertook this act, she shut her eyes and said good-bye to Wasp, the maker of music, and wondered what form Wasp's spirit now would take – bird or tiger, chattering insect or hard stone. She would look for Wasp on her spirit journeys and hoped that she would be skilled enough to recognise the musician's presence when next she did appear. When Skin concentrated on these things, she found it easy to ignore the smell of the black-haired woman's cooking flesh, a scent not too dissimilar to boar. She doubted whether the Thick would find it disconcerting at all. Funeral fires were sacred and meditations such as these eliminated the more mundane interpretations of such odours, thought Skin. The fire had a purging, religious significance.

There were a few shells still left sticking to Skin's palm. The red-haired hybrid crunched these too, sprinkled them over Wasp and stepped back. Wolf was still intoning a prayer, her small stocky body rocking back and forth as she concentrated, her hair falling over her furrowed brow as she grimaced with the strength of whatever vision she was experiencing. The scent of charring flesh became overwhelming, but Skin resolved not to find it distressing. She sensed movement behind her, and glanced quickly at Bat. He walked up to the fire again and Skin could see only the black silhouette of his body as he stood juxtaposed again the bright harsh flames. This dark shadow now reached into his pocket and drew out a long thin object. Skin tried to catch Wolf's eye in alarm, but the dwarf was still deep in a trance: eyes screwed shut, lips murmuring loudly. Skin could feel the heat of the fire from where she stood transfixed, could smell the dark, rich scent of burning flesh. He would not dispose of it, she thought.

But Bat did, though first he lifted the flute to his lips and Skin thought then that he was going to attempt a melody. She could almost feel his breath as it blew out of his lips, past the flute and towards her. But Bat did not touch his lips to the instrument and lowered it. He stretched his hand quickly into the flames, so quickly that Skin had no time to move to stop him, and placed the flute on his cousin's chest. Wasp's body had still not been consumed and the white bone flute on her chest was momentarily illuminated before Bat jumped back, screaming with pain.

Then Skin did move – she ran to Bat and near forced, half-carried, him to the stream where she plunged his arms into the cold glacial water, far out of the scope and light of the fire. He was sobbing and cursing, but it was necessary for Skin to lead him quickly back to the fire in order to see what damage had been done to his arm. Fortunately, due to his speed as he deposited the sacrificial gift of the flute, he was not harmed at all – only shaken. As was Skin, who had witnessed his action, and Wolf, whose trance had been broken by sudden sharp screams. The three said nothing to each other, but stood there watching the flames until at last Wasp was gone and the moon was much higher in the sky. Throughout this Bat seemed more like himself again and perhaps, thought Skin, this cathartic, violent good-bye was what he really needed in order to stop Wasp's voice calling to his grief-stricken mind even while he slept.

Then Wolf offered her arms to Bat and held him as they both lay down and eventually fell asleep, exhausted, while Skin kept watch until at last she dozed before the flames, as well.

At some point in the night Skin woke up. It was still pitch black and she experienced the same disorientation that she had had upon waking in the cave. When she remembered where she was and whom she was with, she listened for the sound of breathing. She could hear Wolf's light snores some distance away, and Skin tried to listen for Bat as well. She heard nothing. And then she did hear his breath: very close to her.

She was grabbed, and a hand was over her mouth, before she could scream. It *was* Bat; Skin wondered whether he had gone mad with grief. She had no time to consider this further, for he thrust his other hand down her cleavage, rough and abrasive against her breasts. She felt danger and lust spike up from her cunt. Her throat went dry; her heart started to pound. He had frightened her, but now it was mainly rage that she felt.

His hand was still over her lips, tight, too tight. She could smell the dirty sweat on him and his arousal. She was aroused too, squirming against his body. Bat seemed like a different person; this was not the slow lust he had exhibited from the cave of the night before – this was something separate and nastier. His hand squeezed her breasts together; her rib-cage felt too tight to breathe. Skin's pussy was wet.

Neither of them spoke.

He ran his hands over her breasts and abdomen, under her robe: impersonal, detached. It was too dark to see his expression. He pulled and twisted on her nipples, moulding them into cones, rubbing them into hard points. Skin hissed at him underneath his palm, then tried unsuccessfully to bite him.

'Bitch!' He swore and grabbed his hand away. The underside of his hand was smeared with her saliva. They stared at each other: she still couldn't see the entirety of his expression, but now she could see his eyes. They were fire-filled. Mad.

'I wouldn't get in the custom of waking me like that, if you value your flesh,' Skin said in a low voice. She was so angry that her head was pounding; it felt as if it were going to explode from the pressure. Her breath was ragged; her chest heaving as she tried to steady herself.

Bat seemed crazy. He was still looking at her; his eyes had turned cold and glinting in the firelight. It was unnerving. Then he rubbed his hand hard across her nose and mouth. She could smell her own spit. Her hand went out to slap him, but he caught it just as quickly. 'You want me.' He clutched her close and hissed the words in her ear. 'You're wet already. I can smell it.'

I could scream now, thought Skin. I could wake up Wolf and stop this if I wanted to. But she could smell herself, too.

She smelled of pussy and rage and sweat: musky, itching, venomous, sweet. Like a wolf-bitch on heat. She was shaking with fury and need. He was still staring at her. His eyes were moving over her body and it felt more like a scrape than a caress.

Though it felt good.

He still stared. They both held their breath. The night ticked on: the fire crackled, the coals smouldered, the stars were dazzling, Wolf snored and turned over in her sleep.

Skin grabbed Bat round the neck and they began to wrestle. It wasn't exactly violent, but it was the next thing to it. As they puffed out their exertion in the chilly air, their bodies began to slide against each other from sweat. Bat seemed desperate, full of lust. And still Wolf slept. The dark-haired Thin tackled Skin to the ground. It was combat and it felt good, and Skin tightened her fingers round Bat's slim waist, tried to lift him. She was pushing him off her with strength she didn't know she had, and he fell backward. He cursed under his breath and she faced him, legs apart, hands wide and stepped towards him, pushing, throwing him immediately off balance. She pinned him to the ground, her hands holding his arms down. For a moment he struggled, but then his head bucked up and his lips caught hers in a kiss. His tongue was vulgar and exciting in her mouth. He was still thrashing about, trying to free himself, but despite the resistance of his kicking and fighting, he could not immediately break free from her strong arms. They tongue-kissed with hearts beating fast, both breathless. Skin relished the feeling of Bat's lithe body underneath hers, her breasts pressed tight against his chest and his cock stiff beneath the reindeer skin he wore, pressing hard and solid against her own groin.

Bat reached behind Skin's neck and took hold of her red hair, wrapping it tightly round his fist. He pulled her towards him. She moved down on him, her scalp in pain and her cunt wet and hot and needy for him. And when she closed her eyes, she felt his gentle kiss on each row of lashes.

This was the moment he had been waiting for. He threw her off, reversed their positions and she was thrust down to the ground by him, slammed to her knees, his hand still tight in her hair – but even as he did this she was grabbing him too, pulling him down with her so that he stumbled down against her. Behind her, she fumbled blindly for his cock, groping for his stiffness, and when she found it and ran her hands over his prick, he grunted with desire. She felt lust all the way from her scalp where his hands tightened to the dampness between her legs. Behind her back, she wanked him, her hand sliding effortlessly over the dry hot column of his sex. She ran her hand over its tip and felt the moistness that had pooled there. He groaned again, cursing, and then released her hair at last. He pushed back her robe over her waist rapidly, exposing her quivering arse and plump thighs as he did so. *Now*, Skin willed him, do it now. Her palms were flat on the ground as she knelt there in the night.

He was sniffing at her crotch, grunting as he slathered his face in her juices. His tongue was rough and bestial before he moved away and left Skin exposed, dripping with need. Then his cock was in her cunt. He pounded into her from behind as she squatted there, thrust her back and forth like she was any other animal he could fuck, his filthy glorious prick wet from her juice, back and forth. Skin felt like a sow as the wild boar takes her: voiceless, trembling with need. She wasn't even able to groan her pleasure as his cock sank between her arse cheeks. She felt his pubic hair bristling her sex lips. His hair would be wet now too, she thought, wet from her own juice. He pumped into her, ramming hard, his hand pulling on her hair, tight, painfully. At last she began to moan a guttural low song – a rhythmic tune that had no words, just a tune that varied whenever his cock hit her hard inside at the peak of each thrust. She wanted this fuck. She wanted it. He had his hand on her backbone now, pushing her down to the ground. She was tasting dirt, face pressed down tight to the ground. Her lip was bleeding and she could taste blood too. Her cunt was crammed full of him; she felt like she was burning up, on fire from his thick cock.

He fucked her and fucked her, slow and thick and hard until they were both grunting with lust and he came inside her. Though the night was black, in the air there was the scent of spunk and juice and their sweat and wet grass.

He withdrew and his come ran down her thighs; he shoved his face to her pussy and licked at her while he fingered her cunt, licked until she came too, her head spinning, still kneeling, her pleasure like a thick liquid that surged through her limbs, making her whole body shudder and shake as orgasm overtook her senses.

They lay there breathing hard and reeking of sex as Wolf continued to sleep. And it was then that Bat got up and moved away, and then lay down next to the dwarf, curling back into her.

Skin found that she was no longer angry – neither at the sudden need that had inspired him to wake her nor his sudden retreat back to Wolf's sleeping body: she felt only pure exhilaration. She wrapped the edges of her cloak around her in a makeshift tent so that the cold air did not intrude and so that her own breath could warm her body. It took her some time to relax enough to fall asleep again, but when she did it was a heavy sleep indeed.

When she woke again it could not have been much later, for the sky was still completely dark and the fire itself had not yet burned itself completely down. Wolf and Bat were still entwined and sleeping by the fire, their hair mixed in layers of glimmering auburn and wavy obsidian-black against the dirt. It was not they who had woken Skin, but she had a very specific feeling that there was some reason that she had been roused, perhaps some sound which had disturbed her. She closed her eyes and pulled her cape around her, trying to listen. Somewhere, far off in the distance, there was a faint noise, and then Skin heard the familiar and horrible sound of the strange flute music, only it was closer this time, very close and right outside the campfire.

'Wolf! Bat!' Skin whispered urgently, reaching out to shake them awake in alarm – but in alarm they started to scream, piercing the air; all around the three of them was screeching noise and fire, so much fire. Panicked, Skin had jumped to her feet, followed immediately by Wolf. The dwarf already had her knife in her hand as she looked rapidly around them, her eyes desperately searching out a source to the flute music and light. Even Bat had risen groggily to his feet in the midst of this cacophony.

'What is it, Wolf?' Skin cried. She had no weapon other than the ceremonial tooth she had used at the naming-ceremony.

'The Valley of Bones,' Skin thought she heard Wolf say, as the dwarf lapsed back into a dialectal Thick word for the valley itself. Wolf was too panicked and desperate to offer Skin any comfort at all – certainly no clarification – and the sounds were getting louder all around them. Painfully loud, tremulous flute music, as loud as if a giant played a flute; their own screeching, high-pitched screams. And flames, terrible flames all around them, as if the entire mountain were on fire.

'What??!' Skin's voice trying to rise above the other sounds surrounding them. 'What is it, Wolf? What is happening?' She could not hear the dwarf's answer, although she did see Wolf's mouth open in response.

But Skin had already figured it out anyway – these were the demons Tooth had always warned her about. They were not stories after all. They were real.

The screaming all around them did not stop, but Skin was unsure whether it was Wolf, Bat or herself emitting the noise; as yet they could see nothing. Worse, there was something deep inside Skin that was strongly convinced that this was what had killed Wasp, too – a horror that wasn't possible to name or see. Wasp had known something was about to happen to her, Skin was convinced of this. It hit some primeval, horrible surge of terror deep within her.

'We've got to do something!' Wolf shouted above the din. Yes, thought Skin, but what? The danger around them was getting louder and there was a new sound, too: it sounded like the trumpeting bay of the woolly mammoth – it occurred to Skin that she was probably going quite mad. But Wolf reacted differently – she cocked her head and tried to listen, gripping Skin's bare arm as she did so. Through the line of fires – were they torches? – Skin could make out a cloud of dust through the night. 'We have to run,' Wolf yelled into Skin's ear. 'Hurry! We have to leave the fire and run.'

Skin looked desperately around her, but as she still wore her caped robe and waist-string and shoes, there was nothing else to take with her. Her heart pounding, she saw that Wolf now seemed to be shouting probably the same thing to Bat. Despite his numbness he appeared to understand, for he nodded and Wolf turned back to Skin. Everywhere there was smoke; the world was made up of smoke and fire and terrible noise, and Skin's eyes watered from the gritty fumes even as she read Wolf's lips, which formed a single word: *now*.

In the split-second before they rushed from the fire, Skin had turned her head to ensure that Bat was coming, too. And perhaps her eyes had fooled her, but it looked as if Bat were holding two black-charred bones that he could only have plucked from the fire. Skin had the briefest impression that one was the flute itself. As the three of them ran away from their fire and towards the line of torches, a chill shook its way through Skin, working itself into a solidified thought: there was a possibility that it was Bat himself who was the murderous flutemaker. His behaviour was certainly irrational.

But then they were running, dashing past the line of torches, and although afterwards Skin could not swear that she had *seen* the demons at this particular point, she certainly *felt* their hot and rancid breath as she and the other two pushed ahead, blinded by the dust, all three holding hands with Bat stumbling in the middle.

The more they pushed forward past the row of lights, the more the dust cleared, but their distance from the bonfire meant that it was again difficult to see into the dark, deep night. The trumpeting sound was even louder and then Skin immediately understood why. Before them was a herd of mammoths – it was difficult to see how many were snorting and stamping in the dark, but Skin had the impression of dozens of massive, moving shapes. She could smell their wild scent. Yet here too the flute music began again, and Wolf clawed at Skin's arm.

'Climb up!'

'What?' Skin couldn't have heard properly. But the wicked music was growing louder and Skin saw that once again the line of torches was coming towards them. And this time she knew she would be able to swear later that she had seen their famed black- and red-striped fringes of hair and teeth winking and shimmering around throats where no human teeth should surely be.

One of the beasts kneeled directly in front of them; Wolf was stupidly leaning into the great animal. It looked as if she were tickling it between its hind legs. And though the light was bad, Skin thought she saw its trunk undulating like an obese wrinkled snake, and the yellow-white flash of its heavy tusks. But really, Skin was moving so quickly that she found herself obeying Wolf once again. She lifted Wolf up first and then climbed up herself before leaning over and giving her hand to hoist up Bat. To her surprise, the pachyderm stood still, heavily docile as she mounted it. But then the great beast began to move in the frightening night, and then they were riding, riding quickly, Skin's nose plunged deep into the wickedly pungent musk of the mammoth, her fingers gripped tightly into its long dark-brown hair, damp with oil secreted from the glands atop its head, and in her eyes a horrible, sinister vision flashing: people wearing human teeth, necklaces of human teeth, flutes of human bone. She knew she would see the demons if she looked up and opened her eyes: terrible demons with deformed eyes, demons with red and black hair and over-wide smiles; toothless gums and all their teeth strung around their necks in ropes and ropes of human teeth, white and glowing. She couldn't look up; she knew they'd be there, riding alongside and laughing, no, now they were singing – no, worse, now it was a melody, a flute melody played on a bone, wicked and piercing and beautiful, just like Wasp's music had been.

Skin buried her head deep into the pelt and tried to will away the vision. They had stolen Wasp's music, and now they were jubilant with it. The mammoth thundered on; it was completely dark now. Wolf and Bat were also still with her, still clinging on to the pelt of the mammoth. Tooth had taught her that all spirituality was good and eventually peaceful, but she thought that this type of demon spirituality was not good. It was living, yes, and vibrant, but it was not good. It was this thing that she had been unwilling to touch as an apprentice with Tooth: the part of her that meant she had to kill for food or to protect herself. She had always figured that the offerings she made excused her actions and she realised that this was still the truth, but what she hadn't admitted to herself was the glee that comes with killing, the surge of power from conquest – the pure enjoyment of blood and power for the sake of it alone. These may have been, she thought, the elements that Tooth had mentioned that she was sorely lacking in. And these figures that were still riding alongside the mammoth, cackling and wild, they were part of her, too.

She couldn't bear to think about it. She buried her head further into the rich brown shaggy hair. She could hear its great thumping heart. Wind whistled over her bare arms, and she could still hear the click-clicking of their rattling teeth necklaces.

'Skin.'

It rattled still. She couldn't bear it.

'Skin.' It was Wolf, who was clicking her fingers to get Skin's attention. The mammoth had quieted, was no longer moving at all. 'Skin, we must get off. Please help me down, and then help Bat.'

Skin turned around. Bat was still there, but his eyes were dull with shock and Skin didn't need to speak to him to know that he could not at the moment answer either her or Wolf. The dwarf was right. The two of them would have to get off the mammoth, and quickly, and then help Bat, for it was suddenly clear to Skin that there was no way he was going to be able to help himself.

They tumbled down off the mammoth and on to the wet sedge grass. As Skin buried her head gratefully in the moist dank vegetation, there was once again the sensation of rumbling earth. Skin caught her breath, but this time there was no earthquake, just the vibrating sound of the mammoth herd, retreating further and further away.

Chapter Four

Despite the season the night was wintry, permeating the three sleeping figures with a chill that was close to polar as they slept through the remainder of the night. Because of the frost and because of the temperature, they slept fitfully.

Wolf woke up just before sunrise.

Daybreak always reached the mountains first, stealing over the peaks with a languid glow. It rapidly turned streaming white and overbright, piercing the eyes of any animal that turned to gaze towards dawn. The valley was next to be ignited. Often, like on this morning, it was shot through with sunlight: the boulders of the lit terrain slipped up through the soft grass of the hillside. The landscape was dotted with a range of rough grey rocks and fringed with high beargrass, a species of vegetation that was half living, half rotting throughout the entire summer, and one could see for a great distance – up to the bordering mountains and across the plains to the stony foothills. Here the beargrass was deep and compact. The sweet, rotten scent of damp old grass becoming mulch bordered on a stench as the plant fibres decayed into the soil. From this soil, coarse rocks bulged – lead-coloured, craggy and scabrous under a tender film of moss. Morning rushed in quickly, and with it a warmth that thawed the ache of Wolf's cold bones, which were still unyielding from sleep. She looked at the hybrid, who slept soundly. And then she looked at Bat.

It was heartbreaking to see him like this: vulnerable. Perhaps at last she could say something to him – somehow let him know how she felt – but she found that she could not. Bat, clutching his two stolen bones to his body under his cloak as he slept. She pitied him, and now was not the time to reveal the depth of her caring.

He had fallen asleep immediately once he had been helped off the mammoth. In fact, they all had: Bat dreaming, no doubt, of his cousin; the bigoted hybrid dreaming probably of her own selfish, tidy rituals where nothing ever went wrong and all was in its proper cosmic place; and Wolf, of course, dreaming of paintings that disappeared upon waking, as impermanent as ever.

The diminutive shaman blew on her hands to warm them, rubbed them until they were ruddy with friction. The valley was still bitingly cold. The ground cracked with frost; it would be some time before it would loosen with warmth and some time before she too would feel the solar heat. Wolf wondered why they had not all cuddled together for warmth, as was the norm for travellers when sleeping in the open. But there were odd barriers between the three of them. And of course the day before had been weirdly gruesome. And though she had held Bat last night, nothing was the norm lately, so it was understandable that sleeping arrangements should follow this pattern. It was important to be close to Bat, to hold and comfort him. But everything was so strange these days, and she did not know how to talk to him, let alone communicate by touch alone. It had taken her several years to overcome her distaste for his relationship with his cousin, but once she had accepted it, she supported it, for Wolf had been very fond of Wasp and saw how happy she made Bat.

Bat was beautiful even when ravaged by grief: his sleeping face full of tension, his eyes trembling violently under his heavy lids. Skin lay near him, her copper braid having unravelled into a fire of colour every bit as brilliant as the fires of last night. She was breathing shallowly; Wolf knew she would wake soon. So Wolf took the opportunity to properly observe her. The hybrid was tall – but then, most adults were usually taller than Wolf – and voluptuous, bordering on stocky. She was moderately attractive, Wolf admitted grudgingly to herself. At least Bat and Wasp found her so. Skin had the remnants of green colour scratched on to both cheeks, evidence that she had performed a naming rite recently. If the ways of the hybrids were in any way similar to those of the Thicks, then Skin would once have had two curving, thick-painted streaks of green paint traced from each ear to either side of her mouth. But Wolf did not know if the hybrids had the same traditions. Some of them looked very like Thicks: powerful, strong, red-haired. And some of them looked more like Thins, with darker hair and frail bodies, and perhaps only a hint of a protruding browridge and the slightest auburn tinge in their curls to indicate a shared ancestry.

They were a strange people. Despised and by turns exploited by Thins and bewildering the Thicks, they had separated into little islands of communities, keeping to themselves. Wolf knew for a fact that there was a community not too far from here. She did not know their specific traditions, but she did know that hybrids were obsessed by heritage and breeding. Something to do with their religion, Wolf thought. Each birth was an accomplishment, as it was said to be difficult for them to breed: large-skulled Neanderthal heads emerging from narrow Thin pelvises often meant birthing trouble. Each birth was considered an improvement, a step towards something better. And though hybrids valued difference, they did not value difference that they considered to be weakness. They bred for improvement, each generation intended to be stronger, more clever, more stalwart than the preceding. They did not value Wolf. They did not value any trait that hinted at weakness, even though Wolf was sure that she was stronger through regular exercise and sheer determination than most of the Mixers that she had ever met. At least, this obsession with improved breeding was the best explanation Wolf could find for their consistent hatred. They were a strange people.

The hybrid called Skin was no exception. Wolf had observed her fighting her distaste every time they spoke together. It was only in the midst of fright and fear last night that Wolf for the first time saw Skin relax in her presence. And after that, things went too fast for Wolf to gauge whether Skin had changed, or whether her behaviour had only momentarily lapsed into friendliness. And yet, Wolf thought, taking a gentler and more fair second appraisal, she was beautiful as she lay there, her long limbs stretched out brown and taut in the morning sunlight. Beautiful. But not as beautiful as Bat.

He stirred first. Wolf's whole being warmed to see that his eyes were clear of the cloudy shield that trauma had caused. He would still grieve, of course, but he would not die of it, as Wolf knew some had done. This was also true: many times she had herself suffered pangs at Bat's indifference to herself. Yet she knew she could not die of it. Bat stretched, and Wolf watched him under her lids. He was slender: Wolf could count his ribs under that delicious pale layer of his skin. His complexion was clear, and the muscles in his abdomen shifted with his stretch, twisting his navel into a deep, unattainable indentation, as unattainable to Wolf as any other, more private, aperture of his: his sweet red mouth, or the darkened tender skin between those elegant, sculptured buttocks. He might not have been eating well lately, but it was obvious from the healthily luminous texture of his skin that he had done so in the not-so-distant past. Wolf wanted him so much suddenly that all she could feel was the wanting itself. And though she was very pleased by the sight of his lovely lithe body it pained her, too: as trim and moulded as a young tawny horse, shaking that head with its gorgeous glossy black hair, unaware of the spell that his body created for Wolf.

Unaware, still, at this early hour of his sun-darkened arms and of where the tan disappeared into pale, vulnerable flesh. Unaware of his morning erection. Unaware of these things. Wolf, however, was very aware of them.

Her response to Bat's beauty prodded at her even now, in the midst of her personal grief over Wasp, a woman she had slowly grown to respect. Her flesh tingled at the mere thought of touching him, despite the tragedy and despite their midnight escape from unmentionable things. Despite Bat's own kind indifference towards Wolf in particular and the devastating sorrow that would hit and overwhelm him before he took another two breaths and remembered the events of yesterday and what dreams had allowed him to forget, she desired him. She wanted him. She could never have him.

Bat yawned, extended his limbs gingerly out to his sides. His eyes were unfocussed, but they were clear with intent and awareness. 'Good morning,' he whispered, his voice a light growl. It was still husky from weeping. He does not yet remember, thought Wolf.

'Good morning.' She smiled at Bat. He tried to return the smile, but although his lips moved upwards for a moment, he did not exactly achieve what Wolf could ever call a proper grin. Still, it was an attempt. 'How are you?' she continued, and this time pressed some herbs into his hands. 'Take these and chew them for a while. They will soothe your throat.'

'I had terrible dreams, and good ones, too,' Bat began. And it was awful, then, to witness his expression change as it became suddenly, horrifyingly apparent to him that the dreams had been reality, after all. He slumped down on the ground again. His teeth were chattering and Wolf could see that he was trying hard not to cry. She was unsure of whether it would upset him if she took him in her arms and told him to cry all he wanted. Instead, she watched him take control of his features and force out the first nicety he could think of in order to distract himself from the fresh pain: 'What did you dream of, then, Wolf?'

Wolf stared down at the ground and patted him on the shoulder. 'Last night I dreamt of nothing, Bat. Nothing at all.' She pulled him gently to his feet again, and looked down at Skin. 'Come. Let us find some firewood before this lazy apprentice decides to wake up, too.'

He moved stiffly, his muscles still unyielding from the cold. He hoped that if he concentrated on walking, one foot lifting and following the other in a predictable pattern, then the thoughts of falling, of painful sudden death and the memory of the dust – powdery, bitter in his mouth – would not come too readily. But already the images were swirling back: Wasp's dead body, the crackling fire and, strangely, that seemingly endless moment when he and Wasp had stood there looking over the valley, holding each other, so happy. The place where they had made love together for hours only the night before. The breath of a moment before the earth shook and everything changed. How could a moment be so short, and yet be so crystal-clear when one looked back and saw it in its unambiguous perfection, right before the world came crashing down in that torrent of grime and anguish? One foot after the other, following Wolf's barely discernible indentations in the grass.

Wolf was chattering nervously. 'I don't know exactly where we are,' she admitted, 'but if you look over there –' she pointed behind them, back over their shoulders in the distance '– you'll see the mountain from where we came. That means that the Lekken camp should be somewhere close to here.' She snapped her mouth shut and stole a glance at him, trying to gauge whether the reference to the mountain upset him. He pretended to ignore her slip, but inwardly he felt the pain of Wasp's death once again. He was aware that this was something he was going to have to get used to: an open sore of a wound that would make him wince whenever it was jostled until at last, if he were lucky, repetition might dull it into a scar instead. He could not believe she was dead. Wonderful, beautiful Wasp. He would never again see her laugh, or even smirk. Or sing, or argue, or open her arms for his embrace.

He decided to talk instead; conversation might distract him. 'How is it,' he began, his voiced somewhat less croaky after swallowing the cool and pungent-tasting herbs Wolf had given him to chew, 'that you knew how to calm and then ride the mammoths? I thought that skill was an ancient myth to amuse children. Or at best a skill long forgotten.'

Wolf looked at him. 'I was told by my mentor Falcon, and have practised it only once before. He told me how shortly before his death.'

'And the demons? The ones that rode alongside the mammoths, playing that awful music?'

'You saw them, too?' Her face tightened. 'I was not sure if you would remember, after all that happened to you yesterday, or even if you saw them. It is as I told Wasp several days ago, before I journeyed to your cave to meet your hybrid: I still cannot talk of these occurrences, or explain what I know of them to you until I know more myself. It is something I must think further on –' she took a breath '– I will inform you of any conclusions I might draw. Look!' She stopped short, pointing on up ahead, through the tall sheathes of grass. 'There is the Lekken camp. They really are the only ones who dare to live in the valley itself.'

Bat shielded his eyes in the morning sun and looked. 'We should go and wake up Skin.'

'Yes. A hybrid is going to come in handy when it comes to negotiating our approach to this settlement. And –' she looked at Bat with some urgency '– I am nearly sure that we can trust her.'

Bat nodded. 'But not yet.'

Skin approached the camp slowly with the others, her eyes alight for new details that would explain their flight and rescue from the horrifying apparitions. But easy solutions were not forthcoming. The other two had said nothing when they woke her, just that they wanted her to look at something. Bat in particular gave no indication that he remembered their sudden fuck in the middle of the night. And Skin did not think he was faking his nonchalance: he genuinely did not seem to recall the incident. He had probably been crazed with grief. She had heard of such things happening before. She resolved not to mention it to Bat ever again. It might just serve to upset him further.

What she saw, when they led her forth, was an abandoned camp: mammoth bones strung together in a dome of a shelter, bound with sinew. The sinew and skeletal supports themselves had been coated with a foul-tasting tincture to ward off hungry canines and even larger predators. She had never before seen dwellings like these. It was most likely a Thin encampment. The effect in the early morning light was eerie; it was entirely silent. Shadows curved along the sides of the blue-stained bones and the mammoth hide stretched over frames that were warped in places from the now-dissipating dew. Along with Bat and Wolf, Skin listened for the scratching of scavenger dogs, but heard nothing. Then she took a closer look at the structures, and blinked in surprise.

She was familiar with two different types of shelters: those of the Thicks, and those of the hybrids. She saw that this camp, like the Kretchen camp, employed both Thin and Thick methods. Like the camp of her own people there was a litter of discarded Mousterian tools, but Thin axes, too. The particular arrangement of the huts themselves into a long vertical progression of hearths was Neanderthal, but the houses were like nothing she had ever seen before.

'This camp is similar to that of my people, the Kretchen, but not identical. I think it can only be a hybrid camp.'

Wolf nodded. 'That was what we thought.'

But Tooth had never told Skin of this encampment, so near to her own community's summer dwelling-place on the other side of the mountain.

'Hello! Is anyone there?' she called out, and was ready to call again when there was no answer when an angry look from Wolf stopped her.

'It's not wise,' said the dwarf, 'to enter a new camp with such bravado, even one you assume will be kindly disposed towards strangers.'

Well, she would say that, thought Skin. The dwarf was probably nervous about the hybrids' well-known distaste of misbreeders such as dwarves. No wonder they went back to wake her up before beginning their investigation. But Wolf had straightened the canine hides she wore on her body, and was staring at the indigo bones of the huts without fear. And Bat said nothing at all; he had not spoken to Skin at all since he had – albeit gently – shaken her awake. Skin gave out a high whistle, lips pursed, and the thin reedy birdcall produced no response either. She looked over at Wolf, finding herself unexpectantly waiting for the Thick's approval before proceeding. The dwarf nodded tersely.

They reached the first hut and stopped outside it. It seemed that it had been empty of occupants for what must have been at least a week now, if Skin was judging correctly from the build-up of blown residue outside its tightly fastened entrance. Wolf ran her small hand over the tense, sprung surface of the tanned hide, and Skin followed her example. The hide was cool to the touch; there was no movement inside. Skin kneeled and twisted apart the rawhide that bound the door, also dyed a deep, lake-coloured blue. Blue: the colour that designated humans in Kretchen lore and art, just as red was linked with animals, insects and birds – everything, in fact, except for humans themselves. Skin's heart began to race. This hut had to have been secured from the outside: there was no way anyone could have tied these knots and still be inside. Unless there were people inside, and someone had tied the knots precisely to keep them there –

But the hut was empty, with only a few bits of detritus – old bits of flint, the odd shard of wood and rawhide, half a tattered sleeping-pelt – to attest to its previous inhabitants. It smelled strongly of guano smoke, a scent that was tolerable in caves but an over-pungent perfume in huts. Skin exhaled in relief – she was not quite sure why she had felt that intense, sudden foreboding. Everything seemed to be all right and generally set to order, as if the hut's owners had left with a fair bit of preparation. There had been no hurried escape. She drew her head back out of the hut, which was too musty to stay sniffing at for any extended time, and Wolf called out to Skin that she had already briefly examined the other ten huts in the encampment. The Thick shaman had obviously grown impatient at one point, for one of the hide entrances had been split with her knife – with similar results. There was no question: the camp of blue mammoth huts was entirely empty. Abandoned.

Bat was still standing outside the vertical line of tents, staring at the trampled grass at his feet, where the effect of occupancy had beaten the beargrass into submission. Skin considered calling him to assist them in their investigation, if only to try to engage the depressed Thin, when Wolf's shout echoed across the camp.

'Skin! Come quickly!'

The hybrid apprentice took off at a run, and came to a halt in front of the largest tent, which also happened to be the one that Wolf had ripped open with her knife.

'I cut it,' the dwarf shaman admitted rather shamefacedly, 'because I had the strangest feeling that there was something inside that I had to let out. But when I opened the hide, I realised that it too was empty, like the others. You saw that, didn't you, Skin? You saw that it was empty.' Skin nodded, perplexed. 'But then I had to come back and check again; I don't know – it felt like there was something drawing me back to the hut, something I've never felt before.' Skin was rather surprised that the dwarf was confiding in her to this extent, almost as if they were friends. But Wolf continued: 'Believe me, I'm well-versed in recognising most kinds of magic. So, I looked inside this hut again, reached my hand up along the inside of the entrance flap – and that's when I found this.' Wolf handed Skin a long thin object that initially appeared to be ivory in the first seconds before Skin's mind comprehended what it actually was. It was a bone flute of two interlocking pieces and seven holes, identical to the one that Wasp and Wolf had previously presented to Skin. 'It was strapped to the inside of the hut.'

Skin stared at Wolf. She couldn't understand anything

that was happening around her; there seemed to be rules and patterns that she couldn't even begin to decipher. For a moment she felt as if not just the flute and huts but everything around her were bone – as solid and inflexible, as equally impenetrable to questions. These bones in her head were shadow-coloured, evening-coloured, the colour of darkened berries and eerie lakewater depths. The same shade as the stains tattooed and painted on to the mammoth structures to dispel wolves and more vicious felines with a venomous flavour. Briefly, Skin too felt a bitter taste on her tongue.

'This flute . . . it's the same as the other one, isn't it?' she asked Wolf, who nodded. But all Skin could think of was that Red Deer went missing, and then was found dead with one of these. And now Tooth was missing, too. Skin shivered. The environment around them seemed more disturbing than ever.

'Let's go back to Bat,' Skin said abruptly. She turned around and walked away from the huts, and Wolf followed close behind. Wolf was nervous; she kept glancing back over her shoulder and was clasping her healing-satchel far too tightly.

They reached Bat and told him the news, but his reaction was minimal. He responded only when Wolf removed the new-found flute from her satchel, and even then it was only to flick his eyes shut again, as if in pain. Skin assumed this was because the flute served to remind him once again of Wasp's death. When Wolf patted him consolingly on the back, he smiled faintly.

'Are we going to continue to seek out who makes these flutes, if the Lekken themselves are not here?' Skin's question was straightforward and she levelled her eyes sternly at Wolf.

'Yes.'

'Together?' Skin added as an afterthought.

Wolf's grey eyes grew wide as she nodded. 'We will have to make our way towards the Thick camp called the Vexlu. Though it is very strange that this camp has been abandoned.' Bat murmured assent.

'Then,' said Skin, 'I suggest we take stock of our supplies and plan our journey.' Her own confidence startled her slightly, but Bat and Wolf did not seem to question her at all as they began to lay out their belongings on the grassy ground. She did not press the matter that she had suspected earlier back in the cave before the accident – that there were secrets being kept from her. She had to assume that they would trust her enough to confide in her, eventually.

Bat's contribution was unsurprising: crimson manganese crayons, ochre, a stone sculpture that looked Kretchen in origin, and one that he placed out for only a moment. There was as well the first bone flute Skin had seen (now charred from the funeral pyre) and something wrapped in the softened skin of a cave-bat – grey and furry, the skin was made of several small hides stitched together with green-dyed sinew. He declined to unwrap the parcel and neither Skin nor Wolf encouraged him, so he took it back beneath his own clothing and brought out instead several pouches of dried mammoth meat, a pendant of an insect trapped in amber and strung on braided rawhide – Wasp's totem, guessed Skin – wild onions and sage bunches and a personal flint kit – as well as several knives: some of obsidian and one of rawhide.

Wolf's inventory, however, was more spectacular. In addition to a wolf tail, a tarp of rabbit skin, a small supply of grains and dried fish, the predictable knives, herbs and poultices as befit a named healing shaman, the latest flute and the pale-orange stalactite which Skin remembered only too well (and with a blush), there were also some surprises: several statuettes that looked like those of the hybrids: round and curved, carved from what looked like ivory, though they were so tarnished and yellow-old with age that it was difficult to tell; a variety of paints and sharp chisels; a collection of at least a dozen different feathers and an odd necklace of what looked like human teeth, painted alternately red and black with manganese and powdered black ash. This last item made Skin shudder, though she tried hard not to let her face reveal her feelings. But the teeth *were* remarkably similar to her visions of the previous night. She had not yet had a chance to compare her nightmarish ride with that of the others, but resolved to do so later. She was unsure of how much was conjecture born of fear and how much had been genuine.

Now it was her turn. She emptied her pouches from her waist-string and dug deep into the pockets of her fur cloak to spew forth their contents. There was not much: owing to her sudden and spontaneous departure with Bat, she had brought no food. But she had many herbs with her, among them the hallucinogens foxglove, datura and cannabis and dried pieces of the fungus *Amanita*. She had one remaining whole mollusc of the type that had so numbed the initiate in the naming ceremony. And lacking an animal totem herself, she had the loaned tiger-incisor from Tooth. But that was all: a few herbs, a shell and an old tooth. But both Bat and Wolf were aware that old teeth were generally much more than they seemed, and by their glances she saw that they accorded the loaned totem a great deal of respect.

'Is that your mentor's?' asked Wolf.

'Yes.' Skin tried unsuccessfully to keep her voice from quavering. 'Yes, it is. He loaned it to me for my first unassisted ceremony.'

'I am sure he is well.' It was the first time Bat had spoken to her since Wasp's accident, and Skin looked at him with some surprise. But he retreated back into himself once again, and added no further reassurances.

'I too am sure,' added Wolf gruffly, and Skin felt an

unexpected gratitude. The sun was bright now, making their various treasures shine brightly; she was suddenly hopeful. They had only a small cache of diverse supplies and she did not know what lay ahead, but she knew that they would find Tooth alive and maybe she would find the answers to her other questions concerning her failures as an apprentice. Maybe she would even find an animal totem. Who knew what the future held? What she did know was that in two days her life had changed, absolutely. She did not want yet to retreat back to the confusion and fright, the lack of confidence she had experienced before the naming ceremony when she marked the snowflake pattern on the boy. Things were beginning to unveil now, she thought, surprised that a simple optimistic comment from a mere dwarf could make her feel so much better.

'Who walks there? Name yourself!' Wolf's voice once again broke through Skin's thoughts. Her head bucked upwards and she saw – it was a wondrous sight – a tall, stately figure walking towards them. Wolf's hand had already retrieved a sharp knife from the grass and she was facing the intruder with bared teeth.

'The shaman Tooth of the Kretchen,' said the stranger.

Skin put a calming hand on the dwarf's arm, took a deep breath and smiled brilliantly. Relief flooded through her, warming her all the way to her fingertips and toes. The feeling of optimism she had just experienced had not been misguided. 'It is Tooth, Wolf. It is my mentor.'

The man came closer, his noble, wise face illuminated by the sunlight, his face as questioning as Skin's own. He was safe and whole. Safe. Safe. Safe.

'Skin.' He hurried up to her and reached to touch her, momentarily holding her face in his hands, grinning like a much younger man. It was him without a doubt, but Skin restrained herself from embracing him or clasping him indecorously. Then he removed his hands, still smiling broadly. 'What brings you here? I thought you would be wholly occupied by the naming ceremony.' He did not seem truly surprised to see her, however, and Skin found this disconcerting.

Skin's thoughts returned rapidly to the cutting, and that beautiful young boy. She could still summon up every stroke her hands had made as they picked out the slender lines of the ice-emblem. 'I *was* occupied,' she said softly, never daring to appear too brash or impudent in front of Tooth, 'but Bat here –' she gestured towards the green-eyed Thin apprentice '– requested that I assist him in seeking out . . . something. And you were nowhere to be found, Tooth. If I have offended by leaving the Kretchen, by leaving our encampment, I apologise, but I worried that you yourself were in danger, and they assured me –'

'Don't fret, Skin. It was fine for you to leave.' Tooth's voice was light, coaxing, comforting, and Skin felt the warmth that came every time she realised that she had pleased – or not inadvertently offended – him. How wonderful to see him again; how relieved she was. She took a step closer to her teacher, a move that she would never consider under normal circumstances, and gingerly touched his rough hands.

'I am pleased to see you whole, Tooth.' She was uncomfortably aware of Bat lurking somewhere in the outer range of her vision, and caught a white flash of what surely couldn't have been the rolling of his eyes. Yet she knew that even if Thins despised hybrids, Bat would wait for his introduction to the shaman. Still, Bat – and Wasp too, before her demise – hadn't seemed like any Thins she had ever met. They did not appear to be bothered by Thicks like Wolf nor hybrids like herself. She pressed hard on Tooth's hand, and was pleasantly surprised when he returned the gesture, his fingers stroking firmly over her own hand. 'They said there were rumours of a shaman-death, Tooth, and this is why I worried –'

'Who said there were rumours?' Tooth enquired mildly, his hands still stroking and dipping between the gaps of Skin's long fingers. 'How good it is to see you, Skin. Come,' he looked around the camp and saw only Wolf and Bat, both of whom were trying to avoid his eyes, 'you must tell me of your journey, and introduce your friends, but first we need a little privacy. In here.' He motioned towards the largest of the tents, the very one which Wolf had cut open and in which she had found the latest flute. Skin was loath to enter – for some reason, it still made her shudder – but Tooth held open the torn flap and beckoned her inside and his expression told her that she had no choice but to obey her master. She wanted to tell him of the flute discovery, but something made her hold her tongue. Instead she watched him pin together the rent halves of the hide panel with an elongated pin of sharp ivory that he extracted smoothly from the inside of his cloak.

When the torn flap was bound, the atmosphere bordered on claustrophobic. Skin looked up to the hut's ceiling; her head just missed the top of it, standing. There, all the bones were tied together to form a near-indestructible knot of ossified material and stretched, tight sinew. Through the smoke-hole at the top, she saw a white bird dip its wings as it flew by in the pale-blue heavens above. When she lowered her head, Tooth was looking at her solemnly, his back bent in order to accommodate the dwelling. 'Who said there were rumours of my death?' he asked her once again.

Skin looked up at him in surprise. 'Bat, and . . . the Thick dwarf called Wolf and . . . Wasp. Wasp, who is now dead. In a rockslide.'

'A strong connection and a strong name: Wolf. This is his – or her – totem?'

'Her totem.' Skin realised she was angry that a simple

dwarf could have an animal totem, whereas one had not yet been attributed to her. At all. There was a faint rustling outside the tent, where Wolf and Bat were doubtless still lingering; Bat, obviously agitated to hear of his cousin's death spoken of so matter-of-factly. But it pleased Skin that the other two were out of Tooth's sight for the moment. Her heart had already been stirred to a fast, certain beat from sheer nervousness and she did not want Bat to embarrass Tooth by bursting into tears of grief while she explained what had happened. It would only complicate her own explanation, and she was already so unsure in the proximity of Tooth. And this particular hut made her skin crawl, especially since Wolf had presented her with the flute. Perhaps this was the local shaman's hut – it made sense; it was the largest – and it was here that he or she had been killed. And now that she thought about it, that flute had looked alarmingly like a human femur. This whole place made her think of human bones, in fact – for to the Kretchen, blue was the colour reserved for humans alone, and red was meant solely for beasts.

'Perhaps then they should have been more concerned for their own well-being than for my own.' Tooth's voice had an unexpected edge, and Skin looked up to see a glint of compassion in his eyes before he lowered his lids. She had forgotten how affected he often was by the pain of others, and wished heartily that she had expressed the details of Wasp's death in a different manner. Some way that would not hurt Tooth with its bluntness.

'They were close?' Tooth raised an eyebrow towards the hut entrance where he must also have sensed that Bat and Wolf were still waiting. He was always more sensitive to others' suffering than his own. Not for the first time, Skin was struck with the elegant, masculine beauty of his face: the sorrowful, light-blue eyes shadowed by his short gold lashes, the faint lines creasing up from his lips and the extreme, defined planes of his forehead, jaw and cheekbones. The hut seemed to cut out all external sound; she could not even hear the other two stirring outside any more. She and Tooth were alone together, private, encapsulated in the enormous hut.

'The Thin and the woman killed were kin. Double cousins; their mothers were sisters and their fathers brothers.' Skin took a measured breath, not wanting to affect her mentor further, but at the same time wanting to reveal to him the facts of the situation. 'I did not know her for long, but she was a most skilled musician. I taught her several tunes on the flute, and she took to it with greater skill than I showed myself. Tooth, this is what I wanted to discuss with you: the others say that –'

'A flute?' Tooth's eyes flickered. 'That is most interesting. How did you say the cousin died?'

'In a rockslide, Tooth. It was terrible –' Skin hesitated, not wanting to sound as exuberant as a child, too ready to relay grotesque details. She wanted to tell him about the flutes; the words were already on her lips, but instead she found herself babbling out the details of her journey. 'We were first in a cave, then journeyed through a long tunnel. And then we stood at the top of the mountain over there – you can see the rockslide at its foot, even from here – and the ground began to shake terrifically, and the two of them fell while the dwarf and I remained on a ledge . . . Oh, Tooth, I am sorry.' She noticed, too late, the wetness at his eyes. A shaman felt everything more than ordinary people, she reminded herself. This was something that she would have to attune herself to more frequently. Her tall mentor stood silent, not weeping exactly, but lost in some lonely, empathetic train of thought. How she yearned, as she always did, to reach out and comfort him, to cradle him like a child and share his pain. This was forbidden; she could not touch her mentor. Even here in this disturbing tent, where no one could see them.

Tooth's eyes were now hooded, his face shutting out any emotion. Once again she had lost her chance to reach out to him. He stood there crouched, a tall tree of a man, but still lonely, and she was a failure of an apprentice, unable to empathise with Bat's loss, unable to comfort her own teacher. There was a strong scent of wildflowers – fireweed – outside the tent. Yet this failed to move her. She was detached from nature. She was as far removed from her spiritual and physical journey as she could be. This, too, she was failing. As she faced her teacher, the mammoth hide covering the tent seemed heavy, oppressive.

Suddenly she didn't care about rules any more. About whether she was permitted to touch Tooth, or not. She put her arm on the sleeve of her teacher's hooded cloak and stepped far closer than she ever had before. And as she pulled her mentor into her embrace, her eyes became as cloudy as the wind-light fireweed cotton itself. She closed her lids on the blinding tears just as her heart began at last to race. A miracle was happening: Tooth pulled her tight into him and she became aware that his heartbeat matched hers in speed.

Through the crack in the hut, Wolf watched the older man. He was certainly beautiful but also quite old, probably somewhere between forty and sixty. He was a shaman, and by the way Skin deferred to him it would have been apparent that he was her mentor even had Wolf not already known this. 'Bat!' whispered Wolf. 'Come here.' Wolf peered in again, trying not to let her slight shadow fall across the opening. She was fascinated by the fact that they stood abnormally close to each other. It was strictly forbidden for mentors to interact intimately with their apprentices. The entire situation had an added twist, Wolf had to admit. She glanced over towards Bat, then curiosity overcame her and despite herself she peered in again. She saw Skin looking up at her mentor's face, and this made Wolf scrutinise Tooth more closely, as well.

His proud nose was dented where it had been broken once or twice in the past. It was apparent, thought Wolf, that the younger hybrid didn't know where else to look. And it was true that his huge, muscled body seemed an impossibility to survey as he discarded his clothes, slowly, elegantly, with a purposefulness of motion not found in younger men. Wolf admired the craftsmanship of the scar carved on his chest, and watched as Skin made herself look at him. Skin's face was already burning, Wolf saw, and this made her swallow hard. Between her thighs she felt disturbingly moist, her body over-sticky. She did not like the hybrid. She did not want the sight of two people who were forbidden to be intimate with each other arouse her. But it did. And Skin was blushing. He was staring at her breasts, and Wolf heard him mutter and then give a low groan, as if he were barely in control. And the thought that he might not be in control made Wolf wet between her legs. She was certain that Skin was equally juicy. And yet Skin, seemingly, could not bring herself to look into his eyes to confirm his gaze. The mentor-apprentice relationship was practically one of kinship. She shouldn't be watching their congress. She shouldn't be getting aroused. But.

Wolf continued her inventory of the shaman's separate parts, heart beating wildly and cheeks reddening. His hands were huge – nearly twice as large as Skin's own hands – leathery, strong. He was crude: a mixed person, with only a blurring of proud Neanderthal traits. Yet his hands were a man's hands, not a boy's. He made Bat seem like a youth. Wolf felt disloyal as much as she felt excited, her body clicking over into a state of sheer arousal: skin tight, palms moist, throat dry, clit beginning to distract her with need. She suppressed the desire to rub herself and kept watching. Skin's eyes were still not raised, but she reached for her mentor's hands, running her fingers over the inside of his palms. This time he sighed, a long heartfelt exhalation. And at last Wolf saw Skin look him in the eyes. He was her mentor, her master. It was forbidden that they desire one another. And yet she wanted him. Wolf understood this sentiment only too well, only it was another that she wanted. It was obvious that Tooth wanted Skin. The joy of reciprocity, unfortunately, was not as familiar a sentiment to Wolf as unfulfilled desire.

They were master and apprentice. They were practically related. Yet Wolf found herself wanting Tooth to fuck Skin, with her all wet and sticky for him; wanted his massive hands squeezing Skin's breasts; wanted to see his lust for her. Wanted to see that handsome, craggy face break into lust. Oh, spirits. Wolf put her hand down on herself and gave in and rubbed, her fingers immediately slippery over the folds between her legs. Wanted to see his eyes glaze over. Wanted to watch him nervously wet his lips with his pink, rough tongue. And then she wanted him to push that tongue in Skin's mouth. Wolf masturbated more and more quickly. A perverse sweetness began to spread out from the point of her clit. It was forbidden, this coupling. He would kiss Skin like he was plundering her, the force of his lust shown by his tongue, scraping against her teeth, half-down her throat. His hands twisting the tips of Skin's nipples into hard, dark little points. His hard cock pressed against her. Not in her yet. Against her. It would be more delicious that way.

And then it didn't matter what they did or didn't do, as Wolf orgasmed on her hand. When she caught her breath, she looked in again. Although they were naked, instead of touching they were speaking. She could not hear their words and reasoned that they could not have heard her, either. Wolf smiled as she walked off to find Bat. All that arousal, and it was obvious that their relationship was a platonic one, anyway.

She was feeling so good that the thought of her mistake amused her.

They had undressed shyly and then talked for a while, discussing only the details of the ceremony over which Skin had presided. Then, exactly as Skin had always hoped in her most private, secret dreams, Tooth motioned her over closer to him. She sat nearby. 'Closer,' he said, his eyes meeting hers. She sat on his lap, squirming with anxiety. Her sex, softened and wet, was almost slipping on to his stiffness; his hard thick cock teasing her furry lips. 'Lie down on your back,' said her mentor. She did so and he proceeded to run his rough hands over the naked length of her body. Her hair was hot from the sun; the light made her squint with its brightness.

Her head was cradled in the soft grass on the floor of the hut, dark green grass that tickled and teased at her back. She sighed, lost in both her fantasies and the reality of the fact that her mentor was touching her, about to fuck her. Even though it was forbidden, it seemed appropriate. More appropriate, in some ways, than it had been with Bat the night before. That was not what agitated her a little bit. No, it was something else. In this weird structure, even as she was caressed by the person she wanted most to caress her, an image kept flickering into her mind at the most inappropriate moments: a bone flute, twisting and twisting in her mind. She pulled away, but then Tooth kissed her and his tongue stroked sensations deep in her mouth; she found herself instead imagining things that they could do together that she had never before let herself imagine doing with Tooth: what if his golden-tanned hand moved down between her legs? What if he were to plunder her arsehole with his beautiful cock: so tight and so satisfying, too.

Skin sighed, and Tooth continued to kiss her deeply. She stroked her hands over his rugged body: his massive chest, his still-firm buttocks. As she bent her head to suckle at his tiny, perfect nipples, beaded and erect, the image of the flute again appeared in her mind's eye. And this time there was a melody, too – the same melody that Wasp had once played; the same melody that the demons had played while she, Wolf and Bat were chased through the night. It took all her will to try to concentrate the flute away, and eventually the picture of it in her head dissolved. But she was aware of a deep sense of danger. It was not in itself untitillating, as little shivers ran all the way up to the nape of her neck and her stomach twisted with nervousness. Her fear made her more passionate for Tooth, and it seemed that he was also being driven by a hunger that he had previously suppressed. Skin looked around the domed interior of the hut, but it seemed blue and uncanny and oppressive all at once – the curving bone supports, the emptiness, the dark green beargrass that she lay on. So she concentrated on her teacher, as her arousal continued to rise despite the odd fear and visions that were coming to her without her willing them to come.

Tooth pinched her clit softly, ran the juice with his fingers all the way up to her navel, put his cock between her lush full breasts and pumped into their valley. That her mentor should be so unashamedly carnal came as a surprise. Skin imagined him spraying over her neck, making it turn flushed and red, and her mouth opened in an O-shape as she groaned. Already the strange visions and forebodings were beginning to vanish. He put his hand between her thighs and rubbed hard, sending a quick pain up through her body. When he removed his hand, it was slick and glittering with lubrication. He wiped it off in her cleavage, moisturising the curves of her breasts. And then Tooth heaved between them, pumping and pumping, his cock already dripping with moisture for her as it slid between her mounds. He stopped, and Skin was aware of him moving away and then moving closer to lick at her pussy. The danger meant nothing. She was so wet for him. He could tell how wet she was for him, and this embarrassed her: he would know that this was how she had felt for him all along, how she had always felt for him. Now he would know; her own juicy sex betraying her only too obviously. She groaned again, running her fingers over his chest, the planes of his muscular abdomen. There was only Tooth. She was so wet for him.

'That's so good, Skin,' he groaned. He seemed more animal than shaman at the moment, as lost to lust as anyone else, licking and drinking from her cunt like a man deprived of liquid for weeks. His very need for her was arousing. He stopped licking her and drew away, motioning for her to turn over and go down on her knees for him like any other animal. Wasp had been right, Skin realised then, it did not bother Tooth at all that this sex was in no way a spiritual experience. And she was not going to let it bother her in the future, either.

Skin did get down on her knees, her entire body trembling, her large breasts dangling as she made herself prone for her mentor and he pushed deep into her from behind. It felt so good; it felt like a burst of lightning rising from the point of arousal all the way up to the sweating back of her neck; it felt so good. She imagined how it felt for him: the feeling running up from his belly all the way to the tip of his prick. She knew what she looked like, she knew how good she looked – her sex like a ripe flower or an opened fruit: soft and rosy, wet and flaming, juicy and hot, its petals beckoning Tooth, urging him to fuck – and then he thrust in her – oh, it felt like she were close to climaxing already, she couldn't help it; he was filling her up, spurting inside her.

She tried to keep her chest lower to the ground, so that her arse was even higher up in the air. At some level she congratulated herself for having overcome the unbidden visions to succumb to this intense pleasuring, even as she reached her hands round and opened up the cheeks of her arse so Tooth could push into her all the more, deep and deeper. Skin began to buck underneath him as his juice spurted inside her, coming out so fast that she could feel it running out between her legs, but no – that was her come, she was dripping wet for him, tightening around his cocklength and then opening again, sighing, pushing up against him. She couldn't get enough, and even though Tooth had just come, it was obvious that he just wanted to keep on pouring into her, his balls at the entrance of the wet hair of her cunt, sex against sex. Then Tooth put his hand underneath both their bodies, so that he was rubbing her to a climax and Skin let him do it, opening her legs wide, selfishly not caring anything more in the world than for her own orgasm, as he fingered and prodded her into wet, extreme pleasure.

But even as she came, her head spinning in orgasm, her sex still spasming, her mouth voicing guttural delight, she saw the flute in her mind once again, rotating in slow, skeletal motion.

She closed her eyes, and clasped Tooth all the closer to her.

They lay there wrapped in each other's arms for enough time for the sun to climb to its highest point. It was not very long. Skin was reluctant to speak – fearing that she would either say the wrong thing, or that she would wake up. She could feel his breath warm on her neck. Never had she been in such close proximity to her mentor. Their lovemaking would have been overheard, no doubt, and Skin wondered how Bat and Wolf would react to the broken taboo. But who could they tell? For the moment, all that mattered was that Tooth himself was alive. He was alive. And even now they held each other.

Eventually, of course, they had to rise, and Skin brushed off the bits of grass sticking to her flesh and to the outer garment of Tooth's hooded cloak, on which they had partially lain. Tooth rose up, again forced to bend in the hut. Although Skin pretended to busy herself with plucking even more of the beargrass off her own cloak, secretly she stole another look at Tooth. A mature man, his body was lanky, though still muscular. His skin was not soft – it was rough from the world – and Skin appreciated this indication that he was not a tender-skinned boy of fifteen: unused to the elements, unpractised. Tooth's abdomen was hard with muscle and the triangular slope of his pelvis was delineated by a soft furrow of hair that curled down to the base of his penis, then spread into a fuzz that covered the large, firm fruits of his testicles. His cock was still semi-erect and moist from their coupling. This last stolen glance made Skin's face turn red, and so she turned her back on her mentor to hide her flushed cheeks. Her legs were still trembling; she still felt shaky.

'Turn around, Skin.' When she did so, Tooth cupped his large rough hands around her face and kissed her deeply, his tongue swimming in her mouth. Skin felt dizzy. He was not made awkward by the contrast between by his nakedness and her own clothed body, but Skin felt self-conscious and drew away. 'There was no shame to what we did,' said Tooth in a serious tone. 'We did only what we felt, and nothing more.'

Of course it was nothing more. How stupid she was to think that it ever could have been anything different. She blinked and turned her head, forced a smile on her lips.

'Look at me.' He was smiling gently, his pale eyes sparkling. Skin looked at the proud beak of his nose, the browridge that attested to his mixed ancestry, the laugh lines crinkling up and narrowing his eyes. His thin, wide mouth opening in a white-toothed grin. He wanted her to be happy. She could be happy for him.

'I know that it was not a shameful thing that we did, Tooth. I know this. Do not worry.'

His smile became even wider. 'Good.' He then retrieved his cloak and leggings rather rapidly, and they emerged blinking into the sunlight.

The other two were not immediately visible, but when Skin walked past the last of the tents she finally spied them sitting in the grass some distance from the encampment. Wolf was braiding Bat's long dark hair into the topknot of a hunter. He lay back in her lap, eyes closed. They both looked settled, well fed and content and seemed mildly annoyed when Skin came up to them, Wolf in particular.

'Been busy?' was all that the dwarf said, however. Skin was startled by the comment but could not detect any insinuation.

'While you have, no doubt, been devouring Bat's dried meat, I've been discussing the events of the last few days with my mentor, Tooth.' There, now she felt more in control, as if she had reasserted herself before this upstart of a misbreeder . . . upstart of a Thick.

'Hmm,' was Wolf's only response, as she continued to untangle the remaining strands of Bat's hair with a rigid comb of toughened rawhide. She silently offered Skin some of the meat, which Skin accepted with as much dignity as she could muster.

'Why are you such a distance from the huts?' Skin took a bite and thought nervously of the necklace of human teeth that had been among Wolf's personal possessions.

'This place makes me nervous. There's something I don't like about it, something wrong. And at any moment now, we're going to stumble along the body of the local shaman, dead like the others.' Wolf paused. 'You're fortunate that your own mentor seems to be in good shape.'

'Would you like to meet him? It is probably best that I introduce you formally.'

Wolf sighed, gently pushed Bat's head off her lap, and got up. Bat yawned sleepily, reaching his hand up to feel his topknot. 'All right,' she said. She looked tired, thought Skin. 'Let's go hear what this precious mentor of yours has to say.' Skin was not entirely comfortable with Wolf's tone – she sounded exasperated – but didn't comment. They walked back to the camp where Tooth was waiting, Bat following some distance behind Wolf and Skin.

Tooth was outside the largest hut, shielding his hands and looking up into the sky, but when Skin followed his example and looked as well there was nothing to be seen, not even a bird. She pretended she was brushing her hair out of her eyes instead and said hurriedly, 'Wolf, of the Rusker Thicks, this is the shaman of the hybrid camp called Kretchen, Tooth. Tooth, this is Wolf.' To Skin's horror, Wolf greeted Tooth as an equal, not even dipping her head in deference. She *was* a shaman, admittedly, but she was a dwarf – a misbreeder – as well. Skin stifled an impulse to grab Wolf and shake some manners into her, though Tooth's only reaction to Wolf's insolence was a tightening of jaw as they exchanged the formal brow kiss and touched hands to cheeks. Skin looked away. She could barely look at her mentor; just the memory of his rough hands moving against her own soft, silky flesh was arousing her.

He was a tolerant man, thought Skin; she knew well his opinions of misbreeders – she had heard them her entire life, after all – but he let the insult pass. When Skin brought forth Bat and introduced him as an apprentice, Bat's behaviour also gave her cause for surprise: he was almost disturbingly ingratiating to Tooth – and Skin knew from everything that she had ever been told that Thins by nature hated hybrids. Though they didn't think much of Thicks, either, she thought, and Bat and Wolf seemed to get on surprisingly well. It was all very confusing. But in the midst of her thoughts, she heard Tooth's low, almost-rumbling voice as he questioned the young man.

'Apprentice? Apprentice to whom?'

Bat was silent for a moment. Finally: 'Sadly, my mentor – Red Deer of the Swathir Thins – passed away of illness a half-moon ago. I had not yet completed my training, and hope to find another unattached Thin shaman with whom I can do so in the future.'

Why is he lying? wondered Skin. His shaman was murdered, or so he said earlier. Or perhaps he was lying to *me*. In which case, on what pretext am I here?

'Is that the case?' answered Tooth in a smooth, sympathetic voice. 'I am sorry. I met Red Deer several times, and she was an excellent shaman and a good woman, as well. A truly diplomatic woman. What illness was it, if I may be so rude as to ask, not wanting to stir up any sadder memories for you?'

Bat was starting to fidget. 'She had swellings on either side of her neck, below her chin, and this persisted for many weeks before she finally succumbed.' He *was* lying to Tooth, Skin realised, and she was sure that Tooth was aware of this, as well – he always knew when she hadn't done the mental exercises he had assigned to her. But why would Bat lie? She looked at Bat: incredibly nervous – Wolf did not look much more at ease, though at least she was not drawing patterns in the dirt with her feet, as Bat was doing. Next to the impressively masculine hybrid shaman, Bat looked frail, almost feminine. Skin sensed that Tooth wanted to question Bat further, but at that moment Wolf spoke up herself.

'Shaman Tooth, with all due respect, do you know anything regarding where the inhabitants of this Lekken community have gone?' Skin was appalled at Wolf's rudeness, but at the same time thought that the small Thick was rather imposing and brave in her own way, her face as serious as death, her long red hair bound up in the same warrior's topknot as Bat's, as she faced the much taller Mixed shaman.

Tooth's expression was grave. 'I am not sure I know the answer to your question, Shaman Wolf. I know that they keep two dwelling-places. Each is the other's mirror: the cave to the hut, the white mountain sheep to the white hare of the plains, the winter wolves to the summer foxes of the lowlands, the dark fish to the bats of the cave. When they have gone hungry from one place and the hunt of an animal is rare, they know that the season is ready to change and that the spirit-doubles of these animals will be bountiful at the other site. I know though that the hares still run plentifully through the grass, so I do not yet understand why they have left. I myself only arrived –' His voice broke up, and the other three followed his gaze, into the tall grass that grew all around the encampment. It had not been cut back by the previous inhabitants.

'Tooth, what is –' Skin began, but her mentor cut her off with a downward motion of his hand as he began to walk slowly towards the tall grass, as if in a trance. Skin exchanged glances with the other two, but all three of them were equally bewildered, although they followed in Tooth's footsteps as he ventured into the tall grass.

When he stopped, and they caught up with him, they were all equally discomfited to see a shaman's customary hooded cloak fashioned from hyena skin lying in the grass. But otherwise there was no evidence of wrongdoing. There was no body to be found, but it was very strange for a shaman to have left without his or her cloak, almost unheard of. Skin forced herself not to look at Wolf's satchel, where the newest flute was hidden. Hidden? That was an odd sentiment, thought Skin, and remembered now Wolf's necklace of human teeth and how Skin herself had refrained from telling Tooth of the flute and the killings. She opened her mouth to tell him now, but saw how sorrowful he already looked as he took up the hyena hide and hid it beneath his own undercloak. Somehow the words stuck in her throat, and Wolf was already staring at her with the strangest expression. She looked about ready to ask something important of Skin, but ultimately, neither gave voice to their thoughts.

If there had been violence here, reasoned Skin, it could not be Wolf responsible. They had been together the whole night. Yet Wolf had found the flute so easily, and she had that terrible necklace stowed away. She could have committed any number of terrible deeds the day before yesterday. Before she appeared on the other side of the cave tunnel. Maybe all three of them, Bat, Wasp and Wolf, had been colluding. And the actions she had attribued to Bat's mad, lustful grief had been madness instead (though the memory still made her cunt wet). Who knew what spirits Wolf was capable of conjuring up? Even that entire episode with the mammoth, which seemed so weird and dreamlike now, could have been a false hallucination imposed on Skin, already terrified by the night-time and by Wasp's death. Skin's head ached, and she grasped it with both hands. All right, so maybe that last supposition was a little far-fetched.

The tall weeds were stroking at her calves and Skin's eyes followed a crane floating on the breadth of its huge, foam-coloured wings up above her. What had this bird seen, she wondered? Removed and safe in the air, impartially observing or perhaps not even caring, a bird would know what had happened in this inexplicably empty settlement.

'Tooth.' Skin opened her mouth to speak, but was irritated to see Wolf staring at her intensely, as if she were willing Skin not to say something. 'Tooth, you said before you didn't know much about this community, but do you know where the people are? Do you know if the shaman is . . . missing?'

Tooth's face was cold – with worry, thought Skin – and his voice gave nothing emotional away, solely information: 'Not exactly. As I indcated, this is the community's summer camp; I know where their winter lodging is. But as it is still high summer, it would be very irregular for them to move from this site. Still, this seems to have been the case. As for the shaman – she is a very ancient woman, nearly sixty, named Pika. This is no doubt her cloak, but it need mean no misfortune. We can find out more, perhaps, if we seek out their winter site in the mountains far ahead to our left – you, Shaman Wolf, will have a difficult time there, I think –' he added and looked closely at Wolf for emphasis. She held his gaze, did not answer and only blinked in response. Tooth, slightly ruffled, hurriedly continued '– if that is where the people are – we can ask our questions then.' As he spoke these last sentences, his voice hardened, became grim. 'But first, I think, we must clean this site. Perhaps a purifying fire. Yes, I think that would be a good idea. We can think about these matters, concentrate on the many in one. This place feels polluted to me; something very wrong has happened here.'

Yes, thought Skin, he is right; I have thought that from the first moment we entered the camp. The four of them drew back from the long grass, leaving a wake of flattened grass in their retreat where they had forged in earlier. It wasn't until then that it occurred to Skin that the grass had not been pressed down earlier. The cloak had been lying in the middle of the tall sedge grass. Someone would have to have thrown it there recently, as Tooth was the first to push down the tall sheaths. And he had known that it was there, too. He had sensed it, somehow. Skin felt uncomfortable, even though she knew that Tooth was a shaman of great ability. She put the inconsistencies of the situation from her mind as she joined the others in front of the largest hut. Although she was the last out of the grass, she did not want to look back, either. She had the disturbing feeling that she would turn to find that the grass was once again restored to its full, untrampled glory.

Tooth had spread the shaman's cloak out on the ground outside the hut where he and Skin had made love, and was now laying on to it a variety of objects and sundries from within the depths of his own cape: dried and powdered *Amanita muscaria* – the white-dappled hallucinogenic red mushroom, one of Tooth's personal favourites – several handfuls of pine needles, uneven crystallised lumps of spruce sap, several seeds that were unknown even to Skin and a hide sachet that, when opened, revealed only . . . dirt.

Skin watched as Wolf engaged herself equally in the preparation of the cleansing ceremony. Skin thought she detected Tooth's lips tightening slightly at the dwarf's involvement, but knew that he would be too polite to object to any interference. And in a way, she supposed, Wolf had as much right to head the ceremony as Tooth, even if she was a dwarf. As for herself and Bat, as apprentices they kept their distance and both sat down at the edge of the hyena cloak, on their haunches so that they would be ready to begin their meditations when it was time.

What Skin saw Wolf doing then was a preparation that she had never seen Tooth himself do. First, Wolf dug up grass with her orange stalactite until there was a huge circumference of dirt all around her. Then with her fingers, Wolf scratched designs into the dirt, complicated geometric designs that made Skin's eyes swim when she looked at them for too long. She had known that Wolf was a healer, but she had not known that Wolf was an artist. Skin briefly wondered whether Wolf's drawings would be sufficiently appreciated when they reached the second hybrid community – the Lekken were famed for their cave painting and artistic skills. One of Wolf's patterns in particular was fascinating – it was the long sweeping wing of a bird, decorated with spirals and flourishes at one end but oddly spare where the disembodied wing would attach to the rest of the bird, had there been a rest of the bird. The effect was one of incompleteness. And to Skin, for some reason, it only served to accentuate her own lack of an animal totem, while all the others were invoking their own.

Tooth had his – she had handed him his tooth back even as he first began to lay out his preparation. Wolf had hers – a yellow canine incisor. Wolf also had the long silver tail, which she stroked intermittently along the insides of her arms as she paused occasionally from her dirt drawing, biting her labret in concentration. Even Bat, an apprentice like Skin herself, had a totem and accordingly the long vertical bundle was wrapped up in the skin of that particular cave marsupial for whom he had been named.

She didn't want to think about it any more. She dragged her eyes from the complex dirt drawings Wolf was effecting with her fingers alone and turned back to Tooth. He had lit a substantial fire of pine needles to the side of the cloak – almost as if he were attempting to signal someone, so expansive was the amount of smoke produced – and was mixing the crystallised sap he had brought with him with what smelled like urine, rubbing it into a paste and spreading it over his face and hands then emptying the powdered *Amanita* on to his tongue.

He crushed the seeds and mixed them with the dirt, rubbing this uneven mixture between his palms. He was also beginning to chant, his voice taking on a high, unearthly quality. A glance told Skin that Bat had also begun his own meditation, his head held in his hands, his body rocking back and forth on his haunches. He too was wailing; it seemed to Skin that his voice had more of a grief-filled quality than a truly spiritual one. Still, that was not for her to judge. But now she lowered her lids, stretched out her arms, palms flat upwards and began to listen to the chanting and wailing around her.

Eventually the sounds seemed to swarm into each other and there was just a thud-thud-thud in her head, and then Skin felt herself begin to float above the sounds in her ears. The pine needles were burning and the smoke was everywhere, touching every cell of her body, curving into her nostrils, filling her ears, between her legs, her mouth, playing on her tongue. It was a vaguely sexual feeling, though not specifically genital. The smoke also had the effect of making her feel faint, lightheaded. She was gliding above her head somewhere, her mind twisting with smoke and chants and she knew that it was now time to start looking for a signal for her journey, a starting point or some sign. The burning of pine needles and the resulting smoke was overpowering; she let her mind go loose and slack and felt herself float out on the smoke she envisioned; the smoke she could see so clearly even with her eyes closed.

At first she saw nothing. In her mind, there were only billowing clouds of violet-coloured fumes, misty and vague. She thought of Wasp and searched for her, but could not sense the musician's spirit anywhere. She thought of Tooth and her desire for him, and tried to direct her thoughts in that direction. This brought no result, either. She drifted on in the vision, seeking anything solid in the diaphanous muddle, but not even the strange flute appeared in the vapour. Eventually, she began to make out a flash of white against the violet-coloured landscape. It would appear and then disappear, so that within her trance, Skin's eyes strained for another glimpse of it. She was, very slightly, aware of someone sobbing outside the extent of her meditation. But she couldn't let herself be distracted now, as the white smear grew larger and larger, and she saw it finally for what it was: the huge wing of a crane. Somewhere in her analytical mind, she compared it briefly to Wolf's sketch in the dirt, but this was no disembodied wing; this was a huge crane, white as unsoiled snow.

Skin felt herself being drawn towards it magically, drifting closer as she realised that this was the same crane who had witnessed whatever had happened to the abandoned settlement where her body still was, rocking and meditating. She drew closer to the crane, reached her hand out to touch it. Her lips formed the questions she wanted to ask the bird, but suddenly the crane was disappearing: first its eyes dissolved, then its head, its body, and Skin was left holding on to a gargantuan wing, on which a blue stain was appearing rapidly, turning the whole wing as blue as the dyed mammoth bones of the huts. Deep in the trance, Skin purposefully began to detach herself – Tooth had warned her of the pitfalls that could occasionally happen while in the grip of a vision – and saw the wing become ghostly white once more, and then a pale pink. She watched in horror as this time it became red, blood red, the stain growing and growing. In the spirit-journey, she shook her head, and the wing turned blue again, then red again, then blue, and then the whole thing was as violet-purple as the clouds themselves and Skin was choking on the pine fumes, choking and strangling, her whole body trembling. Someone was rubbing at her neck, and she could hear Tooth worriedly repeating her name.

There was an acrid, sweet scent everywhere, which afterwards Skin attributed to the paste which Tooth had rubbed on his body. But there were no burning pine needles, Skin saw as she finally stopped coughing and looked at the place where Tooth had burned them. The detritus of burned pine needles was long cold. Even the tear stains on Bat's face had faded, although not entirely.

Skin had been in the grip of the vision for quite some time.

Chapter Five

There were islands of snow in heaps across the ground, but further up the side of the mountain was where the hybrid shaman Tooth had said the winter dwelling was to be found, so up they climbed.

Never mind that they had trekked across half the valley, an entire day's walk at a too-quick pace, avoiding yet another glacier before they reached the peak. Never mind that they were a good distance away now from the first mountain from which they had emerged, though that fatal hill was still visible far across on the other end of the valley. Never mind that it would take them at least another day to get back.

Bat, Wolf, Skin and Tooth were far above the treeline as they walked slowly up the incline, and although there were a few protesting arboreal specimens, most of the vegetation consisted of shrubs and straggly grey-green lichen, although there were also the very infrequent sprigs of purple, velvet-petalled fireweed, lobelia and even delicate pink roses. These flora were in contrast to the bleached expanses of snow growing ever greater as they trudged on upwards. Bat found it extraordinary that a group of people would choose to make their seasonal habitat in a place that was even colder in winter than it was now. He knew well that Thicks were hardier than his own race, but it never occurred to him that those who bore both bloods might choose a settlement that was so foreign to his own people, no matter how much Thick blood ran in their veins.

The blue-boned huts of the hybrid camp below and half the valley away had been similar to those of his own people. Bat had found this troubling: he generally expected everything about the hybrids to be different, and it usually was: his brief survey of the Kretchen initiation rite two days previous had fulfilled all his expectations about exotic hybrids. But the overfamiliar construction of the latest camp was disconcerting; it was that bewildering mix of things foreign and things known from birth. Bat had after many years overcome his prejudices towards Thicks, or so he thought. So hybrids should be easier to accept than Thicks, as their ways and customs and even looks were closer to those of his own people. But this was not the case – instead, the strangely Thin dwellings, the cadence and rhythm of their speech, even the red hair of the Thicks atop heads which looked Thin in almost every other sense – such as the shaman Tooth, who now led them ever upwards – made Bat feel uncomfortable. He was fine with elements different from himself when they remained safely different. It was when they got too close that he began to be nervous.

He glanced over at Skin and Wolf, both laboriously marching along on his right. Wolf caught his eye and grinned. Skin's mood seemed to have been alternating between cheerfulness and deep thought; now, once-again high-spirited, she began to talk animatedly with Wolf. Bat still felt like he was thinking through a fog, unable to make any decision. Unable to clearly focus on why he was now burying his feet in calf-high snow in the first place. The things the three of them – Wolf,

Wasp and himself – had worried about, had been obsessed with, had even tracked down this peculiar apprentice shaman Skin for, had seemed important and pressing ever since Red Deer's death. Now, all seemed inconsequential to him since the death of his cousin. He reached his hand far into his cloak and ran his fingers over the knobbly protuberances at the top of the elongated object that rested against his heart, against his very ribcage. Except for his totem, of course, and except for this. He closed his eyes in pain, felt flakes of snow fall on his shuttered lids and kept walking. His legs were beginning to pain him; the aching heaviness that exercise produced already making his limbs feel weary and useless. Tooth was beckoning up ahead to something and shouting at them, so at least, thought Bat, this particular trek would be over soon.

He was barely paying attention to the conversation between Skin and Wolf until he heard Wolf ask the hybrid a peculiar question: whether she thought that Wolf should camp outside the Lekken cave that night.

Skin gave Wolf an odd look. 'Of course not. Why would that be necessary?' she asked, in the odd up-and-down rhythm of hybrid speech.

Wolf stared at the hybrid as if she were a child with limited understanding. 'I can think of several reasons offhand. Can't you?'

'Not really – not so that you'd feel you'd have to bed outdoors in the snow, anyway.' Skin's voice was light, nearly flippant; Bat could see how excited she was about being reunited with a group that was ostensibly her people. She wasn't really even listening to Wolf's questions, he thought, watching as she bestowed a quick smile on both Bat and Wolf and transferred some leaves of a small tree into one of her satchels, before hurrying on up ahead. But Bat knew she would soon fall into a state of silent pondering; Skin had been in this unpredictable series of moods since she and Tooth had bedded in one of the huts, or so Wolf had reported. But then, Bat could well understand the charisma that the mature and handsome shaman Tooth commanded, even if he was a hybrid.

'Well, that conversation was a waste of breath,' said Wolf.

Though Skin's dismissal of Wolf's fears was irritating, Bat felt that if he pushed the issue it would destroy the fragile – and necessary – trust that was building up between the three of them, and he told Wolf so. She shrugged and walked on ahead. The truth was, Bat was more than a little tentative about meeting these hybrids himself.

What kind of people would choose to live their winter lives in this blank, dull atmosphere? Why would you make yourselves colder than you had to? What kind of food could they possibly find up here, on a bare snow desert of a mountain? The worst part about these strange environments Bat found himself in was having to negotiate their strangeness without Wasp near him, being able to touch her, having his every thought filtered through her and the same for her through him. We are all hiding secrets from each other, thought Bat. The hybrid apprentice Skin was hiding no fewer than Wolf and Bat were; he was still not certain whether they could trust her. She was over-close to her mentor, and now even physically close. This was forbidden, but the ways of the hybrids were not the ways of the Swathir, so it didn't shock him as much, perhaps, as Wolf would have liked it to.

Bat had known Wolf for perhaps four or five years; they met first when their mentors were negotiating a truce between the communities. Bat remembered it still: Wolf was perhaps fifteen or sixteen, though with one of her stature it was difficult to judge, and Bat sometimes had difficulty discerning the age of Thicks in general. They all looked similar to Bat, and of a current age once past the rites of puberty. Perhaps Wolf and Bat would never have become friends if she hadn't been so different from the other Thicks around him, but since they were of a similar age and quite content to talk to each other, eventually their mentors encouraged the friendship, even after the two communities drew further and further apart both geographically and ideologically. Bat would always be thankful to Red Deer for this – and for many other things as well – encouraging the closest friendship he had found outside of his own dear Wasp. And now of those three closest to him – Wasp, Red Deer and Wolf – there was only Wolf left. Bat did not want to think too long on it, for if he did he would begin to weep, and there was so much at stake now, things that would ensure that the losses of both Wasp and Red Deer were not in vain. And surely his tears would freeze as tight and rigid as rock crystal in this cold air, anyway.

Tooth was waiting for them when they passed around the next bend of the snow trail. One by one, they caught up with him. Wolf now walked last, so that the drifts were well pounded by the footsteps of the other three by the time she followed their lead. When Bat came up to where Tooth and Skin stood, he saw a settlement of four cave holes, naturally carved out in the rock, and saw as well that the snow here had been pressed and trampled by a multitude of feet. There were designs in the snow, drawings of green and bright blue woad dyes, but the latest snowfall had lidded these patterns and beneath the thin white shadow of fresh snow he could not make out what the pictures were intended to portray.

As they drew closer to the caves, Bat tried to keep his thoughts inward, so that they showed not on his face or in his actions. Wolf was now there next to him at his side, his dear good friend as she always had been, and her presence gave Bat a certain strength. Her proud, wise face that was quick to grin (but had not given much evidence of this lately) – except for that unacceptable moment when she and the hybrid were shrieking with a near hysteria that Bat never understood – her sturdy body, which was as developed as any full-grown Thick's, just somehow shrunk down to a compact, miniaturised adult body, her feverishly shining hair, bound up in a flaming topknot as Bat's own was after her attentions. She looked like a very small, but still fierce, hunter. She did make him feel better, just by being there. His one consistency in the nightmare of his life as of late. His one stalwart. Bat reached out for her hand. His friend held it tight in hers, and along with Tooth and Skin they reached the caves.

Skin cheered, but Bat did not share her elation. Instead he looked down at the hide which covered his body, the tanned reindeer pelt which Wasp had helped him cure, pressing and tanning it with him for months, smoking it until it was tender to touch. Its interior was soft fur, still glistening with the mammoth-gland oil that they had rubbed into it together, their hands occasionally meeting. He could hear the older hybrid, Tooth, begin a sonorous chant; it sounded to his ears like a chant of greeting and obeisance, but the words did not translate all their meaning to his ears, so he could only guess. Tooth had a powerful and attractive spirit guide; Bat could well see why the shaman was allied with such a potent animal as a sabre-toothed tiger.

Snowflakes were falling and melting on the exterior of Bat's hide now; he watched the little geometric ice formations appear and then vanish as he breathed on them when he held his sleeve up to his mouth. Eventually he tired of this diversion and wondered when Tooth was going to draw his chanting to a close.

He took the opportunity to survey what he could see of the camp. The caves were currently lived in, that much was obvious from the smell of smoke even had they not seen the trampled snow outside. Bat began to dread the appearance of half-a-dozen red-headed half-humans jumping out at him, with their strange scars cut into their bodies, their horrific head-dresses of decorated animal heads – before he caught himself and reminded himself that of course they were fully human, like anyone else. Though he found their mutilations barbaric, to say the least. Thank goodness Skin had no strange arrays of scar markings that usually signified the hybrids, that hideous arrangement of toughened keloid scars on flesh – though when he first met Skin she had worn that bird mask, which was nearly as bad. Perhaps she had not been properly initiated: it was strange that she had not revealed her animal totem to Wolf and him. This was another reason why she was possibly untrustworthy. Bat knew it was a slanted opinion, but he couldn't understand why hybrids did not instead have the more aesthetic and beautifully coloured tattoos that they could have chosen to mark their bodies with. And at least Skin and her mentor Tooth did not wear those ugly antlered head-dresses, as he had heard hybrids did.

He saw that the ice grew over the caves in a thin brittle sheet, so that the rock beneath was visible but also distant, the extra layer giving it a detached and dream-like quality. Icicles hung down like so many stalactites and Bat consciously avoided stepping beneath the largest – one half the length of his own body – for fear of it dropping off and boring into his own head. He had a hard time imagining people living in this primitive cave, even if they were hybrids and therefore had different ways than himself. He had heard that both Thicks and hybrids had an easier time in the cold than Thins did. Perhaps because they were stockier – their physique was, after all, the reason why Thicks were deemed Thicks and, respectively, why Thins had the opposite moniker. The Thin cave sites were neat and cosy and obviously inhabited; certainly they were lower down in the mountains, below the snowline. These caves looked as if no one had made any effort to modify them at all. From the outside, it appeared – he had a difficult time admitting it to himself, but it was true – as if only animals resided there. But of course, they had had no chance yet to set things in order, if they had just moved in from their summer dwellings. He blew his breath out in a thick steam. But these were their regular winter dwellings, Tooth had said. He had said it with no apology, either.

Then, Bat had no time to muse further, for the contingent of red-haired hybrids suddenly appeared. They were of varying heights, weights and types, though there were none as small as Wolf. There was little uniformity to them, none of the visual pleasure that comes with sameness, thought Bat. His hand tightened round Wolf's. He now knew that he was not going to understand this place. He was not going to understand these people.

The hybrids stood silently; it seemed as if they were waiting for someone to appear. Tooth was obviously composing his greeting, as his face was going through a series of controlled movements and he was mumbling recitations of courtesies under his breath. Then at last, someone pushed their way forward from the hybrid group and Bat saw to his horror that this person actually *was* wearing an antlered head-dress of a caribou, just like all the old stories whispered about hybrids. Stories that he himself had tried to dismiss as mere prejudice. And now this horned being was clasping Tooth in a ceremonial embrace, their mouths meeting and tongues playing. That, at least, was familiar – it was often the ritualised Thin greeting, as well, though usually people made do with the more universal cheek-touch and brow-kiss. When the two hybrids withdrew from the clinch, the antlered leader pushed back the ornamental headdress and Bat saw that she was an ancient woman, much, much older even than Tooth; she had to be past sixty years at least. Tooth and the old woman now began a long recitation of kin, greetings and scripted questions intended to impart any fresh news. This too was familiar to Bat and, suspecting rightly that it would go on for a long time, he sighed and leaned up close against the entrance where he stood, pressing his nose against the ice layer. He could see the minerals frozen beneath, the vein running through the rock, shiny and metallic. When he tried to draw back, his nose had frozen fast to the ice with his own breath and he had to tear it away with no small amount of pain. He rubbed at his raw nose, now red with abrasions as well as with cold.

He looked around, bored: both Skin and Wolf had their eyes closed, as did the rest of the hybrids accompanying the ancient antlered woman. These hybrids were heavily decorated: long strings of shells looped around their necks, throats, ankles, thighs and waists; their red hair strung and pulled through a variety of pierced shells: blue shells, pale-green shells, shells as pink as sunsets; their fingers and toes bedecked with ivory rings that caught the light of their torches and shone white as winter ptarmigans as they shifted their bodies, both men and women. They wore stitched hides of fox; underneath these garments Bat could see that those who were not marked with extreme scarification were marked with the blood-like stain of dried ochre – and Bat guessed that these were designated scars-to-be. Many of their rituals involved this type of flesh modification, and he wondered whether he would have a chance to see such a rite during his stay. But again, the upsetting element was that their tools and clothes were that weird blend of both Thin and Thick cultural trappings, as well as many traits that seemed to be entirely their own, such as the scars.

Bat looked down the mountain to the loose-piled

snow on either side of the glacier that they had passed on their ascent. The slow advance and retreat of this ice river was in a type of a valley, but wet snow was found up above the caves, too. There would be avalanche danger; all it would take would be one warm rain. But perhaps they had techniques to deal with this; ways to clear their cave airholes in such events. He did not know their methods. He did not know much about their way of life at all.

But at least he had a moment to himself, a moment to think and consider what that perplexing vision had meant during the ceremony back at the place of the blue huts. It had been so disturbing that even as he stood outside the cave and waited he couldn't help going over its details in his head. At first the vision had been quite predictable; he had rocked back and forth while listening to the chants the hybrid shaman had been uttering, and eventually his concentration had detached itself from the others around him. He had floated up and up, his body becoming lighter as the slight buzzing in his ears became a roar and the movement of his own body rocking had lulled his senses into a kind of sleepy rhythm.

No, thought Bat, running his fingers absently over the ice of the doorway, hearing Tooth and the old woman continuing to talk, no, that hadn't been the disturbing element. It had been much worse than that. He tried harder to remember what happened next.

He had floated on in this way for a while, all the while imagining his totem along beside him. It had been the first time he had felt himself absent of grief since Wasp's death . . . no, since Red Deer's. It had been as if a soporific drug was entering his veins, calming him and dulling all of the piercing pain he had been feeling for the past two weeks. Such a relief. Deep in the spirit journey, he had imagined his hand brushing over the soft, fawn-coloured hairs of his totem, feeling the warm life underneath. They had soared on together in this colourless, comforting world. It was so delicious. Just smooth floating. No pain. No death. Even though Bat had known well at the time that he was supposed to be concentrating on cleansing the odd hybrid camp. But he had intended all along to meditate upon the bone, so precious and sorrowful, that he had retrieved from the fire. A flicker of pain had reached him through the midst of his trance then, but it had soon dulled away.

Remembering the trance, Bat felt the same burst of grief as he had then. His fingers were now numb from ice, and he drew them away and placed them beneath his cloak. Tooth still droned on, so Bat made himself remember even more. He hadn't yet recalled the most horrible memory, not yet . . .

Within the trance, he had intended to concentrate on the bone, but somehow it seemed easier just to float away and not think at all, his bat familiar at his side. No demands. And that, thought the remembering Bat, as he stood facing the ice, feeling like his very face was frosting over, was when he saw the head. A huge luminous head. The head had been normal in most aspects: vaguely masculine, two ears, one nose, one pair of lips . . . and two eyes. Just like any other face. Except – Bat shivered in memory, and it wasn't because of the cold – except the eyes in that face had been very, very wrong. The eyelashes were right, the eyelids too. But when this head in his vision had opened those pale heavy lids, something had been terribly skewed: one eye was completely blank – like snow with no blemish, its white contained no iris. And the other eye, well . . . the other eye had two eyeballs swimming around in it, two brilliantly rose-coloured irises crowding the cool white membrane on which they rested.

Bat had felt himself being drawn towards the enormous face, and in the grey limbo there was nothing he could grasp or brake himself against in order to prevent this slide towards the monstrous eyes – one blinking and as blind as cave-dwelling fish, the other with a hideous surplus. And there had been that strange, dreary lethargy to the whole episode. Shamans usually attained vibrancy and clarity from visions, even under-practised apprentice shamans like himself. As the eye had loomed closer and closer, and Bat had realised that the height of the eye was greater than his own lanky body from head to toe, he had reached out for his totem, desperately searching for something concrete and known. It had been then that his own totem mind-bat – the soft grey animal that always accompanied him on these journeys – had abandoned him. To have a totem disappear mid-trance. This was unheard of for a shaman, even an apprentice shaman.

And then – and this was the worst of all, Bat thought, as Tooth's incantation seemed finally to be drawing to a close – he had seen his reflection in the pupil. Only in one pupil. He could see his whole body reflected in one of the huge, obsidian-black pupils in the one horrendous doubled eye, and then nothing in the other. In desperation he had tried to move away as the horrifying sensation of his own intangibility had hit him. But then the apparition had been reversed; then he had appeared in the other prism-like globe, a black reflecting dot against the same fleshy pink as his own skin, and not in the other. Then even that reflection had vanished, and even as Bat had waved his hands in front of the eye it was as if it had been blind to him, as if he did not exist at all. And he had been drawn in again, lethargy swooping in on him again, and then he had been in a salmon-coloured kaleidoscopic soup, and then in the jet-dark, sticky, inky pupil, and then he had been nothing, nothing at all. He had started to scream and then weep, calling out for Wasp, but she was nothing, too, and she would never come back. Nothing. Never. Nowhere. Even his voice had become wispy, caught in the trance;

he had not even been able to hear his own cries until Tooth and Wolf had shaken him back to reality.

Bat blinked, and turned back to the group. They were staring at him; it was obvious that Tooth had finished his lengthy incantation some time ago. He wondered what grimaces his face had exhibited while analysing the troubling memory.

Tooth cleared his throat for what Bat was sure was not the first time, and said: 'Well, Pika – here we have apprentice Bat, whose mentor and teacher was Red Deer.'

To Bat's surprise, the old woman smiled. 'Ah, Red Deer. A worthy mentor. How is she, boy?' She had the same musical rhythm of speech as Tooth and Skin did, Bat observed.

His voice came out hoarse, and he cursed himself for appearing nervous in front of what was, after all, only a group of hybrids. 'She is no longer with us, Mother.' He added the honorific as a matter of politeness and the old shaman seemed pleased.

'In what manner did she leave?'

Rude! thought Bat, but he answered nevertheless. 'She died of sickness, Mother.'

It could have been his imagination, but the old woman's grey eyes darkened somewhat, though not a muscle moved on the rest of her face.

'I am sorry to hear that. I knew Red Deer quite well,' she said, 'and I know she did much to link the Thin and Thick communities together. The last I heard of her, she was even trying to forge an alliance with the Kretchen – and then maybe our own people, the Lekken hybrids.'

'That is true.' Tooth nodded gravely.

'Yes,' said Bat, warming to the old woman. 'Wolf here was also instrumental in the first discussions between the Thins and the Thicks.' He pointed to Wolf, who was standing in the shadows behind him, silent.

The old woman's eyes glazed over, and Bat was not sure whether she had heard him. 'Red Deer was a good woman, and I have many friends myself in the Thick community of Vexlu.'

'That's right,' Skin entered the conversation with some excitement, 'that is near the same encampment that Wolf is from. Aren't you, Wolf?' She went silent suddenly, and Bat saw that Tooth was looking at Skin quite sternly.

Wolf grunted an affirmation, but did not step out from behind Bat's back.

'Do you know much of this Vexlu Thick community?'

Bat waited for Wolf's response, but to his surprise the old woman was addressing the question to him instead. He felt quite flustered. 'Um . . . I have met them a fair number of times, outside the camp, of course, and it was there that I met Wolf, so I got to know her people through her, and . . .'

'The Vexlu are a fine people,' said the antlered shaman, her voice trembling with age. 'And, for the most part, exhibit fine control in their breeding practices and produce fine strong specimens of people, fine strong specimens indeed. There are some here who are kin to them, several generations back.'

'But –' Skin was staring at the old woman, open-mouthed. She looked over at Wolf, and then back to the headwoman.

'Skin,' Tooth said in an admonishing tone, his voice cool.

Bat thought Skin looked upset. He felt disturbed himself, though for no reason that he could as yet put a finger to. Before Skin had a chance to say more, though, the elderly woman turned heel and started to walk back into the cave interior, nodding back at them.

'You are all welcome to follow.' She motioned, and one of her manservants came forward with a number of hides, handing them to Skin. Skin doled them out immediately to the others. 'It is good to have so many shamans and apprentices present. We shall have to make a ceremony to mark the occasion. You are welcome.' She paused, her forehead wrinkling with thought. 'All four of you.' The leader moved back for a moment, and bestowed a ceremonial lip-press on the foreheads of Bat and Skin, but not Wolf. Bat couldn't see Wolf's expression behind him, but he saw that Skin's face was now bright red, whereas he himself still felt as if he were floating along in a fog, as the four of them followed the shaman deeper and deeper into the cave.

As he strode after the group of nearly thirty individuals, Bat took the opportunity to observe the hybrids. He had never seen so many hybrids in one place, though he had known Thicks for many years and befriended many both in his youth and now in his early adulthood, though always on neutral territory, of course. And hybrids were part Thick, after all. He had met hybrids on a variety of previous occasions and his comfort level was always controllable. He had thought himself comfortable enough with Skin and even with the shaman Thick, whose blend of Thick and Thin characteristics was somehow attractive. Bat realised that, except for the naming ceremony he had witnessed, before he had only met hybrids singly, in groups consisting at the most of two or three. It was he who now was by far outnumbered, in a community full of people with protruding brows and small delicate noses. Or smooth, flat brows and huge, Neanderthal noses. And always, nearly always, with the bright red hair of the Thicks. Though the colour and texture varied from straight auburn folds of hair to tight-curled, bright copper kinks, it was this characteristic that attested to the foreignness of the hybrids. Bat had heard that red hair carried easily from parent to child, perhaps even more easily than dark hair. His people, the Swathir, never had red hair. And when they did, insinuations were put about that there was Thick blood in the family. They were called hybrids, and the term was meant to be pejorative. Now Bat was in an entire community of hybrids. And his ease was not as great as he thought it would be.

But by now they had emerged into a great cavern of a room, complete with an exit-hole to the outdoors and a great many air-holes chipped into the rock of its dome-like surface and a tunnel on the far side, surrounded by a huge altar. This was evidently not the living quarters, and even though he knew that the art of the hybrids could not equal that of the Swathir, Bat was still astounded by the wealth of images. Across the interior was painted a variety of bizarre shapes and fantastical creatures. There were antlered humans with two penises each (one of which looked as if it were sprouting a phallus from its chin, too) and tigers with a surplus of legs – six, maybe seven, extra limbs. The being that caught his eye, though, the rendition that made him stop straight in his tracks, was of an extraordinary flying creature. It was difficult to see whether it was bird, rodent or insect – hiding most of its head behind a bright purple wing. The other wing was snowy white, perhaps daubed on with crushed root or white lead. But below the purple wing was what interested Bat, for it was there that one of the creature's eyes peeped out. And in its case of lids and lashes were set two irises, both as pink as fresh salmon eggs. Bat started to tremble. He had managed to dismiss his peculiar vision of the doubled eye and now here it was again. He didn't want to think about it. He didn't want to think about it at all, so he lowered his head and looked around the extended room, where the hybrids had assembled.

His stomach rumbled. 'Are we going to eat soon?' he asked Skin in a low voice. It was the first thing that guests were offered among the Swathir – food and then eventually beds. Right now, it seemed the best of traditions.

Skin gave him a bemused look. 'After the welcoming ceremony. It always comes first.'

And now it seemed that the welcoming ceremony was commencing, for to his horror Bat saw that an assortment of dried head-dresses were being distributed amongst those present. He did not like the look of anything that covered the eyes or face, and masks in particular had always bothered him on some very basic level. The thought of being encompassed by any animal other than his own totem was nearly blasphemous. How else could you keep your loyalties to your particular totem animal? But now they were being doled out and Bat was not excluded: he found himself holding a pale-tan scaly object, which upon closer examination turned out to be delicate fish-leather. Its scales were dull, however, as Bat turned it over in his hands.

'How can someone allied with one totem stand to wear the mask of another?' He voiced his thoughts to Skin.

Skin's lips pursed and her eyes narrowed before answering: 'It is thought healthy to mix totems in a welcoming ceremony – it symbolises the mixing of guests with hosts, and shows us that in this life we must wear many faces, not just those to which we are accustomed. It is not good to place *too* much emphasis on a totem-animal, I think.'

'Oh.' Skin's tone was so sharp that Bat resolved to keep his questions to himself, at least for the time being. He felt an unhealthy twinge of envy when he saw her mask: a grey, fragile creation of thin raspy layers, stitched together with the finest fluff of fireweed. It had the two holes for eyes and stem-thin sinew to bind it behind the head. It was a wasp mask, a papyrus quiver to hold a face. His cousin's totem. It should have been his. 'Which mask did you get, Wolf?' he asked. It was difficult to see in the room, as the fire was just being lit at this moment.

'None.'

'None?' But just at that moment Tooth appeared in front of Bat.

'Here, let me help you,' the older man said in a gruff voice. His hand easily unfolded Bat's designated mask with its countless scales, and what had seemed dull and brittle now gleamed in the limited light of the cave. Then again, the fire was finally lit, and this could explain some of the fish-mask's current dazzle. For a moment, Tooth's hand touched Bat's and Bat felt a shock run through his body, as clearly as a birch-bark shaving set suddenly alight. Tooth stepped back, blinking, and Bat wondered if the older man had had the same reaction.

'Don't worry about the food, young Bat,' said Tooth, and Bat felt ashamed that this older shaman had overheard the conversation with Skin. 'There will be a great deal of that later. Though I have to wonder whether they feed you at all in your own community. Judging by your frame, it is not a surety.' Tooth's gaze moved speculatively over Bat's body. Bat was mortified at this easy perusal and looked over at Wolf to see if she had marked it. But Wolf for some reason was angrily biting at a thin rope of sinew on Skin's mask, with which she was suddenly preoccupied. Skin had knotted it incorrectly when attempting to don the insect guise.

'Do you want some help with that?' Bat asked Skin, but Skin shook her head so fervently that he drew back startled. When he looked over at Wolf to see what she thought of Skin's behaviour, he was surprised to see that Wolf seemed to be biting back her tears. Surely her task wasn't absorbing or frustrating to this extent? He suspected it had something to do with Tooth offering to help him instead of Skin. Skin's reaction to his favoured status was puzzling. Bat felt slightly guilty about lying about the way in which Red Deer had died, and compounding the lie by repeating it to Pika (Tooth had been there the second time, and Bat couldn't very well say that he had told Tooth an untruth previously), but there had been something that made him question whether or not he could trust the shaman fully – perhaps it was something to do with his over-casual air at the Lekken camp. Bat couldn't worry about it at the moment, though, for despite himself, despite his grief and everything else, his hand still tingled where the shaman had touched him. Since Bat had found himself attracted to hybrid people as of late – well, Skin at least – the pull he felt towards the shaman did not surprise him inordinately. For his whole life, people had talked about the sexual prowess of hybrids. He had never thought it respectful – and now he hoped that he wasn't becoming someone as sexually boorish as his own headman, Jerboa. He didn't think he was – he was fairly sure that most of the reason he was attracted to the shaman was for the sheer power that he represented. That was a universal trait, not specific to hybrids alone.

So Bat turned back to Tooth, who was still standing there – rather expectantly, Bat thought – and smiled. 'Thank you for your assistance.'

The shaman raised an eyebrow. 'Any time you desire it, you have only to ask.'

Bat could sense Wolf looking at his neck from behind, willing him not to respond. She must know herself how charismatic the shaman was, thought Bat. He licked his lips, which were inexplicably dry. He was aware that the tall shaman's pale eyes were still raking over his own lean body and to his great mortification, Bat's cock began to firm. He turned away, his face red with heat, and hoped that the shaman would not be able to notice – but he is a man, thought Bat. Of course he will notice. Bat looked back quickly and gave the older man a slight, embarrassed smile. The shaman was still staring steadily at him and Bat thought he saw Tooth's eyes dilate. This hope that the older man could be equally aroused made Bat's cock stiffen all the more.

But when Bat turned to Skin, there was a look of pure outrage on her face. It was irritating to Bat that she could get that upset over a slight botching of such an unimportant task. When he tried to engage her in conversation, telling her it didn't matter that she had misknotted her mask, she didn't respond, and so they both stood sullenly fiddling with their masks. First Wolf, and now Skin, thought Bat. You would think they would both be pleased that his mood had lifted a little, but instead they seemed as surly as two famished bobcats.

'Bat,' whispered Wolf in his ear, her voice catching, 'I'm not going to watch the ritual – all right? I'm going to wait near the entrance where we first came in, back through the tunnel.'

'What?' Bat was surprised, even in the midst of his preoccupation. 'Why not?' But Wolf had already disappeared, slipped back the way from which they had come.

Skin nudged Bat in his ribs. 'Is she all right?' This concern from Skin rather surprised him; he thought they didn't get along. In fact, it now seemed that her unfriendliness was more directed towards him.

'I think so,' he answered. But he was dizzy with fatigue and too preoccupied to give much thought to Wolf's sudden little tantrum. He was actually quite excited at the thought of participating in a foreign rite. His misgivings had almost entirely slipped away after viewing the expanse of art and beauty to be found, of all places, within a hydrid cave.

So he watched as the hybrids bestowed upon Tooth an old antlered caribou head-dress as well. Even though not long before he had thought the antlered head-dresses peculiar at best and horrific at worst, he found himself admiring how Tooth looked in the pronged ceremonial gear. He looked proud and rather handsome, not ludicrous at all. Virile, even.

The flames were already eroding the rough-ended birch logs away into charcoal as dark as deepest night, and the mixture of black coals and red bursting fire made Bat think, uncomfortably, of the night that Wasp had died, when in the midst of his stupor there had been the strange dreamlike instance in which Wolf had led them through a gloom of mammoth rides and demons with red and black hair – after Wasp had died . . . Bat put a hand up to wipe at his eyes, angry with himself. He felt as if he had spent most of that night and the following day in a type of sleep from which he was only now beginning to emerge. That depressing vision at the blue huts hadn't helped, either. He stared at the fire grumpily for a moment. He had not been ready for a mind-journey, and with two full shamans and one other apprentice present, they certainly should have been aware of this fact. But of course Tooth was a busy, important shaman, with other things on his mind . . .

The stupid idiot. Wolf was shaking with fury. How could he have not noticed? How could he have not noticed the extent to which she been ignored? Was he not aware that all of the perfectly calculated slights by the old witch of a shaman had been directed towards Wolf herself? Or how Wolf had not even been handed a mask with which to participate in the welcoming rite? And then to ask her what was the matter! Even Skin had shown more empathy than Bat had. Wolf walked straight through the cave, her fury transporting her safely back to the first entrance without going astray. The stupid idiot. She twisted her labret as she thought, a habit she had done for years. She was not going to cry. It was a mistake even coming here in the first place, knowing as she did the attitudes of the hybrids towards those they felt to be misbred. She had known this, and still she had thought it important for her to journey along with Wasp and Bat. And now look where it had got them: Wasp dead, Bat a dizzy, self-absorbed fool, and herself, shaking with humiliation. She should have known that he was too wrapped up in his own thoughts – at first she had thought it was grief, but now it seemed to be infatuation for that condescending mentor of Skin's – back when she had held her hand up to him for comfort and reassurance and he had merely given it one dismissive squeeze. She should have known then. *He* should have known how it felt to be her, entering into a very community of hybrids.

She didn't know if it made it better or worse to realise how talented these people were – to be forced to look at their stunning paintings, pictures the like of which she would never be able to paint herself. This train of thought reminded her of the vision – it hadn't even been a proper vision, really – back at the Lekken camp, when she had closed her eyes and all she had seen were the swirling colours of paint, a thousand rainbows and shades, all of them out of her reach. There had been that annoying bird in her vision, too, just one of many beautiful renderings that had swum up before her eyes at the time. It seemed to have mocked her with its pink eyes, as if to say: look at me – this is the type of painting you will never be allowed to create. Then to see that same cursed picture again here in the cave was nearly too much to bear. If she saw it while mid-trance again, Wolf thought, she would send her mental totem snapping at its beautifully painted, skilfully depicted, artfully composed feathers. She would not cry, thought Wolf, as she exited the cave and stood outside, breathing in the cold, rough air.

To make matters worse, there was a variety of stunning snow-pictures dyed on to the drifts when she emerged. She avoided them and walked further out.

There were several hybrids some distance away gathering snow; all were dressed in cloaks similar to those of Skin, Bat and Wolf. This made Wolf feel surprisingly grateful about Skin's dispensing of hide cloaks. The curing on Wasp's coat was unusual; Wolf suspected it had been smoked for softness. But it was warm for early night, and Wolf felt cosy when encased inside it. So warm, in fact, that she became desperately thirsty, having not had any liquid since early the day before. She heard the cry of a wolf. Her own totem, but she did not know how to interpret the portent. It usually functioned as a warning, however, and her senses were heightened. Her head ached. She honestly did not know which was worse, she thought, pressing her hands to her forehead – the obvious flirtation between Bat and Tooth, or Bat's indifference to her own treatment.

She got up and walked towards where the others stood; it was where the cleanest snow was and she was now sorely in need of water to cool her throat.

When she walked the periphery of the hybrids and cut across so that she walked past them – she was not foolish enough to try and go amongst them – she was alarmed to see that a young man followed her. He was just out of adolescence and cocky with it – his naming scar had not even yet healed and was an angry red colour still on his chest, in the shape of a bear paw complete with curling claws. She had to admire its craftsmanship, though; it was very well executed. It seemed an appropriate totem, for he was as aggressive as a bear sow nursing cubs. Wolf turned her back on him, trying to ignore him as she melted the snow in her hands. But she was aware of him behind her all the same. When he shoved her, she was ready. She turned with a certain viciousness and surprised him by having her knife drawn and ready. She had secreted it out at the same time as she had melted the snow. It winked up at him, black and glossy. Its rim was sharp enough to be molecule-thin at the point of its lethal edge. It was a severely dangerous instrument and the hybrid was aware of this fact.

He spat at her, having no other immediate weapon. 'You ugly little misbreeder, why don't you leave? You don't need to stay here and sully our water-supply with your filthy hands. Someone should tear that plug right out of your vile pierced lip, as well.'

Wolf did not answer but touched the spiked tip of her knife, staring him in the eye. Eventually he backed off and walked away, muttering a litany of slurs under his breath. The other hyrids watched silently.

'What's the matter with you?' Wolf suddenly said, rounding on them. 'You all feel exactly the same, isn't that the case? That's why you're afraid to do anything. Aren't you?' She stepped up to one woman, whose lip curled in disgust but who also stepped out of Wolf's way. Some of the others did not appear to share the same revulsion, but they kept silent. 'You're all cowards,' Wolf said with loathing, as she walked over to where the cleanest snow was and now drank her fill, while the others watched from a distance or disappeared back into the mountain with the teenager who had attacked her.

Those whose prejudice was obvious were cowards because they backed away, but it was the other ones whose silence actually bothered her more. They were more responsible, Wolf thought, for they allowed slights like this to happen. And the slights could become more loaded: it wasn't that long ago that a group of young hybrids, drunk on fermented dandelions, had attacked and beaten a young Thin girl from Bat and Wasp's encampment, merely for having a misshapen arm. It was at times like this that Wolf became homesick for her own parents and little brother, back at the Rusker camp. The girl in question had managed to run away regardless, but it was incidents such as these that had made Red Deer's attempts at treaties between the hybrids and others difficult to manage. Though, Wolf thought, remembering what had happened to the two Vexlu shamans eight years ago, it wasn't just the hybrids who had their bigotries.

The Lekken brethren sat in an oval around three hearths, both men and women. There were no children present and Skin assumed this was because it was so late. Bat sat at her left; Skin examined her feelings carefully and decided that she was still irked with him. She knew he was grieving, but that did not excuse his flirtation with Tooth. The very thought of her mentor made her flush again; she was glad that no one could see this reaction in the rosy glow of the fire. She moved down into a crouch and smiled. She was silly to be jealous of Bat. She was with kin – with other hybrids, anyway – Bat's flirtation meant nothing, and all was right with the world . . . well, except for Wolf. She would think more on that later, perhaps somehow try to appease Wolf. For now, she would concentrate on the rite: she stilled her thoughts to her senses, or at least made the attempt. For behind her mask, as grey-rustling as birch bark, she could hear the lament of a distant wolf, and the hair on her body rose.

Perhaps *this* was her totem-animal, Skin thought, and resolved to ask Wolf how she knew for sure her calling when her naming had happened. Through the cave-opening, Skin could see a tree back-lit by moonlight, its dark, radiating spikes of branches silhouetted as she looked out into the blue night.

Skin, Bat, Tooth and the hybrids around them were taking part in one of the most important rites of her own community. Though there were several differences that she noticed immediately: the Kretchen did not designate the shaman by the use of antlered head-dresses, though they did use the mixing and distribution of masks; her own people chanted but not for so long; these Lekken people seemed to keep their eyes fastened on a distant tunnel, whereas her own people closed their eyes in order to better concentrate on the ritual . . .

She looked closer at the tunnel and the altar built around it. The altar was fashioned from bones and stalactites, tarnished and charred with ash, hung with rows and rows of tiger teeth strung on long cords of sinew. The bones were covered with a series of carved Xs, zigzags and an extended line of dots bored out by a chisel. These markings, at least, she understood. The Kretchen used such marks both for ceremonial marking and as a method of tallying food supplies. The altar was huge, rising nearly three times as high as Skin stood. It framed a tunnel, and it was towards this tunnel that Tooth now began to walk, ponderously, slowly. He looked stately and even holy, like an antlered man ready to transform slowly into a stag, slip out of the cave and back down into the trees. Beside her, Bat took his breath in at the sight of Tooth and Skin felt again that inexplicable irritation. She tried to concentrate on the altar. At various intervals along the lengths of tiger teeth were strung chips of crystal, hard gems that looked like little white stars. As Tooth walked closer to the fantastic altar, Skin felt her nipples stiffen with excitement. Beside her, Bat cleared his throat.

Then the miracle happened. There was a hiss like wind, and Skin felt a breeze push back her hair. From nowhere, a tiger appeared, one whose strong teeth were able to crush the head of anyone present. But Tooth seemed to charm the animal as the huge cat watched his antlers sway back and forth in a mesmerising fashion. Tooth kept up this slow shuffle of a dance until the tiger slumped near Tooth. The shaman went even closer to the great cat. Skin's mouth was dry, her heart a knot of fear. No one in the room seemed to breathe as the cat lashed out its tail, bringing part of the altar crashing to the ground. But still Tooth went closer, holding something up in his hand. He was putting his other hand out now, Skin realised with alarm, to stroke at the tiger's fur, and she wondered how all that rich tawny glory would feel against her own skin, plush and luxurious as the soft hair on Tooth's chest. But now Tooth was stroking between the great cat's legs and the animal's purring filled the cavern, resounding in a great rumbling echo. No one moved, nor could tear their eyes away. Skin felt herself go wet, watching Tooth and the great female cat. The scent of musk pervaded the air. Tooth was rubbing rhythmically between the cat's legs now, charming it. Skin wondered if the she-cat were as wet as she, and if there were a great slippery wetness between the animal's legs, wondered what it would feel like to stroke that place on a wild cat, whether their sexes went pink and sticky waiting for a mating or stroking.

Then Tooth brought his other hand up. Skin could see now that he held a vessel – a squirrel skull – in it. The cat let forth a stream of liquid from between its legs, purring all the time, and then Tooth slowly backed away, holding the container tightly. Skin's heart was pounding, and her tongue emerged to wet her lips as she watched the cat rise and then slowly saunter back into the tunnel. Then it turned round suddenly and nonchalantly burst out of the altar's frame and Skin heard herself screaming as it leaped over all of their heads and exited through the opening where she had seen the cool blue trees. Despite her own cry, it was now completely silent in the cave and now, only now, did the other hybrids lower their heads. Skin had never seen anything like the scene she had just observed. She was very conscious of sitting there, wet between her legs and her limbs still trembling. She could not help but notice that Bat beside her was painfully erect, that the muscles were tight over his face. But the ceremony was continuing, so even though her sex buzzed and her skin felt like it was too small for her and she was slippery between her thighs, she made herself sit still for its progression.

Tooth mixed spruce-sap and feline urine into a paste, and once this was blended he added a pinch of crumbled grey *Amanita muscaria* and some violet flower petals which he ground into the mixture, as well. This fungus powder disappeared into the sweet-smelling paste as he stirred it in. The scent reached Skin's nose and the odour was sharp as well as sweet. It made her think of gamey animals, ripe for rutting, and of vernal spruces fertile with sap, sugary resin seeping out as if from a pierced fruit. Her nipples tightened until they were nearly painful. Just the thought that Tooth was there at the other end of the ring of people made her sex damp. His capable fingers, now stirring deeply through the drugged mash, seemed over-sexual. He lowered his lids. His bare torso and its ritual scar were beautifully exposed to the scarlet glow of coals. His upper arms were thickly muscled and adorned with a moderate amount of body hair and his biceps extended and pulsed as he stirred his fingers through the pulp.

The chanting stopped and, startled, Skin looked up. She realised that she should have been paying more attention to the words – she had a reputation to uphold, after all, as apprentice to Tooth. The chant was very similar to that of her own people's, after all, and she should have been more aware of the slight, barely perceptible, rise in cadence that indicated that the incantation was drawing to a close. Eyes were darting towards her; they knew that she was his apprentice and knew as well that she would soon be chosen. She lowered her lashes fetchingly. She had decorated her hair with small, green shovel-shaped aspen leaves, bright with colour and life still, their knubbly thin stems twisted far into her hair. She had done this style especially for Tooth, as he had once made it known to her that he liked her hair arranged in this fashion. And she had done it especially tonight because she knew that in a moment he was going to rise and anoint her first with the paste, just as he had done the other two times. And bestow the ceremonial kiss, too. Though the previous two times it had been platonic, she suspected it would not be on this occasion.

Tooth's pale-blue eyes glittered like iridescent, sky-coloured dragonflies as he got to his feet. In a way, Skin wished Wolf could have been here to enjoy this spectacle, just so the dwarf could see the enormity and importance of the ceremony and fully appreciate the complex religious practices of the hybrids. Wolf had opted out of the evening ceremony, her face curiously indignant. But if so, it was a dulled and beaten-down outrage and what did it matter now anyway, as Tooth raised the squirrel cranium in both hands and began to walk towards her. Skin's heart began to race with excitement; she felt perspiration beading across her brow and her mouth go parched.

'Now,' intoned her master, 'I offer this small skull of vision and dreams to an apprentice and guest here tonight –' Skin smiled modestly '– the protégé of Red Deer of the Thins beyond the mountain, Apprentice Bat.'

Skin's smile fell nearly – but not quite – as quickly as her heart did.

Tooth anointed Bat's forehead with the sacred paste and then his tongue and then kissed him hard; Bat felt the pressure of Tooth's tongue against the smooth crevices of his own teeth; the pressure of both of the older man's hands circling his neck, pulling him forward, forward into his fierce mouth, his lips impacting on the soft skin of Bat's neck. Bat was so erect he felt like his cock would spill forth of its own accord if Tooth gave him one more deep, wet kiss. The hairs rose on Bat's neck, desire already starting to pulse through him as he felt the rock-hard response of the older man. Tooth pressed his lanky body against the younger Thin, and Bat felt himself grow even more rigid against the muscular body he could feel beneath the thin hide, a body that was tense and coiled and equally urgent.

Bat wanted to suck the man, to open his lips wide over what he imagined as his thick moist cock. Thinking this, Bat ground his hips against the older man, running his fingers over his stubble as he did so. He wondered if Tooth would find this reckless and wanton, or even lewd. It was a new experience to give himself to a man so much older than he, and he hoped that he wouldn't seem too young and eager in his need. But this was exactly how he felt: young, needy, over-eager, near bursting with desire for the tall shaman. How could he not be, in the presence of someone so stunning, Bat thought, admiring how fire made Tooth's body glow, the red tingeing the shaman's limbs and highlighting his sinewy body. Even the tiger-claw scar curving up between the shaman's nipples was beautiful. Bat moved against him, pressed his lips ardently against the other man's. But Tooth drew away from the kiss and left Bat breathless, his heart pounding with desire, blood pounding in his cock. He couldn't even speak as the older shaman walked away, seemingly composed, and proceeded to anoint and kiss all the other people present, too. Though none, hoped Bat, with the same fervour as he had been kissed himself. His face was burning with desire; he knew his eyes were glowing and he felt – nearly – happy. As if he was opening up like a flower, or a fruit, blooming in holy colours. This too was a vision. An entirely separate experience from the vision of the blue huts.

Bat's heart was roaring upwards in ease; his self flew up to the dome of the cave and he saw with new eyes the outlandish paintings there, the bird that had scared him so previously. He was dissolving into the paint – this time around the doubled eye held no horrors for him; he was swimming in pink, his head roaring with music and sound. His self skimmed around up there, feeling the cold wind that entered through the air-holes, breathing the smoke that gathered in thin spruce-flavoured clouds. The taste was very sweet, very smoky. He was surrounded by the glorious, female scent of a she-tiger on heat, musk swarming through his lips and nose, the sound of purring escalating in his ears until his whole body was rumbling, vibrating, trembling flesh, opened up, his own beauty exposed in this world of scent and vibration: the sweet heady sugared urine, the perfume of animal musk, Tooth's kiss still reverberating through his whole body. The paintings were flashing out a series of geometric patterns, vibrant rouges and orange-yellows, lurid greens, pinks like watered-down blood. Everything divided into smallest parts: the scent of spruce sap became seedy pinecones and tender spring-green many-leafed needles; the urine, yellow droplets; the tiger, a single tawny animal hair. His flesh was living, all of his body was living and exploding and then he was falling down, down, his body extending and falling, breaking apart in tiny fragments; these pieces each held an equally beautiful part of him and he was falling and falling, back to the floor of the cave, back to his whole flesh, his skin finally full of life and love . . .

Wolf made her way sombrely back through the tunnel, aware the entire time that someone might be hiding around the next corner, ready to attack with a verbal onslaught – or worse, fists or knives. Fortunately this did not happen, though by the time she found her way back to the enormous domed cavern her muscles were tense from stress and her hand ached from holding her knife too tightly. When she rounded the corner to the room, she saw that the ritual had already happened. Everywhere she looked were dilated eyes and beatific smiles. There was a strong acrid odour too, one that slightly turned her stomach. The altar that had been marked with patterns so similar to the scratched number-bones of her own people was now crumbled down; perhaps this was part of the ritual, she thought: they all rushed at their altar in one amorphous mass, crashing it down like the thugs they were. Then they felt closer to nature in all its destructive power. She knew she wasn't being fair, but she was smarting not only from the slight of the old female shaman, but also from the attack she had just experienced outside.

As always, her eyes first went to Bat. He was by himself, looking up at the ceiling. This reminded Wolf of what she wanted to forget, so she swiftly changed the course of her thoughts. Bat was smiling with what looked like genuine happiness. This was good, at least. Skin was at his side, eyes open, staring off towards the altar. Neither of them were meditating, so she went up to them.

'Wolf!' Bat's voice was pleased, momentarily content. 'Where were you?'

Wolf sighed. She would explain it to him, but it irritated her that he did not guess it himself. 'It was made abundantly clear to me that I wasn't welcome, Bat.'

'What?' Bat looked over at Skin, who at least was nodding assent. 'Are you sure? I mean . . .' His brow wrinkled up in thought. 'I suppose you didn't get a mask, did you? But it could have been an oversight,' he finished lamely, looking from Wolf to Skin and back to Wolf in turn.

'Not likely really, is it?' Wolf felt extremely tired all of a sudden. Exhausted. It wasn't the only reason she had left, but she didn't need to tell him that. Just looking at the cavern's paintings had reminded her of her own vision back at that abandoned Lekken camp. And she hadn't wanted to think about that.

'But that's . . . awful. Unfair.' Bat's indignation was as apparent as Skin's shame.

'Yes.' Wolf's response was clipped. 'I do not want to prolong our stay here; I'm sure you understand why.'

'Yes . . .' said Bat uneasily. He is thinking of someone, Wolf thought suddenly, he does not want to leave. She could imagine who was in his thoughts: he did not want to leave the shaman Tooth.

'Look,' said Skin. 'I thought this might happen.' She seemed irritated with Bat, thought Wolf, this too involves Tooth, and jealousy. But Skin was holding her hand now, wonders of wonders – a hybrid touching a 'misbreeder' – and apologising. 'I am ashamed, Wolf. You *are* a shaman, even if you are a little . . . different, and you should be treated with respect. It's just probably that they've never met anyone like you. I hadn't either, and now I feel I know you, a little and . . .' Her voice trailed off. Wolf felt more fatigue than even before. She glanced at Bat. They would have to talk to Skin. Now was the time.

'All right, let's leave that subject for a moment. There are other things at stake. Skin, I want to trust you. I hope that I am right. Bat and I need your help. We need you to ask Pika – or ask Tooth to ask Pika – whether or not they have found any objects other than the flute, whether any artefacts of Thins, of hybrids, of Thicks have been purposefully placed. We need someone who knows the clues and details of each group – well, aside from the demons, that is. We need to ask Pika if she knows anything at all about Red Deer's death.'

'You need me to find this out. All right, I'll ask Tooth.'

'Yet here too is another problem: the answer to the murderer's identity may not be one that you will like. Do you understand what I am saying?' Wolf looked hard at the hybrid, and even harder at Bat. Would the hybrid understand what she was insinuating about Skin's own mentor?

It took a long time before Skin responded. When she did, her voice was slow and measured. 'Yes. I understand what you are saying.' Wolf could see the fear in the hybrid's eyes, as an urge to do the right thing fought with a deeply instilled loyalty. And even perhaps the strong forge of lust itself.

Yet Wolf felt relieved: she could trust the hybrid, after all. She added: 'But this is not a foregone conclusion, either. What we are asking you is to keep your mind open to uncomfortable possibilities. Aren't we, Bat?' But Bat did not fully meet Wolf's eyes. She would have to pull him aside later and talk about this very foolish attraction of his. It wasn't just because of her own feelings for Bat, either, at least she didn't think so. 'You said that the meal comes after the ceremony, Skin. Is it time to eat now, then?'

Skin smiled. 'It is. I was told earlier by Tooth that food is placed in one of the offshoots of the first antechamber we passed by. Come with me.'

As they walked towards this room, they could see Tooth speaking with Pika. Wolf pointed him out to Skin. 'Now's your chance.'

Skin was much more worried about how Tooth was going to behave after the recent changes to their relationship than how he would react to her questions. In spite of Wolf's misgivings, Skin was sure he was not involved in the murder. Weirdly, she did not feel as obsessed with him as she had before the place of the blue huts. She would never have suspected it, but her overriding hope was actually that their relationship could go back to where it was before. What's more, she was a little disappointed by his dismissiveness towards Wolf. And *that* was a sentiment that she never expected to have. And since Tooth had appeared and she did not have to worry about him having been killed, she found herself making excuses as to why it was important for her to proceed with Wolf and Bat – she was curious about Red Deer, of course, and the flute – but the real reason was actually that she had never been somewhere on her own before – without Tooth, gaining confidence. She wondered how he felt about having coupled with her – and how he would feel if she told him she was not sure if she wanted to again. She suspected that he would accept it, either way. She was on a quest now, too – perhaps to find her totem, but mainly to find herself. And going back with Tooth would mean going back to her old life, with its prescribed roles of master and apprentice. Going back to her lack of confidence.

This, then, was what was utmost in her mind when she went up to Tooth. 'I need to speak to you,' she told her mentor as he stepped away and walked into a more private corner with Skin, smiling. 'Did you ask Pika about her cloak?'

'Her cloak?

'The one that we found discarded at the Lekken camp.'

'*That* one.' He hesitated. 'Ah yes. Pika was grateful for its return.' He did not meet Skin's eyes.

Now I will have to tell him everything, thought Skin. About Red Deer and about the flute. And she did.

He was not surprised at all. And when she asked him if he knew of anything else peculiar, he told her that Pika had only mentioned a flute – one which had terrified the group so much that they had packed and left immediately for their winter camp, even though it was high summer.

'But why would a flute be so terrifying?' Skin asked. And Tooth told her that he did not know. 'Does Pika know anything about Red Deer's death?'

'She knows that Red Deer did not die of sickness, as your young friend insisted previously.'

'Then why are you here, Tooth?' This was the most painful question for her, for she needed to know that she could trust him.

'I followed you all the way from the initiation ceremony. I wanted to make sure you were safe.' It seemed, thought Skin, as if he were telling the truth.

'Why did Red Deer mention the Kretchen camp before she was killed?'

'That is a question, Skin, for which I have no answer.' But this time again Tooth did not meet Skin's gaze as he made his response. Then he cleared his throat, and touched her bare arm. 'I hope you feel better now, Skin. I have tried to answer your questions. And now I think it is best that you join your friends and get something to eat.' He led her gently towards the antechamber, in this subtle way re-establishing the relationship of mentor and student.

Skin thanked him and walked away. She touched her arm where his fingers had been. She was still attracted to him, she realised, just not as much. It came as a bit of a relief.

They took their food back to the huge room and ate a meal of crowberries, smoked jerboa and pounded balsam root, cooked as hard and solid as a rock. They stayed apart from the others the whole time. In a secluded corner of the cave they could still see people, of course, and hear the murmur of voices, but this way they had a bit of privacy. Skin was nervous, and Wolf saw this as the natural reaction to a shift in alliances. Wolf had no illusions that the hybrid was not still closely linked with her mentor. But even if Tooth was innocent, this process could only be a good thing for Skin, thought Wolf: she was beginning to question, a natural part of the mentor–apprentice relationship. Still,

Wolf was pleasantly surprised when it was Skin who suggested that they continue on to the closest Thick site to see if they had heard anything of flutes and whether Thick rituals held any clues. Wolf did not think that the signals pointed towards a Thick killer – in fact, the flutes seemed too obvious, as if they were being placed to incriminate the Thick people. But her opinion was hardly objective.

She kept this opinion to herself. Still, it was gratifying to hear Skin say that Wolf's persecution had become too problematic for them to stay much longer at their current site. And even Bat hurriedly agreed with this.

The fires died down low and Skin, Bat and Wolf made their bed in the same corner on a pile of furs that Tooth had acquired for them from Pika. This female hybrid shaman still had not acknowledged Wolf, but the sting had lessened now that Wolf knew for sure that they were going to be leaving soon. There was a bond between the three of them that had not been there previously. Wolf had hoped for this bond, but had not expected it. The atmosphere seemed red, red from the coals and the heat around them. Red, remembered Wolf, was, for the hybrids, the colour of animals. There was a faintly sexual feeling to the general mood, but Wolf had no inclination to press for details. She trusted Bat to tell her if he had seen anything that had pointed towards clues regarding Red Deer's death during the ceremony, and he had said that there was nothing that was of use to their search. This did not mean, of course, that Wolf was not still wary of the shaman Tooth – though Wolf felt a certain degree of relief after Skin had related her conversation, Wolf was not entirely convinced of his innocence.

She was dimly aware that all around them in the cave people were making love: in couples of men or women or mixed couples, sometimes in groups of three or four. She saw in the shadows opposite two people standing by themselves, their hands moving on themselves, their gender indistinct. She could not make out more than shapes in the darkness, but she could smell the sex that was in the air and she could hear muted groans and sighs, whisperings and low moans. It was not exactly public sex, but it was rather implicit that most people in the room were sexing, by themselves, or with others.

She put out a hand and stroked Bat's bare leg, feeling the soft dark hairs on his slender wiry calves, caressing the ridges of his tattoo. It was meant as a gesture of friendship, not a sexual overture, but he pulled her up to him and kissed her softly. Her ears started to burn. This was more than she had asked for; she felt herself melting. And then Skin was there too and they were moving together, all three of them. Her hands became moist with Skin's wetness; Bat's warm erection pushing deep into her own cunt, deep, so deep, her flesh tight around him; this was what she had always wanted and she had always known it. The beauty of Bat's lips in her ear, whispering his need for her. Her own sex slick with arousal. The softness of Skin's breasts. Everything moved Wolf into vibrant emotion, but then she looked up and saw the shaman Tooth watching them. He was fully dressed and standing several feet away. His eyes were glazed with arousal. His mouth was twisted.

She turned away then and her heart fell when she saw how Bat looked back at Tooth, and felt then how Bat pushed his cock even harder into her when he saw how the older man was watching them. She wanted to disengage herself, but she was so meltingly slippery as Bat ploughed into her with his displaced lust that finally it aroused her too to see Tooth watching, to feel how hard it made Bat inside her from merely exchanging a gaze with the older shaman. Wolf looked at the hybrid apprentice; Skin's eyes were closed as she rubbed herself. *She* could not see Tooth. That's a good thing, thought Wolf, but pleasure was shooting up her cunt, wild hellish pleasure, born of jealousy and lust and from Bat's beautiful prick pulsing inside her. Wolf cried out now, her auburn hair loosening from its knot. She clasped Bat with both hands; all she could feel now was fucking. And the weight of his cock pushed into her in jack-rabbit pulses like they were mating beasts.

She didn't care about Tooth watching or how much his voyeurism aroused Bat. She didn't care about Skin unknowing beside her, the hybrid's petal-smooth but now sticky flesh abrading Wolf's own in regular beats as Skin rubbed herself and jerked away in pleasure. Wolf cared about herself. She cared about the orgasm shooting up from her cunt to the two points of her rock-hard nipples, surging into warmth, throughout her body, throughout her mind. For the moment, that was all she *could* care about.

Chapter Six

'Move your foot off me,' groaned Bat.

He was emerging from a spectacular deep dream involving Wasp, Wolf and two hybrids he couldn't place: one young and female, one older and male. The dream was an orgy, all of them rolling around in the snow together, with some more lurid moments involving his fist gripped around the hybrid male's cock, pumping him towards a stiff, hot climax while Wasp and Wolf and the hybrid female watched. Bat was nearly bursting into orgasm in the dream but, as luck would have it, he was waking up now, blinking into consciousness, staring up at an ornately decorated ceiling. He gazed at it for a moment – the pink irises disturbing him as much as they had the day before. And remembered. Wasp dead. It hit him like a rock in the chest. Two hybrids. That would be . . . Skin. And Tooth. But how to explain the languor in his bones that usually only came from exhaustive fucking? Well . . . he struggled to get up, but what seemed to be Skin's leg was pressing him sturdily against Wolf's body, around whom his own arms were tightly drawn. Well. The sex part of the dream might well have been the truth. If only Wasp were still alive, as well.

Wolf's dark red hair unravelled across his chest; her head nestled in the crook of his arm. And Skin's foot pressed against his chest and was attached eventually to the rest of Skin, whose upside-down naked body felt silky and smooth where it wasn't crushing him down. He could now remember everything from the night before. Tooth. The ceremony. And Wolf. How did it feel to have made intense love to such a close friend? Well, it didn't feel that different from making love to someone else he had been close to – Wasp. It felt good. Bat watched Wolf raise her short dark lashes, revealing the startlingly grey eyes, the colour of clouds and dirty ice. She didn't move her head, but merely looked seriously into his own eyes. He felt suddenly warm, protective and aroused all at the same time. He had never felt this way about Wolf before, not as a lover, anyway. As they continued to gaze at each other he began to feel flustered and confused as well. Without shifting his arm, he indicated with his eyes the overhead patterns to Wolf, and whispered: 'They're beautiful, aren't they? Even if they're strange. I've been looking at them for a while. Such bright colours. That pink is so vivid.'

'It's a distilled ochre wash; it's also used for waterproofing,' said Wolf. 'And the yellow is from madder. For headaches, as well. And the blue from indigo or woad. Good for dyeing garments.'

Bat blinked. He hadn't actually been enquiring after the technique of the composition, more the effect. 'This is strange here,' he whispered again. Wolf nodded tentatively. Now he bent down his head and kissed her softly. It seemed easier than talking. Her lips were cool and yielding, and for a moment it felt strange to push his mouth to his friend's, until they both moved so closely into each other that the embrace began to feel more urgent; their lips pressed to each other's lips easily and openly, with more exploratory sensuality than urgency. Bat's excitement was slow to kindle, but now he felt himself steadily stiffening, his penis pressing into Wolf's upper legs. It was sweet to taste Wolf's mouth, and with his tongue he softly explored her labret and then the curves of her mouth, then withdrew and kissed her nose, her brow, her throat. She was trembling. He held her closer, felt her surprisingly full breasts press against his ribs, yielding, warm as a fox pup. And now Skin too began to stir against them; he could feel her flesh moving, taut as a drum as she awakened.

As he and Wolf kissed, Bat felt emotion roaring through him, more than he had felt since Wasp had died; a great thundering surge of feeling, some bad, some good. It was getting mixed up in the sex as well, he thought, as he shouldn't be feeling this much from mere carnal lust. Both Wolf and Skin were groaning and he saw that they both had their own hands between their legs. He saw how Wolf's face became tender when she looked on him. This moved him and it made him worry for an instant that he would grow too involved, that his heart could be torn out again just like it was with Wasp. He would be vulnerable to loss. Above his head, the pink iris was flashing again. He made himself go cold as he kissed Wolf, as he ran his hands over her compact body. He could still feel lust, but now his heart was not involved at all. It was better that way. And when Skin wrapped her fingers around his prick, holding his stiffness, massaging him towards thick, coarse pleasure so that his mouth was dry with desire and blood pounded in his head and he was already thrusting in her hands like his cock was unattached to his body, shooting out, jism spurting through her soft tight fingers, his tongue simultaneously ravaging Wolf's mouth – well, even then he made himself inflexible to emotion. He consciously cut himself from the warmth he had felt upon wakening. He didn't want that type of closeness with others, friends or not. He jerked himself dry in Skin's fist and felt his heart shudder to a slower speed as first Skin and then Wolf climaxed shortly after.

They lay there at first breathing in tandem and, after what seemed a long time, with their breaths staggered. Bat stroked at Wolf's red hair. This day promised to be an unusual one. Alliances between the three of them were shaky, he thought, if closer than they had been previous to the ceremony last night. There was a link where there had been none before. It was just that it felt like too much, so soon after Wasp's death.

Wolf stirred. 'We've got to get going, you know. I know I don't want to linger around this camp for much longer – some hybrid might well end up with a cut throat.' She lifted herself up and began to put her small collection of belongings into order before rubbing red ochre into the leather of her strapped shoes for waterproofing, as she had explained previously. Bat watched as she looked back over at him (he was nearly dozing again) and Skin, who seemed to have fallen much more soundly asleep, curled against his pelvis. 'Surely you've got some things to set order to as well?'

Bat tried to think about what he needed to do before they left. He was grubby, dirty with grime and sex, but felt reluctant to bathe just yet. He felt as if he were hanging on for something; hoping that some other event would take place. He looked down at Skin, but she was still fast asleep, even snoring lightly. 'Well, I wouldn't mind talking to Tooth a bit about his opinion on the rites, see if I can glean out some information as we planned.' He lowered his voice. 'To see if what Skin told us was true.'

'You think that's wise?' Bat nodded. 'Well, in that case it's probably best to do it sooner rather than later.' She turned around and went out through the tunnel.

Bat was annoyed by the fact that she wanted to get going as soon as they got up. He knew that was the original plan but Tooth could still explain many things to him and he wondered whether he oughtn't tell the hybrid shaman the whole truth of their quest. But he had sworn oaths to Wolf that he would not breathe a word of the details of their quest to anyone who was not directly involved, that was to say: Bat, Wolf and now Skin. Wasp would have been involved too, thought Bat, were she still here. The pain upon waking and remembering afresh was not as distressing as it had been the previous day, but he wondered when the nightmare of reality would change to the solid substance of remembrance. It was a process that he did not want to rush along. He was grateful even for those few moments when he believed Wasp was still alive.

Upon Wolf's return, she woke them and they drank a bit of melted snow she had carried back in a bladder-flask, ate some pine nuts and a few small apples, packed their belongings and in turns went out to relieve themselves (far away from the dwellings in the snow, as was polite). Skin accompanied Wolf on the dwarf's own request. Wolf did not explain why she wanted the company, but Bat took it as a personal slight to himself. Though it did give Tooth a chance to come over without Skin giving Bat an evil glare. By this time, Bat had realised that the female hybrid was jealous.

'You slept well?' asked Tooth, laying a hand on Bat's shoulder.

The younger man started to tremble. 'My mouth is dry,' he said, 'it feels like I can't shake my head awake.'

Tooth laughed. 'That's the effect of *Amanita*, boy.'

Bat stared at the shaman, feeling reckless. 'Maybe.'

The older man drew in his breath quickly.

Bat took a step in closer, so that he was very close to the other man's body. He was gratified to notice that Tooth seemed to be having slight difficulty in breathing. That he should so affect the older man was in itself a feat, as breath-control was the simplest of shamanic skills, and one mastered by first- or second-year apprentices. Bat raised his chin and his thick lashes. His eyes came level to the other man's throat, and there he saw the tick of a fast, urgent pulse. And then Bat, too, started to breathe quickly.

It happened more quickly than he had time to register the action. Tooth's head dipped down and he grasped the younger man hard around his waist, breathing a husky voice into Bat's ear: 'You're tampering with me, apprentice. I wouldn't advise it.'

'I'm not.' A rush of heat hit Bat, to think that he could have this influence on such an esteemed shaman. He was making this handsome, mature man in his prime groan like a young man. Bat was just beginning to move towards Tooth when he felt someone tapping at his shoulder.

'We're not interrupting anything, I hope.' Skin flashed Bat a rather wicked and insincere smile.

'Of course not,' Tooth said, unruffled. 'Young Bat was just about to enquire about the flute found in the Lekken camp.' Bat shot Wolf and Skin a look – that, decidedly, he had not said. He looked back up at the taller man, who was gazing at him levelly, with the effect that Bat's heart began to race that little bit faster.

'And what are your opinions regarding that find?' Wolf's tone was also even.

'I am afraid that I have no opinions on that particular subject.'

'Maybe you'd like to explain to us what you mean by that.' Wolf looked incredibly serious.

Tooth smiled. 'No, I don't think I would, actually. Not at the moment.'

'Or perhaps to explain it to me alone. One shaman to another.'

'Again, I'm going to have to defer. Perhaps some other time.' Bat was not positive, but there was a hint of deprecation in the shaman's words to Wolf, masked by the melodious Kretchen intonation. He looked at the older man's dominant, proud face, the rather cruel shape of his lips and felt his cock harden beneath his robe. Since no one could see, Bat slipped his hand beneath and stroked himself, just a little, as he listened to the shaman's words. 'Go on your quest with your friends here, find out if what you seek is really what you find – and take good care of my little Skin. Then, if you still need the answer after a moon-long quest, I will not deny any answers at my disposal.'

For the second time that day, Wolf stomped out of the tunnel. That left Bat, Skin and Tooth staring at one another uncomfortably. Bat could see that Skin was confused, not sure where her alliances should lie: there was more than jealousy involved here, thought Bat, surprised to realise that Skin, at some level, also felt a responsibility to Wolf and himself. If you're confused, Bat thought silently at Skin, think how I feel.

Then it was his turn to feel the poison of jealousy streaming through him, as he watched Tooth pull Skin towards him, embrace her in his thick strong arms. 'Skin,' Bat heard the older shaman say to his apprentice. 'You will take care of yourself on this journey, won't you?' And then it was necessary for Bat to turn away entirely to avoid the sight of Tooth kissing her, crushing Skin to him, his hands caught in the spill of her red hair. Though even when Bat's head was turned he could hear their breath hasten and Tooth's quiet groan.

So Bat was surprised that it was Skin who he heard say, 'Stop,' and who, when he turned back around, was the one who was disentangling herself from the embrace. As Skin gave Tooth a rather formal brow kiss, her eyes were kind and her manner towards her mentor was affectionate, but also dismissive. Bat could not understand it. Then he forgot the matter completely when Skin withdrew to follow Wolf outside and there was only Tooth and himself remaining, secluded in this private corner of the great room.

Bat was not sure who moved first, but suddenly his face was gripped by Tooth's hands and the other man was kissing him fiercely, the older man's tongue almost brutal in his own mouth. Tooth's hands dug into Bat's shoulders. And passion, as quick and ardent and eager as bull mammoths when they mounted one another, their long elephantine cocks sticky with musk, shivered down the whole of Bat's lean body. Tooth's hands undid the rope round the younger man's waist. Bat's cock was so hard it was painful. He saw the hybrid shaman's pale eyes go smoky with lust as he reached out for Bat's cock. And Bat needed this. He needed Tooth to maul him, to masturbate him – a hard, fast wank.

When at last Tooth's hands pressed and stroked between Bat's legs, stroking and stroking and stroking, hard and fast on the tight rigid length of cock, Bat cried out with need, moaning against the older man's mouth. Pure pleasure and a growing, itching gratification coursed up through the younger man's prick and the sensation grew tighter and more aching with every motion. Bat's mouth was wet and slack, his knees weak and ears roaring; he was overcome with what could only be described as lechery, and any time that delayed the moments when he could remove Tooth's clothing and feel the length of his skin against his own was time that was wasted, in Bat's opinion.

Wolf was washing the dirt and clay from her face and body with snow, a sight that made Skin shiver. She went up to Wolf and greeted her. Wolf did not seem surprised, but neither did she seem particularly friendly.

'I left them both behind there; they were quite able to occupy themselves,' Skin added. Wolf grunted in response. Skin took a deep breath and continued: 'I want you to know that I don't approve of how Tooth is treating you, even if he is my mentor and master. It is obvious that he has a problem with mis— that he has a problem.'

Wolf removed her hands from her face. It was ruddy with cold. 'You think so?' she said, in a voice that bordered only slightly on sarcasm. 'It's not that long ago that you exhibited a similar revulsion. Remember?'

Skin flushed. She did remember. 'Well, I just wanted to let you know that I was aware of it.'

Wolf stared at her for a long while, twisting her labret thoughtfully, so long that Skin felt her feet going cold in the snow. 'It's a good thing to be aware of.'

'I also –' Skin started to speak, and then broke it off. She stirred the snow around with her toe. She could probably use a wash herself; she felt grimy from the events of the last two days. 'You know when we went out earlier this morning? And we didn't say much to each other, but just went about our morning tasks?' Wolf nodded. 'Well, there was something I wanted to say to you then, but didn't. And then we returned and I saw Tooth, and the way he treated you made me think, well, it made me think that it is possible for those I have faith in to fail me in small ways. And since I am going to be throwing in my lot with you – now with my master's blessing – I think that I have a right to ensure that my faith and trust are well-grounded.'

'What are you getting at?'

Skin fixed her eyes on Wolf's feet. 'That necklace of yours. I know you have a necklace of human teeth. Just like the demons have. I saw it in your bag the morning after the rockslide. I need to know what they mean, and whether you're involved with . . . demons.' Even to her own ears, it sounded stupid.

But to her surprise, Wolf laughed. 'Let me tell you something, Skin,' she said, her voice gentle. 'You're not a shaman yet, so you don't yet know some of the details of the profession. But there are different ways of going about things. Most shamans are genuine seekers, leaders, people on a spiritual quest, mind-travellers. There are also those who use their prestige to intimidate and control through fear. They receive loyalty based on superstition and manipulation, and they're usually not very good at the rest of it, what really matters: the mind-journeys, thoughtsight, the connection to the spirits and so on.'

'I know all this.'

'Ah, but what you don't know is that this second lot have a whole mythology based on this fear: tales of demons who live in the Valley of Skulls who skin humans for their pretty teeth. If you tell people you can control these demons, then you can control the people, too. Most shamans acknowledge these tales for what they are, stories to titillate and frighten children. It's actually become a bit of a joke amongst shamans, and we often play with the idea. But no worthy shaman genuinely uses stories to control people through fear.'

'Tooth used to tell me to behave or the demons would get me.'

Wolf grinned. 'Ah, well, that's a positive use, you see.'

'Where did you get the necklace from, then?'

The shaman extracted the necklace now from beneath her clothing and handed it to Skin. It was a real work of art: mammoth ivory skilfully carved to look like human teeth. 'I carved this out myself once during a long retreat in my first season as a full shaman; as I said, it's a bit of a private joke amongst those who have gone through the entire initiation to shamanhood. I figured that even if I failed at everything else, I could always fall back on this. I am sure even Tooth, despite his failure in regard to accepting those different than himself, would find it fairly humorous. He never really tried to instil a belief in demons once you were an apprentice and an adult, did he?'

Skin thought about it for a moment and smiled. 'No.'

'Well, then. Here.' The dwarf handed Skin her outer cloak and a piece of red ochre. 'You stink like moon-old fish. After you have a wash, you can rub the ochre into the cloak and then help me waterproof this leather; I'll help you with yours, as well. I think it's going to rain today and I've no desire to look or feel like a sodden grouse.'

Bat was shuddering with need, but he pulled away, even though the rhythm of the older man's fist wrapped round his cock was glorious. For Bat wanted to touch and stroke the shaman first – before Tooth touched *him*. Bat was desperate to feel the other man's skin. He began by pushing back the open folds of Tooth's cloak, by reaching out and touching Tooth's scar. Bat's hands were urgent, but shaking. He couldn't understand how he had ever found the scarring tradition abhorrent. As he traced the pattern with his thumb, he realised that these marks were like a hunter's scars: earned from valour and bravery. It would take courage to withstand the pain at the occasion of such a large cutting. The healed ridges were a web of toughened skin, and with his hand Bat followed a line of the tiger-claw design up to a plump hard stone of a nipple. The curves of Tooth's well-developed chest only served to emphasise this little garnet of sensation – and the scar served a purpose too, as Bat's focus centred on Tooth's nipple. Bat's mouth began to water, as he began to stroke Tooth's nipple firmly with his thumb until it was rock-hard. Again the older man sucked in his breath, as if he were about to protest, but by then Bat was already kissing and tonguing at the nipple. Tooth groaned, and pushed Bat's mouth hard against his chest, his robe falling over Bat's head so that Bat was enveloped in there, squeezed against the masculine, decorated torso; Bat could feel the shaman's rigid hot cock pressed against his own abdomen and this proximity made him suck harder. Then he was biting, growling and grunting, pushing away the creases of the cloak, and his mouth was at the shaman's throat: sucking him, eating him; and then their lips met and they shoved their tongues half-way down each other's throats.

This time when Tooth moved his hand down on Bat's sex and began the rhythmic pull again, Bat did not draw away. He let himself be worked by the older man's confident hand and a steady warm lust began to overtake his mind, in peaks of pleasure that receded and then advanced with each stroke of Tooth's fist on his cock. Bat began to jerk forward, thrusting in the shaman's palm, aware of nothing but the lust he felt and the knowledge of Tooth's body so close to him. The knowledge of the other man's breath on his neck, and then his tongue in Bat's ear. I – want – to – thought Bat, each word coming to him in pulses as his mind matched the motion of a fist curled hot around his prick, I – want – to – fuck – him – instead. Would the older man let him? He voiced this thought to Tooth, his words coming out in jagged breathy grunts.

The older man's hand eased.

He moved away from Bat and undraped his body entirely.

His physique was magnificent and his cock was just as impressive.

Then they were fucking hard. At one point Tooth reached up behind him and took hold of Bat's shell necklace that was dangling down and twisted it in his passion, ready to grab on to any thing. Bat looked down at the solid straining muscles of Tooth's back, from the back of his neck to the slope of his buttocks, and did not complain; he even relished the beads scraping against his skin. If anything, the restricting sensation made him pump even more forcefully into the other man, filling him.

Tooth moaned, a low gravelly sound, and this made Bat even harder; he could feel pleasure rising up through his body, rising up through his cock, terrible and wonderful and still the shaman kept groaning, arousing Bat even further, making him want to fuck deeper. He plunged as savagely as he could into the older man, taking all of him he could get, his hard cock massaged so briskly by Tooth's arsehole. Tooth's scar on his chest was beautiful. Everything was grinding into a rhythm and Bat broke out in a sweat. It was so delicious, sweet lust, delicious friction. He pumped further, again and again, deep into Tooth, and felt the other man tighten around him. Just the fact that he was inside this beautiful older man made it difficult for him to hold back. He tried to, but Bat was gasping now too, a dirty low growl as he stopped himself from shooting out a stream of come. He reached down and wanked the other man, gripping him tightly in his hand. Fuck. It was good. It was too good. Dirty and tight and delicious and Tooth was so hard, just so hard, almost ready to come, and then Tooth shot out and this made Bat fuck him as hard as he could, until they were both pounding and yelling. I love you, thought Bat. I love you. He shuddered as he came. It was then that he realised that he had failed in his attempt to cut himself off from emotion. Tooth voiced his pleasure in a deep groan, but Bat felt it all silently, from his head to his feet to his still-trembling pelvis.

When Skin and Wolf finished waterproofing their outer garments and returned into the main hall of the cave, they saw Bat and Tooth sitting, clothed. They were holding each other's hand, and despite a little envy, Skin realised that Bat looked happy again, as he had during the rite. Maybe this was his way of healing from Wasp's death, she thought. She found that when she was aware of her jealousy, it hurt less: so in an odd way it was less painful to see Bat and Tooth sitting so intimately than it was to imagine it.

Tooth took his leave of all of them equally, though. Skin wondered if this was for Wolf's benefit – for as soon as she and Wolf had come upon the other two as they sat there, Tooth had detached himself from Bat's embrace and stood up, beginning a long prayer to bid them good luck and a successful quest. He knows, thought Skin, that Wolf is in love with Bat, and he is being polite. This made her irritation over his prejudices regarding misbreeders slightly easier to bear. And he had wished Skin well, given her his blessing; she was very grateful for that. Skin felt excitement: she was doing something different, something that she was sure would lead her towards her spiritual destiny – surely towards the acquirement of a totem-animal.

When they finally said good-bye and embraced Tooth, clutching their belongings, Skin noticed that Bat did not meet Wolf's eyes at all, and her own only moderately so.

It did rain, inevitably. Skin and Wolf were moderately better off in their newly protected outerwear. Once, when Bat opened his mouth to complain that his own garments weren't as impermeable, Wolf gave him such a furious look that he said nothing at all. They made their way down the mountain as the snow on the ground turned to wet slush and the rain continued to fall. Once they reached the area where there was more earth than snow, they began to hurry for fear of avalanches, a common result of unceasing downpours just like this one. Wolf said that she knew how to direct them out of the valley to the nearest Thick site, so they followed her lead.

When they did talk, it was to discuss whether or not they thought that the Lekken would have been capable of Red Deer's murder. Skin had no idea – and marked how they looked disappointed with her, as she was a hybrid herself and thus should have more insight. But both Bat and Wolf eventually agreed that it was unlikely that the Lekken were involved: they had seemed genuinely upset to hear of Red Deer's death, and more terrified by the thought of such a foreign object as a flute than intrigued by it. As the landscape became less and less snowy, so it also became more wet, and by the time they reached the flat plains they were dodging puddles. Throughout this period there was a bad feeling within the threesome: Wolf glowering, Skin thoughtful and Bat in a peculiar mood.

Finally, in the midst of a great field where fragrant clover had rapidly become wet compost, Wolf stopped short. 'I've had it,' she said abruptly to Bat. 'If we're to continue, you'll have to cease gloating over your fuck with the hybrid shaman.' Skin looked at Wolf, shocked at her wording.

But Bat squared off to Wolf. 'Maybe you'll have to explain more clearly what you mean. Or do you resent my little bit of happiness? Has Skin been whispering her jealous thoughts to you?'

'No . . .'

Skin was mortified to see that Wolf was biting at her labret. It was infuriating, so frustrating to be in the middle of this. Without thinking, she stepped between the two of them, nearly slipping on the damp grass. 'I'm sick of this. Bat, it's not fair to ignore what happened between the three of us last night and this morning. As far as Tooth is concerned, I'm not too jealous. And I don't think either Wolf or myself wants you to be unhappy.' Bat stared at her, speechless. Skin, in full swing now, turned to the dwarf shaman. 'You, Wolf – instead of pouting like a spoilt child, you ought to tell Bat how you feel about him. I've noticed it. Tooth noticed it. The only person who hasn't is Bat. It's obvious to all that you're in love with him.'

Now it was Wolf's turn to gape at Skin.

Bat turned slowly to Wolf. 'Is that true?'

Wolf looked down at her fingernails. There was an awful pause. 'I suppose so.'

In theory, it should have made everything easier. But it didn't, thought Skin. Now she had to trudge along, not only with Bat and Wolf uncomfortably silent with each other to the point of excruciation, but now also sullenly ignoring her, as well. And though the rain had lightened into just a sprinkle of moisture, there was no such relief within the travelling group. Skin was unsure if she had ever been in quite so uncomfortable a situation. She tried to sing once to pass the time, but they both glared at her.

At last though, as evening fell, the embarrassment began to ease a bit and the conversations necessary to make camp ensued. Even if Bat had been thoughtful and preoccupied since Skin's probably foolish disclosure, she marked that he was now more solicitous of Wolf, even if they were not speaking: standing closer to her, making sure that the rain did not pour down into her neck when her cape hood was down. Wolf, on the other hand, did not make eye-contact with him at all.

When she got a chance – while Wolf was tying a tarp of stitched rabbit skins to three close-standing trees – Skin spoke to Bat in a low voice. 'Look, I'm sorry. I just felt that maybe things should be out in the open.'

'Just because you've thrown in your lot with us?'

'Well, yes.'

'I understand. You want to solve the mystery. Maybe you even want to gain some independence from your mentor. But that does not mean that we all have to live knowing every little secret about each other. You might have been used to that with your master, but it's not the case with us.'

'Yes, *my* master,' Skin said with emphasis.

'Yes, your master,' Bat agreed, unblinking, and Skin's irritation dissipated.

'How can we work together if we don't know these things about each other?'

Bat gave an exasperated sigh and took out his flint set. 'Skin, you're like a child who has suddenly switched allegiances from one parent to another. What exactly is it that you need to know?'

'We're supposed to be chasing down a maker of bone flutes. You yourself hold two bones together beneath your cloak; only one is the flute.'

Bat's face was livid. 'And the other is from Wasp.'

Skin made her voice mild. 'I know that. I saw you take it from the fire. But why do you keep it?'

'Skin –' Bat paused '– you know nothing of Thins at all.'

'That is true.' Skin was beginning to squirm.

'Well, rest assured that I have no present intention of turning Wasp's leg bone into a flute. And that's all you need to know. And now if you'll excuse me, I have work to do.' Bat angrily set to work with his flints to achieve a fire. It was a near impossibility in this weather, but to both Skin and Wolf's surprise, he eventually succeeded in setting alight the pieces of damp wood the three had gathered.

Later, while Bat slept, Skin could hear him calling out his cousin's name in his sleep. But she did not have the energy or the will to comfort him and, she realised as he continued to moan, neither did Wolf.

Wolf was more talkative the next morning, contributing a single conversational sentence. 'We should reach the Vexlu camp before noon.' But the small effort on Wolf's part had loosened Bat's tongue, too, and it wasn't long before the two of them were chatting lightly of inconsequential matters as if they had never argued at all. They're unpredictable, thought Skin. Then she shrugged and joined the conversation. Though once they were hiking towards the camp, Bat fell silent again, at which point Skin asked what troubled him, worried that he might find the question again too intrusive.

'I am thinking of Wasp,' he said quietly, and Skin let the matter drop, as that seemed to be what Bat wanted her to do.

By the time they had crossed out of the valley, he was speaking more frequently. Unpredictable, thought Skin, doesn't even begin to cover it.

Right before the sun hit its highest point, they reached the camp of the Vexlu Thicks. They had walked through a forest of birch and pine, Wolf guiding them effortlessly through a series of notched trees. The Xs and holes were indications, Wolf said, of how many people were at the camp, how long they had been there and how many births and deaths there had been since. Skin said to Wolf that her own people used these marks on number-sticks. But it was a waste of breath, for Wolf merely snorted contemptuously and walked on ahead. 'But we use them for decoration, too,' said Skin, and mentioned also the etchings on the tiger altar at the Lekken cave.

Wolf was still disparaging. 'Those markings have become symbolic, detached from their meaning and used only for ceremonial purposes. Here, there is real and pertinent information that can be imparted, not just pretty scratchings.'

Saintly Wolf has her prejudices too, thought Skin, she can't even credit intelligence where it has its due.

They halted at the beginning of the camp to catch their breath, where they could see smoke rising and people bustling some distance away, and then headed in. Skin felt excited; she had always loved visiting the Thicks as a small child, her grandmother pointing and answering in a kind, patient voice all the questions that had bubbled to Skin's lips. Now she felt a similar anticipation, and when the first Thicks – a man and a woman – walked towards them, Skin felt a warm familiarity. The pair was moving purposefully. They both had their rust-coloured hair bound up in a similar style, twisted together with black hawk feathers; rings of both silver hematite and shiny mother-of-pearl circlets from abalone shells (though the man's hair was balding, slightly). They looked to be of a ripe old age, well into their thirties.

Looking around the camp, Skin quickly saw that others did not have the same hairstyle, from which she concluded that these two were the leaders, the brother-sister team traditional to Thick social structure. But everyone seemed to be equally elaborately decorated: most wore canine teeth through their earlobes and similar canine dental necklaces pierced and strung on cords around their necks; these beads were looped many times around the throat.

Skin wondered whether they were personal animal totems; surely, she had to be the only apprentice ever who had not yet been named to a totem. So far, it seemed that other living groups as well as her own had totemised not only shamans but the general populace as well. Everyone past the age of puberty, really, except for herself. Both men and women wore labrets; all males wore penis sheaths of the same ivory material and most women seemed to be wearing cunnic sheaths, too, just as ostentatiously decorated with bright red ochre and manganese as the men's groin coverings were. Most distinctive, of course, were the many piercings: aside from the usual earlobes and lips, most nipples, noses, navels, labia and testicles were also liberally pierced with trinkets of ivory and wood and occasionally amber.

Some Thicks were carrying hand-axes with fossil shells embedded in them, rippling with natural colours of blues and light purples, lovely and intact – these naturally crafted tools were considered just as worthy as those an artisan had spent many days fashioning.

Skin was not surprised that Wolf was such a skilled artist, either, recalling the sand pictures the Thick had drawn back at the place of the blue huts. The only real difference was that the painted art of the Thicks was always impermanent: on snow, on sand, on wood that was later burned in offering. Not just the art but the tools of the Thicks differed from the Mixers and the Thins as well: some Thicks used a similar tool to that of the Thins. Most Thick traditionalists preferred the older style, more for reasons of tradition and respect for the functional, useful, solid, sturdy objects than anything else. Skin leaned over and asked Wolf whether they would get a chance to see the wood paintings while they were here, but Wolf merely gave her a pained expression, so Skin drew back and continued her admiration silently. The Thicks were an artistic, imposing sight, Skin thought, and it pleased her to be partially related, no matter how distantly, to these people.

Much of the jewellery – pieces of bone, wood and tusk – was marked with the customary Xs and lines to indicate the spear from which it was fashioned or to indicate the specific animal source, Wolf explained sniffily to Skin, obviously wanting to drive her previous point home more forcefully – two Xs, for example, meant a cave bear, and only one indicated that the ornament was fashioned from tiger bone. Thicks, Wolf added quickly as the leader drew near, subsisted both on hunted prey such as mammoth and tiger, horse and bear; and also on scavenged food.

And then the leaders reached them. It wasn't long before they were swarming over Wolf, either.

'Wolf of the Ruskers!' The brother–sister pair called out to the dwarf, and Skin was surprised to see that they knew Wolf. They were effluvious and friendly, and Skin felt like she knew them even though at times she strained to fully understand their dialect. She watched as they fussed over Wolf, clucking their tongues and patting her stomach to make sure she was getting fed enough. 'Little Wolf,' Skin heard the brother say, 'and we only recently heard news that you had become a shaman. Is this true?' He smiled, and then his face fell. 'And is it true as well about Red Deer's death? Kestrel –' 'our shaman', he added for Bat and Skin's benefit '– says this is the case.'

Wolf told them that both occurrences had taken place, whereupon they clucked and fawned over her with even greater fervour, at times alternating between consoling and congratulating her. Wolf stood it all with good grace. Skin smiled grimly, knowing her time would come soon enough.

'And this can't, as you say, be the little granddaughter of Lark?' a voice boomed out. 'Look how tall you are already, with such a tiny nose and frail bones. Well, at least you've got the hair. Look, Ermine.'

And here it came already.

Skin was treated to an endless litany, detailing kinship lists and whether Skin was or was not related to this group by descent. And how Suslik and Ermine's mother – of a similar age, apparently, to Skin's grandmother, though both had passed now, bless their spirits – had as a young woman been friends with Skin's grandmother.

'Oh, the time we had then, at the initiation ceremonies,' said Ermine and winked, though Skin tried hard not to take any notice of her meaning, feeling uncomfortable thinking of her grandmother going through the sexually elaborate Thick rituals she had once heard about, where both an older man and an older woman initiated each new adult. It was similar to a mentor relationship, but of course more explicit. Eventually the attention on her eased and she took the opportunity to look around. Bat, behind her, was looking very confident and experienced, as if he had seen it all before. But then he always tried to look this way whenever he felt unsure, so it didn't mean a thing.

There was much activity; the fires had already been hot upon their arrival, and now children were arguing with each other over whose turn it was to take the long heavy stick and roll the stones from the fires. These fires emitted the familiar scent of burning bat guano as well as wood. A pair of siblings won the argument, a boy and girl with flashing black eyes and their hair braided in a similar fashion who began to guide the piping-hot little boulders to the shoal pits not too far from where Skin, Bat, Wolf and the leaders stood. There, the residue of the morning meal of mushed peas and seeds was scraped away and Skin watched the adults place the meat upon the stones. This was covered with fragile blue iris flowers and deep red rose hips which Skin knew were tart and savoury.

A woman painstakingly put down six or seven pieces of flint and then, on top of these fire-making rocks, a skull, jawbone, femur and a litter of other bones from what looked like the skeleton of an almost-born bear foetus. She arranged these bones roughly into the shape of a skeletal, very schematic bear on top of the meat, then set out rows of vertical bear claws in a circle around this grouping of tiny bones, sprinkled a pinch of red ochre – which looked like dried blood – over it all and then stepped away, crying slightly. The other adults then heaped earth over the pit once again and Skin heard the light beat of a drum start. Skin's eyes widened; she had not realised that this was a funeral feast at first, but the elaborate ritual could be nothing else, and besides her grandmother had spoken of this rite often enough. The meat would bake for quite a while; she turned back to wait for Wolf, who was still speaking. And Bat was staring down at the dirt some distance away, for some unfathomable reason.

When there was a break in the conversation, Skin

whispered quickly to Wolf, 'There is a leavetaking feast today; I saw it being prepared. Perhaps we can ask them about Red Deer and the flute after it takes place.'

'I already asked them about the flute days ago when I was first en route to meet Wasp and Bat. Though we do need to ask Kestrel whether anything else strange has happened since then. And besides, I *know* that there's a leavetaking, Skin. Suslik mentioned it early on in the conversation. He has invited us to partake as well.' Skin felt stupid for grasping too tightly on her limited knowledge of Thick culture – of course Wolf, as a visiting shaman, would have been informed immediately of any rituals. She could sense Bat looking smug and well informed behind her. Well, at least I'm related to them, thought Skin, irritated with his pretensions; that's more than you can say, Bat.

But Bat did not look smug at all when he stepped closer; he looked worried, running his hand through his hair. 'Do they not . . . *mind* . . . too much that I am a Thin? Are you sure they meant to invite me, as well?'

Wolf stared at Bat with her stern grey eyes and answered in a short voice: 'We don't discriminate in terms of background, Bat.'

'I knew that,' said Bat airily.

But, thought Skin, they do discriminate in other terms. She hoped that Bat would have the good sense to keep his mouth shut. Bat and Wolf drifted away, and Skin took the opportunity to walk around the camp, listening to the nasal dialect that was both exotic and familiar, and to the bustle of a camp preparing for a very important feast.

Wolf and Bat walked away from the Vexlu camp. They did not speak to each other at first; the mood was painfully uncomfortable.

It was Wolf at last who broke the silence. 'What Skin said was true,' she admitted to Bat. She looked him straight in the eye. 'I do feel that way for you. And I have for years.'

'I –' Bat started to say something, then stopped. He looks embarrassed, Wolf thought. He attempted again: 'I think that I already knew that. Wasp once told me that she suspected that was the case.'

'She did?' Wolf was surprised.

'I liked the idea even at the time.' They stopped walking and looked at each other: Bat peering down from his vantage point of height, Wolf looking up at him quite seriously. It was quiet where they were standing; there were surrounding bushes that isolated them from the rest of the camp.

Wolf cleared her throat. 'I think we ought to get going; the funeral feast will be starting soon.'

'Why?'

'Because . . .' She couldn't think of an immediate reason. Because what Skin said makes me nervous to be around you now, she finished silently.

'Are you nervous?'

'No.'

'Because that would be foolish, Wolf, considering how many years we have known each other.'

'Yes.'

Without any warning, Bat bent down and kissed her. And Wolf felt herself giving in to the sensation of his pulling mouth. She felt the familiar erotic pull towards him. And suddenly it didn't matter what Skin had revealed – in fact, it made Wolf glad that Bat knew. She felt the tension of the many years she had loved him silently begin to ease away. She kissed him back and then they were down on the grass together and it wasn't as detached of an environment as it had seemed, for she could hear the sound of the camp and could smell the smoke from the food being prepared. She pushed her hands up under the caribou hides he wore and traced her hands over his bare chest, the indentation of his ribs, then down to his stiffening cock. He was doing the same to her, her small breasts heavy in his hands as he caressed her and slipped a hand down her spine. He stroked under the silver pelt she wore, and then further down over the mounds of her buttocks. Down, deeper still between the lips of her sex. Her cunt was wet and she moaned and grasped his body close to hers.

'Get up on your knees, Wolf,' Bat whispered to her.

She did so and he pushed her cloak up to her waist, exposing her arse to him. His fingers were urgent in her, smoothing her wetness up over her anus. She screwed her eyes shut, willing him to enter her. She needed the bodily contact, wanted his cock inside her body.

He was not as huge and painful as she had expected, but he filled her entirely and she rocked back on his prick, her arsehole tight around him, and she was desirous, and wet. He began to move on her, gently at first and then pounding into her. She felt like she was going to crack right open. Her cunt was drenched, liquid dripping down to his cock. She felt very, very good. Her arse was stretched out around his sex and she wasn't sure if she was going to be able to take more pressure inside her, but she managed. He fucked her arse more and more quickly, his breath quickening, and Wolf guessed that he was close to coming. Suddenly it felt like her insides were being squeezed together and then released and she began to pant. She was desperate to come and she put a hand down on herself and built up a friction so quickly that once she had rubbed herself to a climax it nearly came as a surprise that her hand was sopping wet and still busily working her clit. She wrenched out another orgasm and as she did so she felt Bat withdraw. She was hit by a feeling of abandonment and emptiness. She had felt filled and satiated by Bat's cock, happy with his proximity, relieved both by orgasm and by the fact that they had at last resolved their irritation with each other. Now he was no longer joined to her at all. She turned around, still trembling.

She was jolted to see that Bat was holding a strange little sculpture in his hand: a two-pronged apparatus made of stone. She was also stunned to see that a strip of sinew was still tied around his waist and that his cloak was still covering his groin – although not concealing the bulge of his erection. She could have sworn that he was smirking.

'Bat . . .? What did you –' Unfortunately, her mouth was working more quickly than her mind, for as soon as the words exited her lips she realised what had in fact taken place. 'Bat.' She folded her arms and looked at him. Some distance away someone was calling for people to assemble for the ceremonial feast. 'I'm not sure if I find this as amusing as you seem to find it.'

'Don't you? You certainly looked amused a few moments ago.' His expression was cocky, challenging. 'Don't you want to take a look at my little sculpture?'

Despite herself, she did. Her fascination with the forbidden creation of statuettes forced her to move in for a closer look. Bat placed it in her palm. It was heavy. 'Where did you get it?' she asked him.

'It was among Red Deer's belongings, with other artefacts. I think it is Kretchen-made. It looks a bit like a spear-straightener, don't you think?'

'A very strange example of one, if that's the case,' said Wolf, turning it over in her hand. Then she looked at Bat and grinned. 'Get down on the ground, Apprentice Bat. I want your back flat on the grass. Strip off your robe and clasp your knees up to your chest.'

'*Apprentice* Bat?' queried Bat, nevertheless laughingly doing as she commanded. 'You were never one to claim privilege, *Shaman* Wolf.'

'Ah,' said Wolf, as she moistened his arsehole now with her lubrication and inserted one end of the 'spear-straightener' into his anus as he moaned assent. 'But things are going to change – starting now, I think.' She slid down on the other end of the stone sculpture, felt its familiar hard length inside her cunt this time and began to ride him. Hard.

They sat around the hearth, their legs aching from the posture, watching the headwoman and headman and the shaman – Kestrel – dressed in identical leopard-skins. The costumes were whole dried animals draped over their heads: the head with eyes removed, mask-like, so that they could peer out over the group; the teeth shining, the claws and arms attached by cord, bound to their arms; long tawny tails behind them.

Skin, Bat and Wolf had each been doled out hollyhock flowers for the ceremony and had already been told that the young man they were to grieve – Bear – was the most talented of hunters and a fine poet, beloved of his mate Claw and most dearly beloved of his sister Abalone and brother Vole. They knew that Bear had been gored by a wild boar and had not recovered consciousness, dying the same day. They knew that when Bear was a small boy he once ran away and played with a young bear cub, with no trouble or attack from its sow, a most unusual occurrence. They were informed of these things and many more as they sat there cross-legged, legs long past the point of deadening. But – and Skin remembered this well from her visits with her grandmother – you were not supposed to move. If your legs fell asleep, well, you were just supposed to meditate upon the pain. Skin wasn't convinced. But maybe this was where she went wrong with her meditations, too: there was nothing wrong sometimes with just observing and drawing conclusions therefrom rather than forcing them all the time. Skin was actually appalled that Wolf and Bat had run in late for the ceremony, their breath quick from the exertion. It just didn't look right.

The stones had been cooking the meat for quite some

time. She and Wolf both knew what was coming up, but it was very unlikely that Bat did. When the earth was brushed away and the meat was lifted off the rocks, it was smoky, already shredded and seasoned with the syrup of the tenderised rose hips. The flowers had wilted into a brownish sludge, but the meat was now sprinkled with fresh irises, and after the meat was removed from the bone, handfuls of hollyhocks and clover were littered over the remaining bones in a rain of vegetation that piled up in a multicoloured heap as most members of the family came forth with flowers to pile on to the bones. The air was thick with pollen and those who stood closest had a thin layer of yellow granular dust on their faces. The meat was a rainbow of different flowers, completely hidden from view by the time Skin, Bat and Wolf came forward to add their contributions.

'It is the most beautiful funeral feast I have ever seen, and it smells delicious,' Bat whispered loudly to Skin. 'Is it mammoth?' Skin kept her eyes on the ground and pretended that she didn't hear him. The beat of the skin drum she had noticed before was louder now and more imposing.

The Vexlu people were quiet as the leopard-bedecked shaman passed around a stone slab of a plate and each member took a largish piece, broke off a small portion and chewed it thoughtfully. Bat, Skin and Wolf did the same in turn, and then the headman Suslik stood up shakily, and began to speak the praises of the young fallen warrior: 'Bear was the best of men – a fast runner and a good cook, and we give thanks that his spirit is present with us here today.'

'It's just like the Thin ceremonies,' Bat whispered excitedly. 'This is exactly what we do, too. Our communities are more similar than we think; this must have been what Red Deer was getting at all those years.' Skin nodded and again said nothing.

The shaman pushed back the carnivorous feline mask he wore and tore off another little piece of the charred flesh and swallowed it, and everyone copied his motions. This ceremonial gesture was repeated by the headman and headwoman at the shaman's left, with a variation of the compliments bestowed on the fallen hunter, praising his sensitivity and valour, kindness and thoughtfulness. Skin noticed that the headwoman rubbed her calves as she talked; presumably to force the blood therein to flow once more. And so it went around the circle, with people's stock of meat held in their hands being replenished as was necessary, until the addresses got to where Skin and the other two sat.

Wolf stood up gracefully, with no indication that her legs might be cramped at all. 'I did not know this man, but I eat to the memory of his present spirit,' she said, and the group did so.

Then it was Skin's turn: 'We eat to his memory and presence,' she said simply and smoothly, ignoring the tingling pain of her leg muscles, and everyone slowly chewed at the savoury meat again.

Bat looked nervous, but he was game. He stood up as the others before him had done and said, 'We eat to the memory of this warrior named Bear. I only wish that he were really here so that I might make his acquaintance, as he seems to have been a most gifted and kind, strong man.' Bat tore off the ritual flesh and chewed it as he sat down again, quite pleased with himself.

But everyone else was staring at him. This is terrible, thought Skin, truly terrible.

The headman cleared his throat. 'What do you mean, you wish "he were really here"? He really *is* here.' Skin buried her head in her hands. This was going from bad to worse. 'And we eat Bear in his memory.' The headman slowly tore off another fragment of the meat and everyone else did the same.

Everyone, that is, except Bat – whose mouth was still

full of his last bite and whose face had gone extraordinarily pale. His eyes turned helplessly to Wolf, who hissed at him out of the corner of her mouth: 'You spit him out now and you will offend these Thicks so deeply that you will undo the years of work that Red Deer achieved. So think hard before you do it.'

Bat swallowed finally, but Skin couldn't help noticing that his skin tone had now turned rather green. Ha, she thought rather smugly, and you thought you knew the Thicks so well. It looks as if you didn't know everything. But fortunately for Bat this part of the leavetaking ceremony was now over, as there had been only two more people to partake of the food and laud the departed and the ceremony had concluded in the interval. Skin was just grateful that they hadn't done a particular funeral act that her grandmother had once described: the skull of the deceased placed on the ground within a circle of stones, and the back of it crushed to extract the brains for their social communion. That would have *really* bothered Bat, thought Skin.

Now instead there was the music of flutes that three men sitting up near the headman played. The music was so skilled and lovely that it brought tears to Skin's eyes, as she remembered how she would snuggle with her grandmother on just such occasions as a child and listen. She reached out a hand to Bat, who now looked like he had recovered a little from the first part of the ceremony. Wolf walked round and sat on Bat's other side with her arm around his neck, so that the three of them sat there listening together to the divine music. As they sat there, Skin thought of Wasp. And she was positive that both Bat and Wolf were thinking the same thing. She didn't even need to ask.

When the melody ended and the musicians wiped off the mouthpieces of their flutes and secreted them away, there was heartfelt applause from the whole Vexlu clan, who were slapping both thighs, pounding out the sounds of their appreciation. Wolf, Skin and Bat separated their hands to join in, too. When the praise died away, the headwoman smiled widely and called out to them in a booming voice, 'Well, now. What do you think of our leavetaking rituals, now? Not bad, eh?

Bat answered quickly, making up, Skin thought, for his prior insult. 'It was wonderful, so beautiful. I have never heard such lovely music before, not even when my cousin, my lover, played the flute. She was a great talent, but sadly her spirit – like Bear's – has gone on. How I wish she could have heard this recital now.'

If it had been silent when Bat misphrased his toast to Bear, it was nothing compared to now. Even Skin and Wolf stared straight ahead; Skin could not bring herself to break her gaze and even look at Bat.

'Your . . . cousin?' the headman managed to croak out. He looked at his sister briefly, his face momentarily as feral as the pushed-back mask of the cape he wore. His fingers beat a quiet tattoo on the skin drum.

Bat blabbered on, worried that he had somehow used the wrong declension. 'Well, double-cousin, actually. Our mothers were sisters. And our fathers were twin brothers,' he added proudly.

'And also your . . . lover?' This time the headman's voice had an edge to it, a dark smouldering tone that everyone, including Skin, seemed to pick up on. Everyone, that was, but Bat – once again.

'Yes.' The memory made Bat look wistful.

Skin watched as people's lips curled in disgust. The worst was happening. Without thinking, she began to move her arm across Bat to protect him. It was too late though, for the headwoman stepped forward and gave Bat such a vicious shove that he stumbled and fell to the ground. He looked terrified, his nose bleeding, as he tried to stem the flow with his leather sleeve. Skin found that her teeth were chattering with fright.

'You perverse animal – how dare you come here and pollute our ceremony? Get out of our sight.'

Now three or four Thicks rushed at Bat. Skin screamed and tried to push them back as they kicked furiously at his ribs. He was curled up in a little ball, hands protecting his head. Then Wolf was in the middle of the fray, too, yelling out what sounded like a wordless prayer or some shamanic chant. It was only at the sound of her voice that the battering ceased, though tension was still shaking in the air. People seemed nearly as irritated at the guest shaman who had stopped this mêlée as they were hateful towards the victim. Someone spat at Wolf, and someone else threw an ill-aimed rock, but other than that there was no sound at all now. Skin's heart was thumping wildly, her breath ragged. Her waist-thong had been broken and some feathers torn off, but otherwise she was fine. She bent to examine Bat, who had had the wind knocked out of him. He was gasping out breaths that were half-sobs and twisting in pain as she checked his ribs, felt along his limbs for breaks.

The headman, his sister beside him, now turned to Wolf. 'Your friend, Lark's granddaughter, is trying to help a bloodbreaker? She ought to learn some sense and let him rot. What sick acquaintances have you brought into our midst?'

Wolf was struggling for an answer, Skin saw, her normally composed and stern face thoroughly scared.

'Say something,' Skin hissed at her, as she confirmed that Bat was not damaged, only bruised. For the second time in two days, she thought.

But Wolf was silent, and when Skin helped Bat to walk away towards the outer limits of the community, she did not speak then, either. She said nothing to the leaders, neither admonition nor approval, as they turned their backs on her and headed to the camp. She started to say something then to them, but the other

Thicks were already walking away, muttering their repulsion, and Skin did not know whether it was an appeal to them or a concurrence. Wolf stood there, hands at her side, looking helpless and utterly alone. Where, thought Skin, has your love for Bat gone now?

Wolf found them later outside the camp, Skin massaging Bat's shoulders with nut oil. The hybrid had also repaired her waist-thong, though it was now minus a few feathers. They both looked up at her, not particularly surprised but not very welcoming, either.

When Wolf spoke, however, her words were for Bat alone. 'I'm sorry.' She kneeled closer, put a tentative hand to a long red scrape across the side of his face. 'There is no excuse for the fact that I did little to help, and the little I did to intervene was far too late.' Bat looked away. Wolf winced, but continued. 'It's hard to go against my people's customs and the Thick community as a whole. I hope you understand that.'

Bat raised his head now, meeting her ash-grey eyes. 'Understand what, exactly? The beating I received?'

'No . . .' Wolf's cloudy eyes were panicked. 'Understand that what is normal for you is not normal for them. Surely you must remember this from Red Deer; surely she informed you – that Thick society is based on brother-sister leadership, shared equally. The entire structure would crumble so quickly if that link, that bond, were in any way threatened by questions of jealousy or intimacy. This is why any traces of familial sexual intimacy are abhorrent to my people. Brothers and sisters, most especially, but cousins too. You might as well have said that you killed that young man yourself and threw away his unblessed flesh as carrion.'

'And was this how you felt about Wasp and me?'

'I admit it was a problem for me at first.'

Bat turned away from Wolf. 'So this bigotry – the simple fact of its existence and approval by everyone –

this makes it all right to kick and curse? This means that it is deserved and justified, and that those who do not approve are kindly tolerant?'

'It is wrong to hurt, that's obvious,' Wolf muttered. 'I was very worried for you.'

'That's not what I am saying. I am not asking you whether you think it is wrong to hurt; I accept that you want no pain for people – I am asking you whether you think it is wrong to think that way.'

Wolf did not answer.

'It *is* wrong,' Skin interjected. If Wolf was not going to say anything, then she would. She felt like a different person these days, daring to say what she actually thought. 'Your love is as right as theirs, Bat, not foundering on some lower level to be merely tolerated.' She glared at Wolf; she knew her eyes were flashing, angry.

'Yes –' Wolf let out a huge breath of air that she had been holding in '– I know that Skin is right on this occasion. And I am sorry for my cowardice, very sorry, Bat.' Tears were glittering at her eyes. 'There are many ways in which our peoples differ, Bat. I know you would wish for everything to be the same everywhere; easier to understand, but this is not the case and this will never be the case. Thins differ from Thicks. Both differ from the hybrids. And even separate hybrid groups – the Kretchen and the Lekken, differ from each other. Red Deer was aware of these differences, and this was what made her such an important ally between the various groups of people in this area. You have yet to understand this, I think. For example, I suspect that you consider what you observed – and participated in, I should add – tonight as simple cannibalism. We see it as caring for our relatives and ancestors, an extension of the deep brother-sister bond – a sign of respect.'

'Caring for your relatives?' said Bat. 'What do you *mean*? You *eat* your relatives, in the name of all spirits. You *eat* them. Oh spirits,' he clasped his head in his hands, 'even *I* ate them. It is murder, bad as that which was done to Red Deer.'

'How dare you?' Wolf's voice was as sharp as a newly hewn obsidian blade. 'We kill *no one*. A life has never been taken for a leavetaking ceremony. It is only those who die *naturally*. It is a mark of *respect*. An *honour*.' Wolf's face was so red with anger that Skin thought Wolf might flare up like a lightning-struck tree.

'At least my people don't beat people simply because they love someone who is inappropriate.'

'No.' Wolf's voice was now icily sarcastic. 'Your people are *most* tolerant. You'll have to ask Skin her opinion of their kindness after we have the opportunity to visit and see whether they are the ones who killed off your dear shaman, as I've satisfied myself that the answer is not to be found here.'

Bat opened his mouth to answer sharply, but then he saw a Thick male coming towards them intently, and flinched.

Chapter Seven

'It's all right.' Wolf patted Bat's arm and went forward. As Bat's head was bent, only Skin could see how much Wolf's legs shook with fright as Wolf walked up to the man in her idiosyncratic gait.

It was the Thick shaman Kestrel who stood there. He was a young and kind-looking man without the leopard cape. He also looked tongue-tied and unsure. 'Sister Wolf,' he began, 'I have come on my own accord. It was shameful what happened back there. I want you to know I had no part of it.'

'Where were you when the beating was taking place?'

The man hesitated. 'I was watching from a distance. I did not want to be involved.'

'Evidently.'

'I noticed that you, too, did not do much to intervene.'

There was a very long pause. Skin expected Wolf to retort immediately, but she did not.

The young shaman began again. 'We do not all feel that way towards blood-breakers, Sister Wolf.' But Skin noticed that the shaman did not look at Bat. 'I will try to talk to my people, to see that next time in a similar situation this can be handled in a better manner. With no violence at all.'

And it was then that Skin realised that this Thick shaman might deplore the violence, but that at some level he still thought that Bat had committed a serious insult to his beliefs. She sighed. There did not seem to be easy answers. This shaman was probably making what he felt was a risky and humiliating trip for himself. And yet it did not go nearly far enough in rectifying what had happened.

Nor did Wolf immediately accept the other shaman's words. There was another uncomfortable silence.

It was Bat who broke it. 'What do you know of the flutes? Has anything peculiar happened here of late?' and then, in an aside to Skin, 'We might as well get some good out of our brief stay with the Thicks.' It occurred to Skin that they had not even managed to stay half a day and that they would be camping out in the cold yet again that night.

'Which flutes?' Kestrel looked perplexed. Of course, thought Skin. They have many.

'The ones Red Deer had in her possession.'

The shaman's voice was shaky; Skin could see how nervous it made him to directly address a blood-breaker. Once he started talking, he managed admirably. 'There have been no particularly extraordinary flute incidents here lately – the only strange occurrence was that a hide painting was found; it was immediately destroyed upon presentation to Ermine and Suslik.' He looked sad for a moment. 'I advise you to leave and search further. There are two flutemakers in the next valley beyond and often a quest for spiritual meaning has ended at their hearth.' He looked as if he wanted to turn and talk to Wolf instead, but continued gamely onwards, speaking directly to Bat. 'Do you know the great glacier, near where the Kretchen live?

'Yes,' said Bat, his face impassive. 'I have been near

there, once.' Yes, thought, Skin – when he first went to fetch me. How many things have happened since.

'You will find the couple there beyond the glacier,' concluded the shaman.

'But –' said Skin. Everyone turned to look at her.

'What is it?' asked the Thick shaman.

'No one has ever been across the glacier. It is desperately unsafe to do so; precipices of ice fall off constantly into the lake. Now that it has been raining it will be even worse.' And there was a little part of her, too, that did not yet want to go home. It felt like the search was tailing around on itself like a wolf pup, ending up right where it started.

Kestrel shut his eyes in thought, wrinkling up his forehead scar. Then he said to Bat, 'Nevertheless, I think that is where you are likely to find your answers. Perhaps even answers to questions which are more personal. This couple that lives there, they are brother and sister to each other. They are –' he hesitated '– lovers, I think. That is not *why* I direct you particularly to them,' he added with some embarrassment to Bat. 'But I think the three of you should leave soon, regardless. And I will do my best to soften these . . . attitudes . . . in the future.'

At long last Wolf spoke back to her kinsman. 'Good.'

Bat led them back to his own Thin camp. He limped for half a day, and then his leg seemed to work much better having walked out the pain for a while. How strange these two are, thought Skin, watching Wolf and Bat walking alongside each other. They have been through a vicious day of mutual antagonism. Yet for some reason they seem friendlier after all of it. She knew she would never truly understand their bond, but suspected that it was mainly one of friendship, with love and sex thrown in for good measure, occasionally. She also had the impression that Wolf was trying to keep her distance in some ways from Bat – perhaps so Bat did not become too dependent on Wolf simply because Wasp had died, and because he was alone and lonely.

In order to trace their trail back to the mountain, they walked through plains still damp with water. The closer they got to the mountain, the quieter Bat became. It wasn't necessary for Skin to enquire why. But she did enquire whether there was any chance of Wolf charming a mammoth again, solely so that they didn't have to walk the whole agonising distance back. Skin had no idea that they had ridden so far originally on the great, trunked pachyderms. But when Skin asked Wolf this, the dwarf laughed shortly.

'I can't whistle them here, Skin. They just happened to be there at the right time.'

In time to save us from demons, Skin thought. Wolf had brushed off the existence of demons in their conversation together, but now it came back to Skin how clearly scared the Thick shaman had been too, at the time. She is still hiding something, thought Skin. I know it. At the very least, she is unsure about the demons. Still, there were no mammoths to be charmed, and so the three had no choice but to hike back to the imposing mountain. On the other side lay both Bat's community and Skin's own. In the course of their walk it rained again; the wind blew, and when nightfall came they fished out several salmon from a creek. They cooked and ate them, and then for the second night in a row huddled together for warmth and not sexual comfort.

When she woke up in the morning Skin was very thirsty. She crept away from the other two and crouched by the stream, drinking her fill of the cold glacial water from her hands. She looked up and saw the mountain looming up ahead of them. Behind it was the great glacier. They would reach the mountain by noon today, she reckoned. These features seemed ominous and indecipherable, as if they represented every one of her unanswered questions. A hill or ice flat cannot represent all this, Skin scolded herself. But still, she was not sure.

They obviously could not go through the tunnel this time, so instead they had to forge over one of the foothills to the left, and this resulted in cold feet from the damp moss and bad tempers, too.

At one point Wolf started to sing, and the beautiful Thick melodies made all three feel lighthearted. This universal good mood lasted until they came within sight of the Thin camp. On the last stretch Skin had had to restrain herself over arguing the best path to take along the plains, since once they were over the foothills she was as familiar with the terrain as Bat was. She tried to hold her tongue since she knew that it was now she and Wolf who were the guests.

Soon she had no time to think at all about such niceties, for as they reached the settlement a little black-haired child spied them and ran scampering off, and then suddenly they were being borne down on by twenty or thirty Thins, all poking and hugging at Bat. He looked at Skin and Wolf and shrugged his shoulders as if to say, I can't help it if I'm this popular. Both Skin and Wolf tried to keep their distance from the exuberant group. It was the first time Skin had really been a true outsider – the Thicks didn't count so much, as she had visited so often as a child – and she experienced a little insight concerning what it must have been like for both Bat and Wolf recently.

She had not expected them all to be so heavily tattooed, but they were. She remarked on this to Wolf, but the dwarf merely gave her a look and told Skin that she still had a lot to learn. So Skin looked closely at the Swathir group, resolving to learn quickly. Apart from the spiralling, multicoloured (mainly blue) tattoos detailed on most parts of the adult body below the chin – a chaos of design and fanciful illustration – the Thins wore more jewellery than either hybrids or Thicks. This included the children too, who were not yet tattooed (Skin had to assume that this type of body decoration occurred at the puberty rituals). There were bracelets of bone and wood: countless rings looped around the arms of the older men and women. The Thins wore pendants and necklaces (Bat's was not unique, Skin saw, although it was made of precious shells) and chokers of stitched-together ivory beads and beads of pale-blue talc. This type of ornamentation only served to accentuate the colourful tattooed designs beneath, Skin saw. One woman, whose body was covered in the swelling waves of a dark-blue river tattoo, undulated as sinuously as the lapping flow of water itself as she walked, and Skin watched her more than the others just for the pleasure of seeing her move.

Yet Wolf and Skin stood back. Though they could not hear what was being said, it now seemed that Bat was telling them of Wasp's death, for the group surrounding him had grown sombre. Several men and women stroked Bat's arms in sympathy; some of them began to grieve themselves. And then Skin saw Bat withdraw the bone from beneath his cloak, the long bone he had carried with them since the night of the fire after the earthquake. The bone which Skin now saw he must have been secretly oiling and polishing, for it gleamed like teeth, like snow, like the white of an eye.

Is it right to display the dead so? thought Skin wildly, what will the shaman say about that bone? – before she realised that of course Red Deer was dead and it was Bat who was the next ranking priest. He will become a shaman soon, she thought. She watched Bat's consolation until a youngish-looking man with hair as dark as Bat's came along the periphery of the huts – blue-stained huts that looked very similar to those in the Lekken camp, as a matter of fact. But hair colour was where the resemblance ended – he was stockier, barrel-chested, with much more of an air of authority, leaving absolutely no doubt in Skin's mind as to his position in the community. This kind of authoritative person usually filled her with dread and drained her confidence – he was the type of man who would come up and thump someone vigorously and painfully on the back and try to pass it off as friendliness, or would boast about his sexual prowess in an over-loud voice, so that those around him could not help but hear.

In fact, Skin could see him thumping Bat on the back already. And now the headman – for he could only be a headman – was motioning towards Wolf and herself, evidently asking when Bat was going to bring his friends over and introduce them. Oh no, thought Skin and when she turned to Wolf she could see that her friend felt exactly the same way.

'Wolf and Skin,' said Bat, coming up to them with the other man in tow, 'this is the headman of the Swathir, Jerboa.' The other man exchanged the greeting with Wolf and Skin, with a variation of the brow-kiss when he tried to tongue Skin's mouth, as well. He pressed Wolf's cheek respectfully, but when he turned to Skin and ran his eyes up and down her body, she did not like the look in his eye.

'You did not tell me you had brought a hybrid,' Jerboa whispered loudly to Bat.

'I can hear you,' Skin said, suddenly ruffled and uncaring as to whether it was rude to respond. She was conscious of Wolf standing behind her, watching.

'And a feisty one, too.' Jerboa reached out his hand and for an unbelievable moment Skin thought that he was going to fondle her breasts, but he let his hand drop when Bat said something to him under his breath that Skin could not quite make out. 'Well, you are both *very* welcome here, I can assure you.' His eyes told Skin that he meant particularly her. She felt uncomfortable and as they walked towards the camp she kept her distance from him. It was difficult, however, not to hear the other comments Jerboa was making to Bat: 'Have you *slept* with one? What is it like? Is it true what they say, that there are ritual scars on their sexes as well –' But here the headman broke off his questions, for Bat had accidentally tripped Jerboa. The headman had to shamefacedly get up off the ground, and he had lost a little of his aplomb. Bat apologised profusely, but the headman shook him off and swaggered ahead to the camp. Skin's face was burning. When Wolf gave her a commiserating clap on the shoulder, she could not even bring herself to look at the Thick shaman.

They trailed through the camp – there were perhaps ten or so huts – towards, Skin presumed, the headman's hut. This large abode, when they reached it, had wind-sculptures hung outside it – an array of bones that swayed in the breeze and clinked melodically. But the merry sound did not cheer Skin at all. Upset by the headman's attitude, she fervently hoped that they would be able to move on to the glacier as soon as possible. She would tell this to Bat at the first possible opportunity, as soon as he enquired whether anything unusual had happened since he left.

But she didn't even get a chance to give him a pointed look.

'There's something I need to attend to,' said Bat and then to the headman, 'Can you come with me?' Even a headman could not refuse an apprentice shaman's request, and abruptly Bat left with Jerboa in tow. She and Wolf, Skin realised, had been more or less dumped outside the headman's tent. Presumably they were meant to enter. They did just that.

Inside the headman's hut, Skin was pleasantly surprised. It was clean, with blue-dyed sand scratching satisfyingly against her leather soles when she moved. She could not see far into it, however, as the sun only truly lit the area by the door. Like the outside, there were objects hanging from string from the ceiling: curiously carved figurines, some of which looked like Kretchen carvings. They were nothing out of the ordinary as far as she was concerned. Wolf, however, seemed enthralled, and reached up to some of the lower ornaments so that she could run her fingers over their curves. There was a rounded stone woman, small and compact, hanging from her feet. That, said Skin to Wolf, was so old that Wolf could not conceive of it. It was older than the hybrids, or the Thicks or Thins. The skills to make it had been passed from mother to daughter to mother to daughter, Skin told Wolf, yet now people were forgetting how to make them. Wolf said she was pleased that the hybrids had at least retained this ability. Yes, Skin had said, they were growing rarer and rarer. Skin was slightly bored with her own recitation.

There was also a huge statuette of a lion the length of Skin's arm with a prodigious if flaccid penis and an ibex laughing back at its upturned buttocks attached to a long bone dowel. 'A spear-thrower,' murmured Wolf. Skin privately thought that it looked a good deal more like a female pleasure tool; it too looked Kretchen-made and that was their primary use. The most stunning hanging piece, however, was a little flute of reindeer horn that managed also to portray a wild cat. It was not a Kretchen piece. Wolf cooed and stroked it. There were five holes in it and Wolf fingered these.

'Is it a Thick flute?' asked Skin.

'No,' said Wolf. 'It is not technically a flute really, being more a vessel-flute. We make these sometimes out of wood, but prefer the more traditional shape. I've always found them quite charming.'

'It's also known as an ocarina.' Skin and Wolf spun around at the sound of a woman's voice. Someone – no, two people were emerging from the shadows, which gave Wolf and Skin quite a fright, as they had thought they were alone in the darkened hut. 'The others you were touching – the lion and the woman – were recently presented to Jerboa by our late shaman, who had received them as gifts from a hybrid camp. Though Jerboa was not alone in doubting that the hybrids were capable of such sculptural mastery. Is this true?' The question was directed at Skin.

'Of course we are,' she said indignantly, 'we're famed for it.' The man and a woman, who must have been silently listening to their conversation, introduced themselves as the two spouses of the headman: Civet and Grouse. The family had three children, apparently, although only these two adults were inside. They looked kind, thought Skin: an older man with grey-shot dark hair and a chest covered by warm curly fur, and a younger, rounded woman, Civet, with serious hazel-coloured eyes that were nevertheless welcoming. After some light chat where neither she nor Wolf gave anything away, Skin and Wolf were given some wild carrots to eat and Grouse went to light a fire. They both chewed gratefully on these vegetable roots and sat on the blue sand, which rasped whenever they shifted. Skin tried her best to keep still, but when she saw that Grouse and Civet were smiling, she laughed too, and so did Wolf.

Once a fire was lit, Skin and Wolf could see that the entire interior of the hut was painted; there was not a bit as long as Wolf's knuckle that was not covered with paint. The portraits were mainly of aurochses and horses, though there were a few bison and salmon thrown in for good measure. After she finished the carrots, Wolf wandered around the hut, marvelling at the paintwork.

'She too is an artist,' Skin informed Civet and Grouse.

'We didn't realise that Thicks painted on hide,' said Civet in a husky voice.

'We don't,' Wolf said abruptly. 'Snow, sand, wood to

be burned, yes, but not anything that has any sense of permanency.'

'Why is that?' the man enquired gently.

Wolf shook her head and Skin could see this subject was one that bothered her. 'Art is considered to be something offered to the spirits, to nature itself. Those beautiful paintings, such as those we saw when we were in the home of the Lekken hybrids,' she added for the benefit of these Thins, 'those are thought to be vain, done for show and boasting alone. But I,' she added shyly, 'do not care. I think that they are beautiful.'

'Do you yourself paint on other things than snow?' Skin asked. She felt foolish not knowing the answer, as if there was some integral part of Wolf that she had not even suspected.

'Wood, mainly. In as many colours as depicted on these hides.' Wolf gestured around her. 'But you see, wood is always meant to be burned. What's more, it is always the duty of the shaman to do so.'

The two Thins clucked in sympathy. 'Don't worry about the paintings, dear,' said the woman, whose fragrant curves were more than a little distracting beneath the fur top and fur bottom she wore so that her midriff was exposed. She was not a small woman in any sense, and such bounty did make it difficult to concentrate on commiserating with Wolf, Skin thought. 'You should try to relax,' said Civet.

The older man nodded his head in agreement. 'That's what we try to do.'

Skin understood then that even though they were the spouses of the headman, their status was limited. Pleasure-spouses – that's what they were called. They might have the privilege of being wed to the most powerful man in the group, but in exchange they usually stayed indoors to be of service in terms of sex or domestic duties.

She had heard this before about the Thins. This had to be the case. Yesterday while they were walking she had quizzed Bat about the truth regarding pleasure-spouses in Thin society. He had brushed off her comments, but there now seemed to be some veracity to the rumour. She guessed that this was one of the reasons why Bat had beaten such a hasty retreat from Jerboa's home – he had not wanted to admit to his lie. Instead he had left them here outside a foreign hut. Though it did not smell foreign; it smelled of pine smoke: comforting and familiar. Skin closed her eyes and tried to think of home and Tooth. Though she was geographically much closer, it felt so far away. In reality it was probably less than half a day's walk. How strange that the Kretchen and the Swathir did not meet more often, in that case.

'So, do you want to relax?' the young woman asked shyly.

Skin tried not to look shocked; Civet certainly couldn't be implying what Skin thought she was implying. 'We can pay for both of you, you know,' the woman continued, 'we have access to a variety of marine shells.' Skin and Wolf looked at each other, realisation beginning to dawn on them both. Civet went and fetched a whole string of tiny pierced shells and brought it back to Skin. Shells were precious so far from the sea here, just as they were for the hybrids. Some people from Skin's camp had gone to extreme attempts when they had none, falsifying them by carving them out of ivory or bone or limestone.

Was this woman really trying to barter for their sexual services in some way? Wolf was smirking at her side. Ah well, this is it, thought Skin: Wolf has been in Thin camps before, of course, and now it is me who is the outsider; I suppose she finds the whole situation amusing. Wolf probably knows very well that hybrids use the little marine shells as meditation points, not for sexual bartering. A snicker from behind her confirmed this.

Skin ignored Wolf and answered politely, 'I don't believe in exchanging sexual favours for shells.' There, that ought not to be *too* rude; they were probably used to thinking of sexuality as something done in exchange for something else.

To her surprise the woman beamed. 'Oh, even better.' She grabbed at Skin so quickly, roughly, that Skin had no chance to protest before she was being kissed deeply by the other woman, who also had her hands beneath Skin's shirt and was enthusiastically feeling her breasts. In spite of her misgivings, Skin felt a flare of excitement at the thought of being desired by Civet, someone who surely was much more well-versed than herself in the art of love. Even if it was slightly insulting to be offered shells for her favours.

'I'm . . . not sure I want to,' Skin stalled. Although there would be evident pleasure in being seduced by the headman's comely wife behind his back.

'Oh, you'll want to, all right,' said the woman, taking Skin's hand into her mouth and licking at it, sucking at it, playing at it with her tongue. Her dark hair reminded Skin of both Wasp and Bat. Her hazel eyes looked like those of a great wild cat, unflinching. And her curves, hot against Skin's breasts, were so clearly voluptuous and sexual that Skin did want her too, right there on the blue sand floor.

'What about Wolf?' Skin said to the woman in a low voice, not breaking her gaze.

Nor could the woman stop staring at Skin. 'She'll be fine, I'm sure.' And when Skin turned, from the corner of her eye she could indeed see that Wolf was otherwise engaged with Grouse. This freed her up. But Civet made her nervous; she reminded her quite a bit of Wasp in personality: direct and forceful. Perhaps all Thin women were like this. It was quite attractive, Skin decided, undressing. But if the woman succeeded in making Skin feel inadequate and inexperienced, Skin knew that her newly found confidence would begin to slowly dwindle. And, too, Skin was tired of being exotic, different. It was, she decided, the last time she would be made to feel an outsider.

So it was Skin who grabbed the woman suddenly by her hair, pulled the dark lengths tight with her hands; it was greasy and fragrant with flower oil. The woman's pupils dilated and instead of shying away in fright from the younger hybrid, her eyelids dipped, her mouth was full, and she pouted. She was lush. Skin knew in some part of her that she was just another hybrid to the woman, easily bedded, but she was relishing every moment and Civet's hand was suddenly between Skin's thighs, pushing up into Skin's cunt, intense and fiery with just a tiny amount of pain. Skin groaned with pleasure. This wasn't going the way she wanted it to go. But now the other woman's fingers were pounding out a rhythm in her pussy, hard, the digits flexing out as large as any cock and then dwindling again.

The other woman withdrew her hand, shimmering with juice even in the dimly lit hut. Then she pushed Skin over so that Skin was on her knees and the woman was fucking her from behind with her hand, deep, fast, filling and Skin, despite herself, was spreading her legs as wide as she could, her large beautiful thighs open for the woman's fucking hand. So Civet could fuck her even deeper, even more tightly.

Skin ran her hands over her own breasts and pinched her nipples violently. She wanted to be in control. She wanted to cuckold that boor of a headman. But she wasn't doing either of these things at present. She wasn't going to climax either, she realised, for she was over-excited, but it felt so good to be filled this way by a woman's hand. With the last of her will, Skin twisted herself out of that position. She felt like her cunt was going to explode; tight and coiled and wet. She rose quickly to her feet. She wasn't going to let a Thin get the sexual better of her.

She glanced quickly at the Kretchen phallus hanging from the ceiling and considered its potential. But no, she wanted to do this with her own hands, her own flesh. First, though, she began to lick at the other woman: the taste was rich and savoury and made Skin's own cunt tingle with excitement. Civet grunted with delight and Skin slid her tongue all the way up to the other woman's stiff little clit. She began to suck at it, but the other woman protested and Skin knew that this was too intense a feeling. So instead she licked around the little jewel, her mouth wet with saliva and the other woman's moisture. She did this until Civet started to thrust back against Skin's mouth, shoving the hybrid's face tighter against her cunt.

But now it was she who pushed the other woman to her knees, she who crammed three rigid digits between Civet's legs. Skin hadn't really fucked another woman hard for some years and the feeling of power was intense. Her desire was stoked even more by the sight of the other woman's beautiful dark-red parts, already slippery with excitement, lips wet and petal-like as she kneeled with her arse to Skin. All of this treasure was an intoxicating and fertile scent, smelling of the sweet musk; all this aroused Skin so that when her fingers slid into the other woman's cunt she fucked her as hard as she wanted to, just feeling the incredible sensation of cunt folding around her fingers, soft, alive. She might have been able to come after all, if it were not for the fact that she suddenly became aware that there was more light in the room than there had been previously.

She didn't turn around immediately but fucked the woman until she came, and when the headman's woman had finished sighing, Skin kissed her once and turned towards whoever had walked in.

Not surprisingly, it was Bat and Jerboa. And while Skin did not resent Bat's very obvious erection, she did not like the look on the headman's face at all. He strode forward confidently with an air of arrogance. Jerboa patted Grouse's arse lightly as he walked by towards Skin and Civet. It was obvious that Wolf and Grouse had been having sex, too, but Jerboa's attention seemed particularly focussed on Skin. 'I've always wondered what it would be like to have a hybrid woman,' he said, leering at Skin's naked body. 'But Bat won't indulge me with the answers to my questions, no matter how I ask. You aren't going to deny me something that my own Civet has experienced, are you? A pretty sight the two of you were. Well, everyone says you hybrids are sex-mad; that you fuck all the time with anything: Thicks, Thins, everyone. I guess that's how you got to be hybrid in the first place. Is that true?'

Skin was frozen with mortification as he moved closer.

'Are the stories true?' he said again.

And it was then that Skin punched him, as hard as she could.

They had to leave rather hastily through the camp. They stopped only once, and that was in front of a tent that Bat said was his own. While they waited for him, Skin noticed a new necklace of bright blue shells around Wolf's neck. The Thick shaman saw her looking and grinned. 'Don't look at me like that,' she said. 'I have no scruples about accepting presents. It was fun in a boring way with Grouse – but it was certainly sweetened by this.'

Skin was preparing her appalled response when Bat returned, already finished with what he wanted to do. And the only thing he did upon his return was disentangle a hanging bone wind-chime that was outside his house like all the others. Skin saw that it was made up of a polished bone and a flute, but she didn't get a close look before Bat had spirited it away.

'I put this up in memory of Wasp,' Bat said, 'but if we're going so soon, then I want to take it with me, too. Its installation was why I left you at the other hut, to assemble and then hang these bones.' He added, 'I'm sorry for Jerboa's behaviour – I thought that since he followed me it would be all right. But he quickly wanted to go back, and I didn't want to let him go alone.'

'Is his always the Thin attitude towards hybrids?' Skin asked.

'No . . . yes, I suppose it is,' Bat admitted. 'People say things.'

'Was this why you and Wasp slept with me initially?'

'I don't think so,' said Bat slowly. 'It was curiosity, I think, but not curiosity solely because you were a hybrid.'

'And Tooth?'

'Tooth.' Bat looked at Skin and smiled. 'He too was a beautiful lover. I do not think it was because he was a hybrid, either. Tooth was because I needed something out of my system. I wanted to fuck and not to feel. The problem was, I felt with him, too. I think the word is infatuation.' He paused. 'I don't think that hybrids are any different from Thins,' he said. 'And knowing you reminds me of how alike our peoples are.'

'Good,' Skin said shortly, and left it at that. 'So this is why you kept the bone,' she said, changing the subject.

Bat's smile was radiant. 'Yes.'

It was a beautiful idea, this memory of the dead, Skin thought, as Bat tucked the bones once more inside his cloak and they began to walk away, the concept that people's ancestors were making music with the wind – here, in front of their homes. It was the best impression Skin had received yet of the Thin community, actually.

She rubbed at her knuckles as she, Bat and Wolf moved as quickly out of the habitat as they could. Her hand still smarted but she hadn't felt so satisfied in a very long time.

It didn't mean she would be coming back any time soon.

Chapter Eight

The glacier loomed out before them, a vast blue sheet. How was it, wondered Skin, that when lakes froze, they froze clear and white and grey, no matter how blue their depths? But glaciers somehow froze blue and remained that way – glossy, right from the initial freeze until they melted into lakes again.

Skin had never been able to understand it.

They had circled round Skin's own village, and even though both Skin and Bat had looked wistful when they decided not to go into the Kretchen community, Wolf had been adamant that they should forge on straight ahead to find this couple of whom the Vexlu shaman had spoken. It was reasonable though, Skin acknowledged, thinking of how Wolf had been treated at the Lekken cave dwellings. And besides, Skin was eager to find these shamans, too.

However, reaching the glacier shamans was another thing altogether. It was dangerous to cross a glacier – when she had said this to the Vexlu shaman she had not said it idly. At first the three flirted with the idea of somehow concocting a raft to cross the lake so that they could then reach the frozen mass directly but, as Wolf had pointed out, they had neither the time nor the tools nor the materials to enable them to construct a raft, at least not one that would be certain not to drown them in the frost-cold waters of the glacial lake.

So at last they realised that they would have to climb the cliffs and then carefully let themselves slide down the other side, down to the edge where the ice licked at the bottom. And then to hope that it was not too brittle or slippery for them to stand there for a moment, before they ran to where the ice was compacted much more thickly.

It didn't seem to Skin to be the best of solutions. Still, she didn't know what else they could do. To climb the cliffs and attempt to do this in the twilight was suicidal, however. By common consensus they decided to wait until morning. They made their way halfway up the cliffs and Skin showed them the same small cave where she had meditated before the initiation ceremony. It was too small, of course, for more than one to fit inside, but the ledge over their heads added some degree of shelter for the three travellers. There Wolf and Skin sang a few old Thick songs (Skin's grandmother had taught her the words) while Bat whittled away at what seemed to be an old piece of wood some distance away. Then they regrouped and ate a meal of fresh fish, which Wolf had coaxed from the stream that ran near the foot of the cliffs, as well as a small roasted rabbit, before they bedded down together. This time they did make love, as deliciously as they had at the Lekken caves. In an odd and quite poignant way, Skin was dreading the end to the quest and the inevitable leavetaking that would take place. So she curled up tight into her friends' warm bodies and dreamed instead of what the next day would bring.

The next morning they rose early to finish scaling the cliffs. It was here, thought Skin, that I saw the mammoth and its great eye, the same day that this entire adventure began. She mentioned this to Bat and Wolf.

Bat laughed. 'I saw you up here, you know, walking on your own before the ceremony. You looked so vulnerable – that was the only thing that made me think you might agree to come along with me.'

'Really?' Skin tried to remember how it felt to be so scared, to have no confidence in her abilities whatsoever. But she was gratified to discover that this was difficult for her to do. She was smiling to herself as they crossed to the other side of the cliff and she was still smiling as the three of them, one after another, began to pick their way down the ice-covered side of the mountain to the greater mass of ice below. Miraculously, all three reached the bottom, but here they teetered on the little ledge of ice, for only an arm-length away was the cruelly frigid lake. If they fell in that, they would never survive, thought Skin. It was just too cold. But another arm-length out was the brittle edge of the glacier, and it was this frozen extension that was their goal.

Bat was first to jump over and waved cockily at them from the glacier; Wolf and Skin looked at each other with relief. Skin squeezed Wolf's hand hard, said a quick prayer to whatever totem she might someday have and took Wolf up on her back. Then they leaped as well. At first it seemed fine as Skin's feet hit ice, not water, and she breathed a sigh of relief. But then Skin struggled with Wolf's weight on the thin ice, stumbled and the ice began to crack.

'Skin!' Bat was pulling at her. 'Walk further in.' She went a few more steps and knew that the ice was thicker there, would support her weight. Though the day was hot, the air was incredibly cold, her nose already like a block of ice, her hands numb where she was clutching Wolf's legs.

'All right. You can let me down now,' said Wolf in Skin's ear, and Skin bent to do so, quite thankfully. They hugged each other once Wolf was down and laughed. But when Skin looked up to see why Bat wasn't joining in the laughter, she saw that he was staring up to where they had climbed down.

He turned round suddenly, his eyes level with Skin's. 'Run,' he said, 'run towards the centre.' His voice was so urgent that Skin looked up and saw that the whole great side of ice where they had half-climbed, half-slid down was loosening: ready to calf. Without thinking, she scooped up Wolf, knowing that there was no way Wolf was ever going to move as quickly as Bat and herself, and then Skin ran faster than she had ever run in her entire life, Wolf in her arms, Bat at her feet. She could already hear the great cracking sound as the side of the cliff began to rip apart from the mother cliff and then she heard the reverberating crash as it hit the water, flooding the glacial lake to the extent that the area where they just had been standing – safely, as Skin had thought – broke off into the water, too. Although they were in too far to be affected, it did make Skin very nervous.

She placed Wolf down and apologised for picking her up with no warning, but the shaman only gave a shaky laugh in response. Skin, Wolf and Bat looked back at the cliffside. There was no indication of the violence that had just occurred. The glacial lake was as peaceful as it had been before, though it had now swallowed a substantial chunk of the cliff. It was beautiful, cerulean, cold and grim.

The only thing they could do was to continue their hike along the glacier itself. They could see occasionally where the ice held ancient grass and rocks, slowly grinding them together. There were places too where the ice had hidden holes that went down forever into the depths of the glacier, and Wolf walked ahead and reported to the other two where these slashes were, so that they could avoid yet another version of a cold death. After the sun rose higher, they began to see in the distance a nook in the cliffside where there was earth instead of ice – and what looked to be a thin column of smoke rising.

Skin was flooded with relief, having had visions of walking on this ice plain until their feet froze off, with no way to return now that the glacier had broken off so far from the edge of the cliff with only the lake in between. Not that it would have been easy for them to shimmy their way up again, in any case.

As they got closer, they could also see a hut made of tanned leather and a smaller hut behind that one. And as they drew still closer, they saw that the glacier went right up to a bridge of bound sticks, a bridge that linked the glacier to the houses. And by the time they had reached the bridge itself, they had noticed that here, too, were intricate ice carvings that were very similar to the Thick and Mixer snow drawings. Wolf pointed this out first, but both Bat and Skin insisted that they had seen the resemblance already.

Wolf went first across the bridge, being the lightest, and pronounced it sturdy enough for the other two as well. And so it was that they all found themselves at last stepping on to a stone inlet, then on to a beach full of smooth, glacier-carved cobbles and several small pine trees. The glacier was receding from this particular lagoon, that much was clear. Past the houses, a trail led up into ice-free cliffs, along a well-trodden trail all the way up to a smallish forest at the top of the incline. Skin closed her eyes in thanks again. Until she saw this path, she really did have doubts about their return.

'Hello!' Wolf called out, walking up ahead of Bat and Skin, as she was always the bravest of the three.

The three friends did not expect an immediate response, but there was one.

From out of the hut came two Thicks, a man and a

woman. Both were extraordinarily beautiful: the hair of both had been bleached by the sun from the typically dark-red shade to a lighter strawberry-blonde. They both wore matching labrets of smooth brown ivory. Their bodies, which of course differed in respect to sex, were similar in that they were both quite wiry and muscled. It was difficult to tell their ages, but Skin would hazard a guess that they were between twenty and thirty years old. And they both had clear grey eyes, eyes like Wolf's, that stared at the newcomers with neither ire nor surprise.

Then the woman smiled, and it was like the sun itself. Her eyes crinkled up with good humour. 'Come inside,' she said. 'You must have travelled far. I am Lynx, and this is Raven.'

It was only after all five of them were sitting in the warm sun, sipping a cold but potent stew of fermented blueberries and munching on dried currants, that the entire story began to clarify.

First of all, it transpired that Wolf recognised the two Thicks. 'I know you,' she said suddenly, then reddened. 'You were banished from the Vexlu, weren't you? You are . . . half-siblings.'

'And I do too,' said Bat, 'though I can't think of where from.'

Skin felt slightly grumpy, being the only one who *didn't* know them.

Both Raven and Lynx kept smiling calmly, giving no indication that their banishment had been a negative occurrence. 'That's right,' said the shaman called Lynx, her smile becoming even gentler and more beatific, 'but that was not the only reason we were banished. We were also banished because we disagreed with Suslik and Ermine – are they still there?'

'They are,' Wolf assured her.

'Oh. I had rather hoped they'd been deposed somehow. Never mind – we disagreed with the limitations placed on us as shamans. It was eight years ago. At that time we were participating in a series of talks with Red Deer, meeting often with her –'

'That's how I know you,' Bat said.

Lynx waited patiently and then continued '– and at that time we were exposed to many different types of thinking. You can imagine how it was, all these shamans meeting one another – being introduced to Thins, to hybrids, to ideas and concepts and customs we had never heard of before, some good and some bad. You can imagine how it felt for us – incredible.'

Skin nodded. That was true.

'Suslik and Ermine had by this point already forbidden us to paint on hide. I suppose we had got in the habit of doing just that with our friends, and when Suslik and Ermine found out that we were lovers – well, you can probably guess what happened then.'

Skin stole a glance at Bat, but his face was unreadable.

'That was the long and the short of it,' said Raven, entering the story. 'That was how we came to be banished. And we haven't had a hard time of it at all, actually, these last eight years. We paint whenever we want; we love each other freely. But,' he said, offering the bowl of fermented mush around once again, 'there's more to it. That was not the end of our association with Red Deer, not at all. You see, Red Deer continued trying for years to unite all people in peace. She had recently gained a hybrid ally, and I believe there was hope that some of the antagonism between the communities would begin to dissipate.'

'She was my mentor,' Bat inserted. He sounded shy.

Raven took Bat's hand and held it. 'Ah, you see, I knew that already, young Bat. She was so proud of you, too; it was difficult for her to stop constantly singing your praises. It must have been so hard for you when she died.

'When she was *murdered*,' Bat corrected politely.

Raven looked at Bat for several beats, then said softly, 'No, Bat, she was killed in the earthquake a little over a half-moon ago. I saw it myself.'

Bat began to pull at his wild mass of hair. 'But the flute. Her heart – I thought –'

'I know,' said Lynx, interjecting with a tentative look at Raven, 'how difficult it must be for you to accept that death. But sometimes there are no mysterious explanations at all; tragedies are as banal as anything else. That is both the beauty and horror of our world.'

'But her heart and lungs –'

'There is an explanation for that, too,' said Lynx. She and Raven exchanged a glance. 'We took them ourselves, after we found her body.'

'You took them?' Bat was aghast.

'To do tribute to them. She had once asked us to do so, many years ago. She knew that it would be an honour – and I think that it was also her way of reaching out to us. Do you understand how Thicks honour their dead, do you understand that we do not kill?'

Skin was still poring over the ramifications of this admission when she was surprised by Bat's answer.

'I do understand.' Bat turned to look at Wolf. 'I have been to the Thicks myself and I began to understand there, a little. I think I do, anyway.'

'Let Raven continue,' said Lynx, 'and see what you think about what happened next.'

Raven looked sympathetically at Bat before he took up the story again, twisting at his labret for a moment just like Wolf. 'As I was saying, Red Deer had been continuing her work. She had the inspiration that perhaps if we shared our arts with one another, then maybe we could all understand that everybody – Thicks, hybrids, Thins – made things of value and beauty. So she tried to negotiate with the shamans of various groups to introduce these differing arts. She would give flutes to the hybrids, she thought; painted hides to the Thicks; those beautiful hybrid statuettes to the Thins. But she did not get very far in this ambition and it was already backfiring. The Thicks burned the cave-hides immediately –' 'Yes,' said Wolf, looking ashamed, 'that is true.' '– the Thins refused to believe that the hybrids were capable of such sculptural mastery; and the flute given to the Lekken hybrids frightened them so much that they retreated back up to their winter caves.'

'But their exodus was long after Red Deer's death,' said Bat, who had been listening carefully.

'Yes.' Now Raven looked quite remorseful. 'Well, their departure was actually our fault. By that time we had taken over her work and thought we would try a different strategy.'

Lynx continued in a soothing tone. 'We wanted to continue Red Deer's work. We thought that if people wouldn't pay attention for the sake of mutual respect, well – we might as well make good use of an old superstition. And playing on people's superstitions at least seemed logical, since their own prejudices seemed to be built on an equally flimsy base of beliefs. We were new to this idea of negotiation, and perhaps we were mistaken. Along with the hybrid shaman –'

'Who?' said Skin.

Lynx smiled indulgently. 'I think you know who. Along with the hybrid shaman Tooth, we planned to continue placing these artistic pieces, but with an added touch. We thought we would convince the shamans of each community to use the fear of demons – the one superstition that all groups share – to encourage people to bind together against a common enemy. Once they had, the "demons" would disappear. The plan needed complete collusion to work. We had a chance to gain that from the Lekken camp, and Tooth had gone to warn the shaman in advance. He didn't reach it in time. Raven and I had already placed a flute in the camp and then made an appearance as . . . well, as two demons. They were frightened so much that they retreated up into the mountains. So then it was necessary for Tooth to go and explain it all thoroughly to Pika. And I, of course, was upset because in the course of dressing the part, I had managed to lose my best cloak. But by a smoke signal, Tooth had indicated that we were not to come back. We were already far away by that time anyway, nearly in the foothills.'

That explains things, thought Skin, remembering back to Tooth's quick retrieval of the garment and the subsequent fire that he had built under the pretext of meditation.

'Did that work?' said Wolf.

'No. The Vexlu shaman – Kestrel – has agreed, and Pika too. Tooth, of course, is in favour – and I assume,' Lynx said, looking pointedly at Bat, 'that the apprentice and acting-shaman of the Swathir is, as well. We have not yet asked the Rusker shaman, however.'

'Well, in a way you have,' said Wolf; it took only a moment for Raven and Lynx to understand her meaning.

'What do you think, then?' Raven asked Wolf. He deferred to her politely. 'Do you feel that this is the way to solve things?'

'No, I'm not sure that fear is the best way to control things,' said Wolf, hesitating.

'It's not fear, exactly,' said Raven. 'It's more an extension of the myth of the demons.'

'I never felt too comfortable about that ruse in the first place.'

'What do you suggest we do instead?'

'I'm not sure. We could try to meet again with all the shamans and devise a plan that does not depend on subterfuge – or subtlety at all. I know that Red Deer tried to introduce new customs in a non-intrusive way. Perhaps this was too tentative. But we could instead have one large gathering once a season, where all peoples are present, if all the shamans, headmen and headwomen are willing. If this does not work, well – then, we keep on trying after that.'

'Well, that's a variation on the same theme, but probably one closer to Red Deer's original intentions.' Lynx paused. 'Do you agree then to meet with Tooth, Pika, Bat, Kestrel and ourselves to negotiate a plan of sorts?'

'If it doesn't involve terrorising people half to death. That nearly happened to us when we were travelling to the Lekken camp and had bedded down for the night.'

'That was you burning the body?' asked Raven in surprise. 'We actually thought that a murder had taken place. Imagine burning like that out in the open without a leavetaking feast – we were trying to frighten those involved into not repeating their actions.'

Wolf cleared her throat and grimaced. 'As I said, I am not in favour of manipulation for the sake of peace, nor of scaremongering to terrorise.'

'That,' said Raven, 'is good enough for me.' He laughed. 'You, Wolf, are wise beyond your years.'

While Wolf had been talking, Skin had been thinking: this is true leadership, this ability to say what you think even when pressured to say otherwise. Wolf had all these traits of a leader – courage, intelligence, kindness. Because she had travelled with Wolf so much lately, Skin had forgotten in some ways that the woman was already a shaman and more spiritually advanced than herself – she had appreciated Wolf's qualities in terms of friendship. Now Skin was seeing Wolf in a different light. Her friend Wolf, Skin thought, could never be anything other than a shaman, a leader. When she is older, she will be even more of a formidable woman.

And then for the first time it occurred to her that she no longer considered Wolf ugly, or even strange-looking.

The person who had previously seemed misbred and out of place now only revealed another human Skin had come to care for – and even love.

The three of them passed the rest of the bright day quietly in personal meditation or simply exploring the small camp. They still had not had the answers to their personal questions, thought Skin, as the Vexlu shaman had intimated that they might. But the older pair had told them that they would be undergoing a ritual of sorts the next day and Skin hoped that this would bring enlightenment. Her stomach rumbled; with the exception of the currant berries, they had been offered no food at all. And she knew it was not from lack of supplies, either: Raven and Lynx had everything they could possibly need there, from a cache of food to heaps of wood to burn – and, as they pointed out, an abundant supply of fresh water. Skin was nearly successful in suppressing a shudder when she came across a basket woven of sedge that contained two familiar wigs of black and red-dyed mammoth hair. She had poked inside a bit and discovered a necklace of teeth. It was at this point that she decided to stop stirring, not certain whether she wanted to find out whether the human teeth were falsified, as Wolf's had been – or not. Instead, she emerged blinking into the glaring afternoon day again. They were all still lying there on the cobbles – Raven, Bat and Lynx – and Wolf, who was playing at the flute she had secreted from the Lekken summer camp.

Lynx was massaging Bat's shoulders and it looked like he was enjoying her touch, but after a while he broke free and got up to withdraw something from his cloak. Then he handed the object to Wolf. 'Play this for a while instead.' It was Wasp's bone, Skin saw, the same one that had been briefly hanging outside his Swathir tent. What she hadn't seen at the time was that it too had been carefully fashioned into a flute.

Wolf's small hands were shaking as Bat handed her the instrument. 'Are you sure?'

'I made it for you to play,' said Bat. And Skin saw then that the holes were closely placed so as to ensure that they were within the shaman's reach.

Wolf's music was unearthly, completely different from that of both Wasp and Skin. It sounded like a person whistling, Skin thought, and when people whistle and sing, these sounds are animal sounds: these sounds are warbling like birds, humming like insects. Skin lay back, her head cushioned by the warm rocks, letting the healing sun warm all parts of her body, letting the music seep through her body like Raven's fermented berries, warming, stirring, lulling. It drained her hunger away like a nourishing hot drink. It was so bright out that everyone seemed to be covered in a brilliant white aura, a luminescence – but perhaps that is because the sun is blazing and everyone seems generally relaxed, thought Skin – even I, and I do not have my answers yet, though we are nearly at our journey's end. Even the edge of her hunger was starting to ebb away. She was sad, she thought, but happy, too.

Through her hooded lids, she was dreamily aware that Lynx's hand was working smoothly on Bat's cock, that Bat was moaning softly, that Raven was smiling, watching them, and that Wolf was continuing to play her extraordinary music. The four other people glowed as the sun played on their varying hair colours, on their shoulders and on the rest of their bodies. Lynx was still wanking Bat in an increasing rhythm and his sighs and groans had increased to the extent that they met the music and blended into the melody; or perhaps it was Wolf who was modifying the melody to incorporate his sounds of pleasure. All this Skin was aware of, to some extent. But when the flower petals began to fall upon the beach – a slow rain of fireweed, violets, apple blossoms, hollyhock, soft purple ceanothus, slivers of dandelion petals, frothy blooms of wild celery, fragrant sweet rose petals drifting down from the over-bright sky – Skin was no longer able to tell whether she was asleep or dreaming.

She closed her eyes, feeling the flowers fall upon her cheeks, her lips, her throat. It didn't even matter, she thought, which it was. And the music continued to play, as flowers fell from the bright sky.

Later, Lynx told them that the flowers were a common enough occurrence. 'I think they blow down from the cliffside,' she said. But Skin wasn't so sure: the flowers, the bright sun, the magic of the afternoon, the eerily isolated lagoon – it all seemed untouchable, somehow removed from the rules of the everyday world.

It was Wolf who broached the subject first, very politely, later in the day. 'Except for the currants, we have not eaten all day and half of yesterday,' she said. 'Would you be insulted if I were to go up the cliffs and forage for our evening meal?'

Skin had never been so grateful for Wolf's customary directness.

'Oh no,' said Lynx with concern, 'you must not eat at all. How else can you be prepared for your answers?'

I am so hungry, thought Skin. And Bat actually said the words out loud, upon which Lynx and Raven merely smiled. 'What's more,' said Raven, 'you must not sleep at all, but merely rest yourselves on these leaves and ponder things the whole night through, examining your feelings and your quest. You must think both good thoughts and bad, both prayers and fears.'

'Don't worry,' Lynx added, seeing how their faces had fallen. 'We will prepare a ceremonial feast and you will be able to dine after the visions of tomorrow.' Skin hoped this meant a *real* meal – often a meal consisting of ritually invested food was disappointingly scarce.

And with that, each of the three rested on beds of alder, birch and mint leaves which both Raven and Lynx strew around the hut. Skin found herself glancing in the direction of the other little hut more than once. There was little chance that she would have been able to sleep anyway. She wondered what Wolf and Bat were thinking as they lay there, what puzzles and worries were going through their minds. For her own part, she felt vaguely discontent: she had gone on this quest, solved the mystery of the flute, found out the circumstances of Red Deer's death, regained her confidence, was probably reacquainting herself with Tooth tomorrow, and despite all of this she still had no animal totem. Once she began to think about this, she lay there twitching in a state of worry, her stomach growling with hunger. The comforting scent of the mint herbs was not much solace. She was certainly looking forward to that ceremonial feast.

When they rose in the morning after the silent sleepless night, Wolf told Skin that her eyes were bloodshot with fatigue. But both Bat and Wasp's eyes were the same.

'Your eyes are all pink, too,' Skin whispered to Bat. He gave her an odd and nearly violent look. It is the lack of rest and food that makes us feel so unstable, thought Skin. I am sure of it. She felt lightheaded and removed from everything, almost giddy. She was not sure if she was enjoying the sensation or not. Her body smelled of mint, as if she were ready to be dropped like a butchered hare into a stew. She was nearly hungry enough for it, too. She recklessly considered making a joke about this to Wolf, and then decided that Wolf might take it as an insult directed towards Thick customs.

But Skin's worry about her lack of totem had not

gone away. She had rested on now-wilted leaves the entire night from sunset to dawn and no new insight had come at all. Skin was well aware that deprivation was a common technique; mind-journeys were often enhanced by it. It was the opposite of the shell meditation she had done on her own in the cave, which was based on the interconnectedness of everything. Deprivation was a way of stripping the body down to the first layer, the most primal skin: the spirit itself. Like the bud of a rose whose petals were plucked off bit by bit, what remained was what was important: the stamen, the pistil, the soul. Like a flower. Like the marrow on the inside of a bone, the richness is there after the superficial case is peeled away.

Skin felt as if she were slightly crazed from hunger. She was fixating on details, instead of letting herself be opened up by the experience. But how thankful she was that Tooth had never been particularly fond of deprivation techniques in his training of her.

It was then that Lynx came into the room and began to speak. 'I want you to lower your heads and listen carefully,' said the female shaman. I hope they are genuine shamans, Skin thought suddenly, I hope they are not hoaxers. But nothing Skin had done so far had solved her lack of totem, so why not try this as well? Lynx cleared her throat, waiting for Skin to listen, and then continued. 'You will each take turns going into the back hut, on your own. Think of what you want the most. You will sit and look carefully and there you will see whatever it is you have been questing after. I promise you that. It will be difficult, but you must stay in there as long – or as short – as it takes. All three of you have been brave. It is this experience now that will give you your strength for the future.' Lynx took a breath. Her face, Skin saw, was friendly and her own suspicions eased: these two wished them no ill. She could see that now. If only her head didn't feel so dizzy, then she would be able to concentrate more on what Lynx was saying. 'Who will go in first?' Neither Bat nor Wolf said anything.

I might as well get it over with, thought Skin. 'I will.'

'And second?'

'I will go last,' said Wolf. It was clear how much she was dreading the experience. They all were, thought Skin. Is this type of self-scrutiny always so difficult?

'Good,' said Lynx. 'Then it is decided.' She looked pointedly at Skin.

Skin rose unsteadily and started towards the smaller hut, walking rapidly and closing the flap behind her in a brisk motion so that none could see her reluctance to face her fears and her unfulfilled desires. Once she entered, she looked straight ahead. It wasn't at all as mysterious as she had been led to believe.

When Skin looked at the wall, she expected to see something quite ornate. Yet this was not the case. One wall was painted, the other was completely blank, white-blank, consisting of smoothed-over chalkstone on the inside, draped with hide on the outside. This was all there really was in the room: two walls opposite each other. Skin didn't have the faintest idea of what she expected to see. A piled heap of cloud-white flutes rattling in the corner? Or maybe even an elderly shaman sitting there cross-legged, elderly, ready to impart wisdom? Skin felt confused. But there was no guru sitting there and Skin did not have Tooth along to explain things to her. She would have to look, as Lynx had said, but Skin didn't know what to look for. She stared at the painted wall. Then she froze. It was there again, that same crane with the weird eyes and two differently coloured wings, one red and one blue. This was the third time she had seen a crane, although it had always had one purple wing and one white.

Skin stared at it until her eyes began to sting and the

colours blurred together and then she kept staring, trying to make sense out of her entire journey. Think of what you want most, Lynx had said. Skin had immediately thought of her lack of totem, but now she began to doubt her first instinct. What do I want most? thought Skin. Are there other things? Do I want Tooth? No, she decided. Even three days ago that might have been her answer, but it wasn't that any more, nothing as simple as companionship or affection or love. And the other thing I wanted, Skin thought slowly, was confidence. And I have that now already. Adventure, excitement? Perhaps, but there was still something that she knew she wanted more. A totem. She had been right the first time, after all.

Skin stared at both wings now, taking in the whole of the bird, blue and red together. Try as she might, she could not conceive of this bird as her totem-animal; she did not feel the spiritual link with it that everyone had said was necessary. What was it trying to say to her? She gritted her teeth so tightly in concentration that her jaw began to ache. The colours were blurring together. She walked up closer to the painting, was close enough to touch it. Give me a totem, she silently prayed. Now. But no revelations came. I have the confidence now, she told the bird, I have changed; I am mature. But still she felt no insight. She ran her fingers over the cracking paint, feeling the daubs and thickness where it had been applied. Wolf was always going on about different paints; this looked like cranberries to Skin. She wet a finger in her mouth and touched a bit of the red paint to taste it. It was. Then she moved to do the same with the blue paint on the other wing, but when her already-rouged moist finger touched the blue, she began to shudder. She rubbed the red into the blue, harder, wetting her fingers in her mouth, licking both hands with her saliva and rubbing her palms all over the painted bird. Purple. The blue and red together made purple, of course, she knew that. Blue – like the humans; red – like the animals. And mixed, they made, well – they made her, the individual human Skin: beautiful and unique. They made Tooth. They made Wolf. They made Bat. The shade of purple was a colour all its own, not something that was half of either and inferior. She stood there dazzled, her violet-stained fingers outstretched, feeling the glacier wind cold on her neck as it lifted up her hair.

She saw clearly something that she was sure all those around her – Wolf, Bat, Tooth, the glacier shamans, the Mixers, the Thicks, the Thins – had missed. Skin's head was whirling.

At last, after so many years, she finally knew which animal was meant to be her totem.

The look on Skin's face when she at last exited the room was one of such relief that Bat was terrified that he would be exposed as an impostor when he entered the small hut and saw nothing, nothing at all. His head was already numb with hunger and fatigue. When Bat did enter the room and look about, he saw immediately the painted bird with the strange, pink eye. He couldn't get away from it. Perhaps this was exactly why he needed to confront the image – there had to be a reason why he was seeing it everywhere: at the Mixer blue huts, at the cave high in the mountains, sketched in dirt outside the Vexlu camp, even as a figurine in the headman's hut in his own Swathir camp (he was thankful that Skin and Wolf had not seemed to spot it). It felt like the bird's eye was following him, displacing even his totem when mid-vision, as if he had an unwanted twin that he couldn't quite manage to lose. And now here Bat was again, being forced to look at it. Well, perhaps it was time to do just this. Lynx had said 'look carefully'. That was exactly what he planned to do.

He sat for a while, but all he was aware of was his

own solitude. It was difficult being here all on his own. He realised that he had been with people constantly since Wasp's death, surrounding himself with sex and friendship and even indignation, all so he did not have to feel. And in a way it added to the numbness. And now as he sat staring at the bird with its doubled pink eye, it occurred to him that the truth was that he was absolutely terrified of being alone. Of being without Wasp. Her sardonic face came back to him, her beloved, intelligent beautiful face, as clearly as if she was sitting now with him. And it hurt terribly. He was not even convinced any more that he was going to be able to go on in the world with this loss, so intense was his grief. That was the truth of the matter. There were things he could do, ways he could destroy himself: herbs, knives; he could ask Wolf for poisons under the pretence of something else. As he stared at the pink-eyed bird, Bat began to weep, tears rolling down to his throat. He was without Wasp. Without her love. It hit him as it never had before. How had he managed to numb this pain out through the last three days, he would never know.

The bird's inscrutable eye looked back at him, giving him no solution whatsoever.

At last Bat turned away and got up, numb, shattered. This couldn't have been what the shamans had wanted him to know; surely it was better to keep this kind of pain inside and not ever let it out to be felt. He stared blankly ahead, his eyes meeting only the white wall opposite.

And it was there on the pale wall, where there were no paintings at all, that he saw the after-image of the bird again. Its blue and red wings were strangely reversed. It had green eyes instead of pink. Green, like his own eyes. Like Wasp's had been. Bat spun round and stared hard at the painted wall, and then back at the blank wall again. Yes, there was the magical effect again; the pink colour became green if he then looked immediately at a white surface. He saw two green irises in one eye, and thought about what this could mean. It meant sight. It could also mean two people seeing together. It could mean that Wasp could see as well. Her face was with him once again in memory, her green eyes shining with love. She was not lost for ever. She was here with him, inside his mind, on his spirit-journeys, in his heart, in his blood, in his cock and his skin. He could go on.

She had not left him. She had never left him.

Through his tears, Bat finally began to smile.

When Wolf got to the hut, she took one look at the walls and shut her eyes. She tried not to think of Bat's tear-stained face as he had exited; she forced herself not to feel envious of the look of relief on Skin's face when she had returned from this room. And most of all, Wolf did her best not to look at or think about the paintings. But as she sat there with her eyes closed, Wolf's head began to fill with the type of paintings she would like to do herself, the caves she would like to fill with sketched animals, the animal hides she wanted to lie down on during summer days and paint to her heart's content, without having to worry that someone was going to come along and burn the hides so that there was nothing left, nothing left of the joyful things she could create. She thought of the sculptures that she would love to carve, not out of wood to be burned but of polished stone that she could keep, look back on years later, recall then what she had been thinking at the time of creation. Art was memory too, she thought, not simply sacrifice to be burned. Not simply vanity. Not simply anything. And she did not know how she could go back and make the approved designs, give her heart to them and then watch them be sifted or burned away.

Eventually, Wolf knew what she had to do once she returned from this lagoon. She opened her eyes. It was finally then that she was able to look at the illustrated walls with peace and not envy; it was the first time she had ever let herself appreciate their full beauty. Wolf was moved so thoroughly that she was thankful that there was no one else there, simply so that she did not feel the pressure to speak.

For there was no way that anyone could possibly understand the degree to which Wolf, Shaman of the Rusker Thicks, had been touched. Touched and inspired by the sheer possibilities that now lay – wonderfully, amazingly, unbelievably – ahead of her.

Once Wolf had exited the hut, the three of them were trouped out by Raven and Lynx into the chilly morning air. It was so hot yesterday, too, thought Skin. This lagoon does not follow the normal rules of nature.

'Have you found out what was necessary to know?' asked Lynx. One by one, they nodded. The day was bitterly cold; Skin found herself surprisingly eager to return home. It is odd, thought Skin, but just as the answer to the flute was not as expected, so too was the totem revelation. Like the weather here, it seems nothing is concrete; everything is fluid. The world, myself, the future, everything I know.

She looked over at her friends to see if they shared some of her sense of liberation. They were contemplative, Bat and Wolf both quiet but cordial. Skin wondered what they could be thinking; she was curious what they had discovered about themselves while in the hut. She also knew she would probably never satisfy this curiosity unless they chose to tell her.

Questions of the type that one voiced alone to oneself in a hut were the primal, unspoken forces behind each of the three's journey in the first place – not the flute, or a shaman's untimely death. She was sure of this.

'Well,' said Lynx when she joined them again, 'I suppose you are hungry?'

They were, of course.

Skin moistened her lips. Revelation or not, she was ravenous. She felt lighter now, freer, more connected with her body since the hut – and this actually served to intensify the feeling of hunger.

They sat together, Skin, Wolf and Bat, out on the cobbles. Today was still as frosty as yesterday had been balmy. It was plain that there was less tension between Bat and Wolf – Skin guessed that Wolf's own wish had something to do with Bat. If this were the case, it seemed to have worked. Bat kept looking warmly at his shaman friend – often when Wolf was not aware of his scrutiny. He may well be falling for Wolf, Skin thought, but he himself is not aware of this yet. And then, remembering Bat's propensity for sudden infatuations, she grinned to herself. Still, there had been that loose, light expression in his green eyes ever since he exited the hut, so who knew what he experienced and wished for in its shelter?

Nevertheless, when Raven came out to say that their meal would be ready soon, Skin saw a spark between the older man and Bat. She caught Wolf's eye and they both laughed. Again, who knew? And anyway, at last Raven and Lynx were bringing them their ceremonial feast, contained within an enormous wooden bowl that Lynx held up, whose contents Bat and Skin and Wolf could not yet see. Skin's stomach growled and she pressed against it with her hand. What would it be? Nettle stew with yams and onions? Mushrooms cooked with liquorice root and sorrel? Wild boar seasoned with sage and cooked with fern roots? As Lynx set the great bowl down, Skin's mouth was already watering.

It was a bowl of hearts. A wooden bowl of hearts laid out for their delectation. They had been frozen, a glaze of ice melting on them still. Skin looked deep into the bowl of muscle. She knew full well that this was to be the ceremonial meal, and the end to the quest.

'We have kept them stored in ice for quite some time now,' Raven volunteered.

Wolf looked sceptical. 'How did you know that we might be coming?'

'We have our sources,' said Lynx – and Skin knew then that she meant Tooth. He must have guessed. He too is wise, she thought. 'There is a silver-wolf heart here, a cave-bat heart and another heart for you, Skin,' Lynx added.

Skin looked at Bat first, to ask his full permission. Though he had never looked so serious or grave before, there was no hesitation when he nodded.

Do them honour, Lynx had said. Think on your totem spirit and give thanks. As Skin reached out for the heart, she knew this was the fullest initiation that she would ever experience. She was full of her totem's spirit, baptised in it, fed by it. She would receive the totem scar on the back of her neck when she returned and that would make it more official, but Skin knew deep inside that this experience would always be for her the day that she first knew her totem. And as she gave thanks, she vowed she would give this animal in general the respect that it deserved.

In actuality they only ate a sliver of meat each, cut off from the sacred organs, a slip of a bite that was swallowed. That limited taste was delicious. Then Lynx and Raven removed the bowl and the ceremony at last was finished.

Chapter Nine

They walked up to the top of the cliffs and then looked down again over the great glacier. Unless one knew exactly what one were looking for, there was no way to see that anybody lived down there; the lagoon wasn't visible from up above and the trail was hidden even at the top. The three friends looked down, and then walked further out on the plateau. They all knew that the time had almost come for them to part from each other. But still they dawdled on, procrastinating through chatter. First Skin wanted to rest a bit, and then Wolf insisted on cooking a meal, as they still had had nothing else than the merest taste of heart. ('Something a little more substantial,' she said). So Wolf managed to spear a rabbit and they ate it cooked with apples and some groundnuts that they had picked up along the way. They talked of the weather and at last fell silent.

They knew it was time to go.

Skin wondered what it would be like with Tooth on her return. He was difficult to work out: he had done so much to help Red Deer and the glacier shamans with their efforts, and yet Skin hadn't been imagining his distaste of Wolf. Maybe a shaman can still learn things, she thought. He is not all-knowing nor all-wise. Even if her totem was accepted by Tooth and her training considered complete, she herself still had a great deal to learn. Skin groaned inwardly. Tooth would no doubt force her to memorise that endless list of herbs and plants all over again. 'Well,' Skin said, 'I can't delay this much longer. We have to say farewell sooner or later, and I probably need to get back to Tooth so I can complete my training. I don't want him to begin to worry. What are the two of you going to do?' she asked, stalling.

Wolf looked at Bat quickly, and then answered. 'I am journeying with Bat to the Swathir, where he's going to introduce me to the artist who does the hide paintings. So that I can be taught the skill.'

Skin's eyes grew wide, knowing as she did that it was forbidden for Thicks. 'Will there be trouble when you return home?'

'I doubt it,' Wolf said, 'I am after all the shaman and have a certain amount of power. I am also on good terms with the headwoman and headman in my camp, so that helps, of course. That had not been the case with Raven and Lynx. But if there is trouble –' Wolf looked at Bat again '– then Bat and I have arranged that I will come stay with him until it is rectified. At the Swathir, of course, I can paint to my heart's content and not be forced to destroy what I create.'

'You might enjoy it,' Bat assured Wolf. Eagerly, thought Skin. Wolf seemed more measured, as if she were assessing Bat's affections. That is probably wise, thought Skin. And as for me, I won't be planning a visit any time soon – and just as she was thinking this, Bat added, 'Of course I could come quite often to visit you, Skin – and Tooth.'

Skin laughed. 'I thought you would be more likely to visit Raven this time.'

'Oh yes,' Bat agreed quickly. 'But let's not forget about Lark, either. I'm sure she'd like to see me again, too.'

'Of course she would,' said Skin. 'And so would I – though not necessarily in that sense,' she added teasingly.

Bat stared at her, bemused. 'For a hybrid,' he said, 'you're being disappointingly cautious.'

'Maybe you shouldn't believe everything you hear of hybrids.' For a moment she considered mentioning their very incautious coupling the night after Wasp had died, then thought better of it.

'Maybe I should. It would be a lot more fun that way.'

'Take him away, Wolf,' said Skin. 'Keep a good eye on him.'

Wolf gave Skin a wicked smile. 'Oh, I will.' She took a big breath, then said: 'We will still be linked, Skin, even when we are far apart. I will often think of you, my friend: Skin of the Kretchen.'

The three travellers held each other in the early morning. At last Skin pulled away and started off towards the Kretchen camp.

She didn't look back once. That did not mean her eyes were dry.

It was time. Skin could hear the shouts of the community. Skin wasn't sure how she felt about the crowd. She wasn't sure at all – and though she was more confident than before, her stomach still lurched with nervousness. She supposed she could learn to deal with it by Lynx and Raven's method: inside-out, her concentration on herself, not them.

She took a breath and tried this, and as she relaxed she felt a warmth beneath her skin, above her belly. For Skin knew then that as sure as there would be those who lived for the group, so would there also be outsiders and those whose thoughts were individual, questioning, creative. That was the type of shaman that she wanted to be. People were as individual and unique as herself – and when she thought of it this way, she did not see the crowd as a blurred amorphous mass. As she looked up from her meditation cave to the hilltop where she would be officially initiated, she began to see the individuals: she saw Frog, with his hearty laugh; old Eagle, with her aching back but lecherous mind; silent, slender Aurochs, who had broken his arm last year and never said a word since. She even saw the boy called Mammoth, the same one she had initiated herself. Tooth was there too, already waiting with his sharpened sabre-tooth knife. She knew she would be safe in her mentor's hands; this helped to ease a little more of her nervousness.

This then was her duty to the community: not as mentor to the whole, but to the individual. The realisation pleased her. Then at last, slowly, Skin began to ascend the cliffside trail, up to where they all were waiting. As she walked the last part of the path, she saw young Mammoth off to the side again. He blushed up like a salmon when she grinned and gave him a wink – and she then walked on.

The shaman walked gingerly, as if the path's blunt rocks were sharp on her bare feet. Beneath the hood, no doubt, her neck was stinging and still bleeding where her mentor had cut her totem. But the shaman's whole face seemed to alight and glow from within. Her heavily decorated eyes were wet with tears, but the tears did not fall and a strong, true smile remained on her lips, which were heavy with red berry paint. She kept her eyes wide open, lashes up, and her gaze was bold as she looked over the community. She was still caped in her mentor's tiger hide, her body caught inside those huge leathery folds, her totem not yet revealed to the crowd.

Then the drums began to sound again. They were reverberating for great distances, telling all in this valley and the next that a shaman had been anointed. Some of those watching recalled the first rite over which the new shaman had once presided: the mammoth kill and the smell of the hunt. How long ago it all seemed now.

The shaman reached the cliff-stone, raised the great flapping arms of the tent-like cape and the murmuring crowd began to grow silent, although they still shuffled; some children still whispered with excitement. The shaman lifted off her cloak – but not its hood – and her eyes were fixed ahead. When finally she lowered her lids, those closest could see the intricate artistry of the eyes painted on her lids, the delicate fronds of her lashes surely a mastery of artist's skill: each dark line a spider's leg drawn with narrow perfectionism. A huge dark-brown iris was portrayed on each lid, and the effect of double eyes was nearly perfect. It was a strange ornamentation, one which the community had never seen before.

It seemed now as if the shaman were watching them perpetually, with only a momentary husk slipping over as she closed her eyes to pray, arms outstretched, and the artificial eyes of paint looked out over the crowd. The hood was still pulled tight over her ears, framing the angular planes of her face as she began to vocalise in the traditional low thrumming tone. At first, the people didn't notice what was wrong with the shaman's song, but it soon became evident that – despite singing the traditional melody – the shaman was . . . improvising. It sounded like a Thick melody now, yet no one was entirely sure.

Then the shaman raised her head, opened her real eyes, drew back her hood and let the entire leathered tiger hide drop to the ground.

Her head was bald, the red mass of hair shaven smooth as a bird's dark egg, all the way down to the slight curve of bone at the back of her neck. There was a fresh cutting there of a human hand, still scarlet with blood, and she wore a necklace of human teeth (which looked to be faked out of limestone). Her garment, however, was made of rich red hair, and there were only a few in the crowd who did not immediately deduce the material source for the shaman's new raiment. They stared at the auburn shirt, as the shaman once more raised her arms and began her song. Long rich strands fringed the light weave of the shaman's clothing, and the breeze began to softly move the human locks.

The shaman was a shimmering, spiritual creature. On each of her fingers and toes was bound what looked like a small painted blue crescent, and the effect was that the shaman appeared to be wearing bits of sky on all her digits. But those closest saw that these small blue chips looked remarkably like human fingernails and toenails. And the shaman began to dance then, arms held high, the red curls of her hair shirt swishing coolly against her bare legs as her hips began to sway, her smooth scalp shining in the glittering sunlight, her song never once dipping into silence.

BLACK LACE NEW BOOKS

Published in September

DEVIL'S FIRE
Melissa MacNeal
£5.99

Destitute but beautiful Mary visits handsome but lecherous mortician Hyde Fortune, in the hope he can help her out of her impoverished predicament. It isn't long before they're consummating their lust for each other and involving Fortune's exotic housekeeper and his young assistant Sebastian. When Mary gets a live-in position at the local abbey, she becomes an active participant in the curious erotic rites practised by the not-so-very pious monks. This marvellously entertaining story is set in 19th century America.

ISBN 0 352 33527 0

THE NAKED FLAME
Crystalle Valentino
£5.99

Venetia Halliday's a go-getting girl who is determined her Camden Town restaurant is going to win the prestigious Blue Ribbon award. Her new chef is the cheeky over-confident East End wide boy Mickey Quinn, who knows just what it takes to break down her cool exterior. He's hot, he's horny, and he's got his eyes on the prize – in her bed and her restaurant. Will Venetia pull herself together, or will her 'bit of rough' ride roughshod over everything?

ISBN 0 352 33528 9

CRASH COURSE
Juliet Hastings
£5.99

Kate is a successful management consultant. When she's asked to run a training course at an exclusive hotel at short notice, she thinks the stress will be too much. But three of the participants are young, attractive, powerful men, and Kate cannot resist the temptation to get to know them sexually as well as professionally. Her problem is that one of the women on the course is feeling left out. Jealousy and passion simmer beneath the surface as Kate tries to get the best performance out of all her clients. *Crash Course* is a Black Lace special reprint.

ISBN 0 352 33018 X

Published in October

LURED BY LUST
Tania Picarda
£5.99

Clara Fox works at an exclusive art gallery. One day she gets an email from someone calling himself Mr X, and very soon she's exploring the dark side of her sexuality with this enigmatic stranger. The attraction of bondage, fetish clothes and SM is becoming stronger with each communication, and Clara is encouraged to act out adventurous sex games. But can she juggle her secret involvement with Mr X along with her other, increasingly intense, relationships?

ISBN 0 352 33533 5

ON THE EDGE
Laura Hamilton
£5.99

Julie Gibson lands a job as a crime reporter for a newspaper. The English seaside town to which she's been assigned has seen better days, but she finds plenty of action hanging out with the macho cops at the local police station. She starts dating a detective inspector, but cannot resist the rough charms of biker Johnny Drew when she's asked to investigate the murder of his friend. Trying to juggle hot sex action with two very different but dominant men means things get wild and dangerous.

ISBN 0 352 33534 3

To be published in November

LEARNING TO LOVE IT

Alison Tyler

£5.99

Art historian Lissa and doctor Colin meet at the Frankfurt Book Fair, where they are both promoting their latest books. At the fair, and then through Europe, the two lovers embark on an exploration of their sexual fantasies, playing dirty games of bondage and dressing up. Lissa loves humiliation, and Colin is just the man to provide her with the pleasure she craves. Unbeknown to Lissa, their meeting was not accidental, but planned ahead by a mysterious patron of the erotic arts.

ISBN 0 352 33535 1

THE HOTTEST PLACE

Tabitha Flyte

£5.99

Abigail is having a great time relaxing on a hot and steamy tropical island in Thailand. She tries to stay faithful to her boyfriend back in England, but it isn't easy when a variety of attractive, fun-loving young people want to get into her pants. When Abby's boyfriend, Roger, finds out what's going on, he's on the first plane over there, determined to dish out some punishment.

And that's when the fun really starts hotting up.

ISBN 0 352 33536 X

BLACK LACE BOOKLIST

Information is correct at time of printing. To check availability go to www.blacklace-books.co.uk

All books are priced £5.99 unless another price is given.

Black Lace books with a contemporary setting

THE NAME OF AN ANGEL £6.99	Laura Thornton ISBN 0 352 33205 0	☐
FEMININE WILES £7.99	Karina Moore ISBN 0 352 33235 2	☐
DARK OBSESSION £7.99	Fredrica Alleyn ISBN 0 352 33281 6	☐
THE TOP OF HER GAME	Emma Holly ISBN 0 352 33337 5	☐
LIKE MOTHER, LIKE DAUGHTER	Georgina Brown ISBN 0 352 33422 3	☐
THE TIES THAT BIND	Tesni Morgan ISBN 0 352 33438 X	☐
VELVET GLOVE	Emma Holly ISBN 0 352 33448 7	☐
DOCTOR'S ORDERS	Deanna Ashford ISBN 0 352 33453 3	☐
SHAMELESS	Stella Black ISBN 0 352 33485 1	☐
TONGUE IN CHEEK	Tabitha Flyte ISBN 0 352 33484 3	☐
FIRE AND ICE	Laura Hamilton ISBN 0 352 33486 X	☐
SAUCE FOR THE GOOSE	Mary Rose Maxwell ISBN 0 352 33492 4	☐
HARD CORPS	Claire Thompson ISBN 0 352 33491 6	☐
INTENSE BLUE	Lyn Wood ISBN 0 352 33496 7	☐
THE NAKED TRUTH	Natasha Rostova ISBN 0 352 33497 5	☐
A SPORTING CHANCE	Susie Raymond ISBN 0 352 33501 7	☐

A SCANDALOUS AFFAIR	Holly Graham ISBN 0 352 33523 8	☐
THE NAKED FLAME	Crystalle Valentino ISBN 0 352 33528 9	☐
CRASH COURSE	Juliet Hasting ISBN 0 352 33018 X	☐
ON THE EDGE	Laura Hamilton ISBN 0 352 33534 3	☐

Black Lace books with an historical setting

A VOLCANIC AFFAIR £4.99	Xanthia Rhodes ISBN 0 352 33184 4	☐
INVITATION TO SIN £6.99	Charlotte Royal ISBN 0 352 33217 4	☐
PRIMAL SKIN	Leona Benkt Rhys ISBN 0 352 33500 9	☐
DEVIL'S FIRE	Melissa MacNeal ISBN 0 352 33527 0	☐

Black Lace anthologies

WICKED WORDS	Various ISBN 0 352 33363 4	☐
SUGAR AND SPICE £7.99	Various ISBN 0 352 33227 1	☐
THE BEST OF BLACK LACE	Various ISBN 0 352 33452 5	☐
CRUEL ENCHANTMENT Erotic Fairy Stories	Janine Ashbless ISBN 0 352 33483 5	☐
MORE WICKED WORDS	Various ISBN 0 352 33487 8	☐
WICKED WORDS 3	Various ISBN 0 352 33522 X	☐

Black Lace non-fiction

THE BLACK LACE BOOK OF WOMEN'S SEXUAL FANTASIES	Ed. Kerri Sharp ISBN 0 352 33346 4	☐

-------✂--------------------

Please send me the books I have ticked above.

Name ....

Address ....

....

....

.... Post Code ....

Send to: **Cash Sales, Black Lace Books, Thames Wharf Studios, Rainville Road, London W6 9HA.**

US customers: for prices and details of how to order books for delivery by mail, call 1-800-805-1083.

Please enclose a cheque or postal order, made payable to **Virgin Publishing Ltd**, to the value of the books you have ordered plus postage and packing costs as follows:

UK and BFPO – £1.00 for the first book, 50p for each subsequent book.

Overseas (including Republic of Ireland) – £2.00 for the first book, £1.00 for each subsequent book.

If you would prefer to pay by VISA, ACCESS/MASTER-CARD, DINERS CLUB, AMEX or SWITCH, please write your card number and expiry date here:

....

Please allow up to 28 days for delivery.

Signature ....

-------✂--------------------